"*Scratch* is not only a ripping tale—of dreams and darkness, humans and houses, and the creatures those houses are meant to keep out—but a contemplation of the beautiful dark mysteries of nature. Like a strange old story you overheard when you thought you were alone in the woods, *Scratch* is beguiling, haunting, and wild."

—KATE RACCULIA, author of *Bellweather Rhapsody*

"*Scratch* finds Steve Himmer doing what he does best—putting a magnifier to the fine line between human and beast, between what is tame and what is red in tooth and claw. Then he sets fire to any old platitudes about nature and man, creating a new mythology out of the ashes and shadows."

—AMBER SPARKS, author of *The Unfinished World and Other Stories*

"Steve Himmer's particular genius involves giving the minds of his characters room to roam. His take on literary horror might usefully be compared to that of Benjamin Percy or William Gay, but its roots reach back much further, through Shirley Jackson to Hawthorne and Poe. This book, this gift to us, is an absolutely essential reminder that every story starts at the edge of the forest."

—ROY KESEY, author of *Any Deadly Thing*

STEVE HIMMER

SCRATCH

DARK HOUSE PRESS

PUBLISHED BY DARK HOUSE PRESS,
AN IMPRINT OF CURBSIDE SPLENDOR PUBLISHING, INC.,
CHICAGO, ILLINOIS IN 2016.

FIRST EDITION
COPYRIGHT © 2016 BY STEVE HIMMER
LIBRARY OF CONGRESS CONTROL NUMBER: 2016949233
ISBN: 978-1940430843

EDITED BY RICHARD THOMAS
DESIGNED BY ALBAN FISCHER

MANUFACTURED IN THE UNITED STATES OF AMERICA
WWW.THEDARKHOUSEPRESS.COM

The bird would cease and be as other birds
But that he knows in singing not to sing.
The question that he frames in all but words
Is what to make of a diminished thing.

—ROBERT FROST, "The Oven Bird"

The true border is always a tangle, always difficult to cross.

—C.L. NOLAN

SCRATCH

WE'LL WEAR THE SHAPES OF COYOTES, TO SLIDE UNDER THE scrub and travel close to the ground. You'll keep up more easily on faster legs than your own, with a coat that blends into the bushes and sharper senses attuned to all you might otherwise miss.

Why should we look like coyotes? Why not something else?

These bodies are fast. They're strong for their size, but small enough to avoid being noticed. And if your kind should see us, so what? What are two scrawny coyotes to be alarmed by, slinking along at the edge of the woods? We could wear rabbits, or butterflies, but neither of those would command your attention. You'll listen to a storyteller with teeth and a growl, so long as it's something you think is less fierce than a wolf. Coyote's shape has worked for me many times, has worked so well he's been blamed for my mischief, so there's no reason his body won't suit us for this story, too.

Follow me now. Get down on all fours. Use your forehead to push the low branches aside as we move toward the border between the town and these trees. This story begins on the edge of the forest as all stories do.

1

THE DOOR OF THE TRAILER SWINGS OPEN WITH A CLATTER against the exterior wall, and its echo stirs starlings into the air. Martin Blaskett, the man responsible for this clearing in the forest and for the houses to be built upon it, descends a folding staircase to muddy ground and leaves the door open. He steps into his story as easily, as suddenly, as those blue-black speckled birds invaded this forest from elsewhere, generations of theirs ago. I watched them arrive as I've watched others and now watch this man, this Martin, descend. Already he's in the habit of leaving doors open, years of city noise rising to his locked windows wiped away by a few quiet nights, but if he knew all that winds through these woods—if he only knew how nearby we are, watching—he'd close it and lock it, or he might go back inside and stay home. As close to home as he comes.

His arms swing like windblown branches, and his body stands straight as a trunk, but uprooted and always in motion—a constant impression of stillness and movement at once, of being both where he is and somewhere else all the time. Martin moves like a man who knows where he's going and knows he'll arrive, a man who has no idea—and would never believe—that in a few hours' time he'll be pinned to the ground with the claws of a bear in his chest.

This morning he arose with an urge to go walking. He dreamt all night of a life not his own—two cars, two children, two well-worn dents in a couch—and emerged with a real sense of loss. I've heard in talk around campfires and through open windows that dreams have no place in the world and no place in your tales, that they're cheap and confused and a residue stuck to the ends of a day. But dreams bounce through this forest, no more abstract than your radio waves. They crackle and hum almost as loudly as your black power lines and the great metal masts that carry your voices from one part of the world to another.

Dreams are true stories told in the only moments you're willing to listen. And because he did listen, because he did dream and because that dream hurt—or if not the dream, his waking from it—Martin is setting off for the woods near his trailer at the insistence of his restless legs, despite mizzling rain and a gauze of clouds over the sun. He's walking it off the way he's been taught.

His gaze slides across this space cut from the wild, space he will refill with acres of bright green backyards. He doesn't see the hills emptied of trees or the grim yellow excavation equipment, at rest and crusted in mud. He only has eyes for the houses he's going to put here, imagination made real in sheetrock and wood. He sees families moved in, assembling for ballgames and barbecues, neighbors who are friends with their neighbors. When Martin builds, he sees into the future, and that's why he's done well for himself—his buildings are meant to have lives lived within, not to be spaces complete in themselves.

The houses here aren't even holes yet, just marks on the mud in the shapes of foundations to come. Ground will be broken tomorrow, but men in orange vests and yellow hard hats have swung shrieking chainsaws for days, and have toppled tall trees from the high cabs of heavy equipment. The forest was cleared in swathes to make room for thoughtfully located Japanese maples or a single mimosa to punctuate each sculpted yard when the lots have become more than mud.

Trunks were bundled and dragged in chains to the road, where they were piled on more trucks and hauled off to mills, swallowed by bellows, chewed up by mechanical teeth. Stumps were torn out. Acre after acre of oak, ash, and birch, of maple, hemlock, and beech, all ground into pulp and pressed into molds by machines, shaped into the components of bureaus and chairs and pressed into paper for printing assembly instructions that make only half-sense. That furniture and those instructions will be boxed up and shipped off to stores or else sold online and those wandering trees will make their ways home to clutter the rooms of these houses yet to be built. Those signals, those sales, will slip through the forest along wires and masts and thin air—buzzing in my ears like the loudest of bees, because you are all like me now, like this forest, waiting for all the world offers to come your way without leaving your homeplace to find it. You've made your world fast enough that you can sit still, and can keep the rest of us moving.

Time was when trees put up more of a fight, snapping sawteeth and breaking arms. They took as many of your kind as you took of theirs, and furniture never traveled so far. Now houses go up in days, one after the other, identical stalks in a field full of corn, and decades-tall trunks can come down without being touched once by hands, only by engines and blades. You can eat at a table, palms flat on the wood, without remembering it was a tree.

Things took longer, a long time ago. Even telling my stories was slow, when I could unwind them out across years because I knew their parts would stay put. But we've had to adapt, we've had to catch up, as the world has grown faster around us. It's the way of things. Glaciers crept in and crept out, leaving these woods with only a lake almost too small for the word. Stones crawled up through the ground, winter after winter, freeze after freeze, and a new group of people drove out the ones who were already here so they might carve the woods into farms for a few generations and pile those stones into walls, then pack up again to raise new walls somewhere else. And now you're trickling back in, with the starlings and loosestrife and empty beer cans. One layer laps over another. Everything is devoured as soon as it's born.

But let's not get ahead of ourselves. Martin's houses here aren't even built yet. These homes of the future began with a sheet of white paper, then black lines demarcating driveways and gardens and pools. He had never heard of this town when he started, when all he knew was he wanted some acres that weren't too expensive or too remote for potential commuters. It's a half hour drive to the highway, then a short trip to Portsmouth or Portland or Boston and to New York a few hours on. The other way, to Montreal. To a city more or less like any other, with restaurants and offices and tiny apartments housing people who dream of escaping to places like this one he's found. People he's hoping will move into the houses he's going to build, who are deep enough in their own dreams that a sagging economy and an uncertain era aren't enough to deter them, who put away money to buy these homes years ago, locked it in for the purpose as he did with the money to build them. People whose most secret dreams are too big to fail.

Speculators and risky borrowers aren't his demographic. That's not who these houses are for, though they've been kind to him in the past—he built the houses he was asked to build, for whoever could pay or get someone else to, and all that money he made is now paying for this, for these houses he'll build for deep-dreamers.

"Now?" his business partner asked, months ago, when Martin said this project would move ahead, never mind the downturn. It's a bet on the future, not the present, Martin explained. These would be houses for people who only look forward. And the money was his own, not their partnership's, so the risk would be his alone, too.

"But why not wait?" his partner asked the next time they talked on the phone, and again over drinks one of the rare times they spoke face-to-face. And again Martin told him he'd already waited and now was moving ahead.

And so here he is, moving but barely away from the trailer when a booming voice calls, "G'morning, Marty!" There's a house across the road from the construction site, a house that began life as two rooms, up and down, but over time and across generations grew rambling additions: new bedrooms and gray shingles and indoor plumbing, a sugar shack and a mudroom and a covered porch off the front. On that porch sits Gil Rose, the only neighbor Martin has for the moment, in the folding lawn chair that seems to be his permanent perch. He was sitting there when Martin returned to his trailer in the small hours of morning, and doesn't look to have left the spot since. He's still wearing the same dark green work pants and white T-shirt, his face red as always despite the shade of an orange hunting cap that may well be affixed to his head. The beer cans the two men drained together last night still litter the porch and the brown yard around it, spilling toward the driveway where Martin's own black sedan sits beside Gil's mammoth, multihued pickup. It's an arrangement they reached after a few days of rain left Martin's car stuck in the mud, its city-sleek shape too close to the ground to roll free without a tow from Gil's truck. Empty chairs cluster in various states of collapse, and Gil reaches out to pull one of the less ramshackle ones close to his own. He holds aloft a battered steel jug and says, "Come on up. I got coffee."

Martin takes a few steps across the cracked, cratered asphalt between them but stops at the dashed line in the center. "That's all right. I thought I'd take a walk this morning. To see some of the woods."

"Woods won't go anywhere. It's Sunday. I'll cook us some eggs."

Martin advances to the foot of Gil's stairs. "I need the exercise. I haven't done any hiking since I got here."

"Gave up exercise when I retired. Can't blame you, though. Mild day like this, I would've been in the woods before dawn, a few years ago." Gil takes a drag on his cigarette then coughs through a closed mouth so the glowing ember dips toward his chin. "Course, I would've been paid for it instead of tramping around for free. This late in the summer, weekend warriors are desperate to shoot something before their vacations run out." Smoke unwinds from Gil's rosaceous nose, and he smiles. "Preferably something big."

Martin slides his palms up and down either side of his waterproof jacket, and notices a hole worn through one sleeve where, he supposes, it rides over the metal band of his watch. "I, uh, I should start walking before it gets hot."

Gil squints at the hazy sky as if his eyes are following something. "Won't get hot today." He grips the chair meant for Martin and pushes it toward the stairs. "We'll get the grill going and make a day of it. You breaking ground over there tomorrow?"

It takes Martin a second to grasp the new thread of conversation before he nods.

"Well. You'll have those houses of yours up in no time."

"I'm hoping to get people moved in after school ends next spring. Onto the first few lots, at least."

"Be nice, kids running around." Gil takes a mouthful of coffee from the jug. "You oughta keep one of those houses yourself, Marty."

"Maybe," Martin mumbles. He leans his weight away from the porch, away from his neighbor, but doesn't take a whole step. He tries to remember the whole night behind him, how much he drank and if he told Gil of his plans to settle in town. To move into one of the houses. All through the planning stages of this development he imagined himself walking from room to room, his mind lifting each house from the paper into three dimensions as he tried to decide which of them would someday be his. But he's sure he hasn't said so to Gil or to anyone else.

"What you oughta do," Gil says, shaking his cigarette in Martin's direction, "is call up that Evans girl you got working for you. Spend the day with her. Both of you need it."

"Alison? She's my foreman. Forewoman. She works for me."

"And that could work for you too, huh?" Gil laughs so hard at his own joke it hunches him over, coughing into his fist. He's hoarse when he says, "That one's a catch. Give her a call."

Martin slides up the torn sleeve of his jacket to look at his wrist before remembering the rule he set for himself about not wearing a watch on Sunday. "I'd better get started if I'm going to hike."

"Bet she'd go. Bring her son along, too. Be good for you. Good for all three of you."

Martin's face gets hot. First the lucky guess about his desire to move into one of the houses, and now Gil is urging him toward Alison, too. Either he's easily read, or he told his neighbor more than he meant to and more than he remembers. Lately he's been drinking more beer than his body is used to, and—at Gil's insistence—more whiskey than he's had in his whole life until now. The hangovers have been slowing him down in the morning and he suspects he's putting on weight. But it's part of the project, part of getting these houses raised: Gil's a loud voice in town, he's the only neighbor the houses will have, and apart from all of that, Martin genuinely likes the old hunter. He's never known someone even remotely like Gil before.

"I think I'll go alone today," Martin says as if this will be an exception.

"No good to spend so much time by yourself, Marty." Gil scratches his head through his hat then adds, "Be careful, though."

"Of what?"

Gil pops the cap off his head, and plays with the band of plastic snaps at the back. "Well. End of summer, animals can get a bit strange."

"Strange how?"

Gil's face tightens and he says, "Ah, I'm just talking." He slides the hat over his thin white hair and settles it back into place. "It's nothing. Elmer Tully's tellin' folks he saw a mountain lion up at his farm, but, hell, you've met Elmer."

Martin nods and recalls the night last week when, as he and Gil talked and drank their beers on the porch, a ropy old man—no older than Gil, but much worse for wear—wound his way down the road like string on a breeze. An unlabeled brown bottle dangled at the end of his arm. Gil called out, and waved, but the man moved by without looking up and as he passed Martin overheard a stream of incoherent muttering. Gil said it was only Elmer out for a walk.

"There are mountain lions around here?" Martin asks.

"Not for a long time. Elmer sees things when he's drinkin'. Still. You be careful." Gil lights another cigarette and slurps from the jug. Martin waits for more explanation, but at last the lingering dream in his legs makes him antsy and he says goodbye to Gil before crossing the road toward the woods.

Last night, Gil told him how important it was to keep hunting, to keep the forest in check. It struck Martin as paranoia or cabin fever, maybe a townie playing it up for a city slicker new to the woods, and he assumes this new warning is more of the same, the imagination of an old man who's lived alone on the edge of the woods for too long.

Still, he can't complain about his new neighbor. When Martin first came to inspect the site, he spotted the single house across the road looking as if it had been there forever, part of the landscape almost, and he anticipated a long, expensive struggle to get his development built. He expected the old-timer to hold out until the price became painful, and to recoup his loss by building additional houses on that side of the street. But before he'd had a chance to approach him, Martin was shocked in a town meeting as Gil spoke up in favor of the construction proposal and told the selectmen he'd be glad to have neighbors. That as long as there would still be room for him to go hunting—only sometimes, because he's retired, he reminded the crowd, drawing laughs all over the room—then he wouldn't mind the new houses. And once Gil had spoken, opposition dried up and the permits came through. The town could use some new revenue, it was argued—a bigger tax base was good for them all, so long as they didn't get pressured for sidewalks and services that might have a place in the city but never out here.

Martin has imagined, already, what his buyers will say about the sound of Gil's guns in the woods near their homes. For most of them this forest will be an overgrown city park—a safe space to send their children to play. They'll hang salt licks in their yards and will watch from the windows as deer approach for a taste. They will shoot them with smartphones rather than rifles or bows. He hopes Gil has thought through what the number of houses, and the types of people most likely to buy them, could mean for town politics. That it won't erupt into big problems later. Those sidewalks are practically paving themselves even now, and the streetlights sure to be demanded in time may as well sprout from the ground.

These changes are always a trade-off. If enough trees are cleared, your kind make hunting illegal because the shots come too close to your homes, but if too much of the forest comes down those of us living in it might as well have been shot anyway. It isn't much of a choice.

It's not that I'm against hunting. I survive on it myself. But there are no tools to keep my hands—or paws—clean, and I don't have any walls to mount trophies on. There's no one to tell me I can kill this but not that, to draw lines too fine to be seen. Eat or be eaten is a nice theory, but it would be easier to swallow if the balance were between tooth and claw rather than bullet and bone. Some of the shapes I've worn at one time or another were slain by your bullets while I was in them, and though it didn't kill me, the experience isn't one I recommend.

Still, there are advantages to wearing a body that takes you along when it dies. There are times I wish I could walk out of this forest and there have been times I tried, but I always end up where I began. There can't be much I've missed in the world, there can't be much that hasn't passed through these woods at one time or another, but I get curious from time to time. And the more men like Martin clear this ground for their homes and the homes of others like them, the more often I find myself on the edge of the forest when I'm standing in places once at its heart. I've been through this before, the forest creeping back and forth at its edges. It's the history of this place, that's this land's nature, but it happens so much faster these days and there's no time to adjust. There's no time to reshape our lives—and never mind our stories—before the next changes come. There may not be enough forest left for me to stay here much longer, whether I want to or not.

I've watched your power lines stretch down mountainsides and carve treeless gullies through forests. First single wires, then three and four side by side, then those skeleton pylons veined with black cables that hum and crackle so loudly I can't hear the world where they run overhead. We learned to avoid them, to plan our routes—when we could—to cross under those wires as rarely as possible, then the air filled with a hum that doesn't need wires and we hear it wherever we are, filling the forest the way only dreams did when your signals still needed to follow straight lines and avoidable wires. It's hard not to wonder what's at the other end of those wires, and it's harder now not to ask where those signals come from. They've made the world seem so much bigger, even as the forest tightens around us.

2

A T THE EDGE OF THE FOREST, MARTIN SPIES A LONG OR-
ange body slipping through shaggy green grass. It's the first fox
of his life so he gasps, and the animal stops short at the sound
and turns yellow eyes toward the man. Martin takes a step forward
then waits a few seconds before taking another, but the fox—perhaps late
heading home after a night spent in town, running riot in trash cans and
amongst the buffets left beneath picnic tables—bolts for the scrub and
Martin watches a white brush of tail vanish into the woods.

The rain has increased from soft mist into hard, stinging drops, but the
change has been gradual and he only notices now that he's still for a moment. He wants to follow the fox; it's a strange urge, hardly conscious, the
way a tongue needs to test a loose tooth, and before he thinks about what
he's doing his feet carry him into the woods. The wet mud of the building
site gives way to the crackle of leaves, and cleared ground is overtaken
by trees. The forest thickens around him as smoothly as waves swallow
shores and glaciers retreat to leave valleys behind, and he pauses just once,
to crouch when a glistening white shard of china catches his eye in the
mud. It's part of a plate, not enough to make out the whole pattern but
there's a gilded rim and a design of bell-shaped pink blossoms—they're
twinflowers, but he doesn't know that—and he can make out only the
opening "1" of the date on the back. 19? 18? These fragments look old, but
they've been in the ground, scoured by stones and soil for who knows how
long. They could be ancient or they could have fallen at a picnic in this forest last week, for all Martin knows. So after inspecting them for a moment
he rises out of his crouch and hurries in the direction he thinks the fox
went, though now the animal is out of his sight.

The sticky heat and muffled sound remind him of lying in bed when
he was eight years old and living in one of many cramped apartments he
shared with his mother. He listened to adult voices growing louder in the
next room as she fought with the man they were living with then—the

one he remembers as only a walrus mustache—and Martin knew that in the morning they would move somewhere else the way they always did after that kind of fight. Despite the dead, city heat in his room, he pulled the bedclothes up over his head until the voices were almost drowned out. Soon he was dripping with sweat so he peeled off his pajamas and pushed them out of the bed, and then pulled the rattling box fan from the window into the tent of his blankets and sheets. Naked and clammy in that mechanical breeze, he sang to himself through the blades of the fan and pretended he was a musical robot instead of a boy beneath a pile of blankets.

Eventually he fell asleep, and when he woke up the fan was back in the window and his mother had already packed his few things. His small suitcase of clothes stood on the floor with his baseball glove perched upon it. The incomplete series of wilderness adventure books one of his mother's earlier boyfriends had bought him at a flea market—the one with the green van, perhaps, or the one who got great baseball tickets?—were stacked to one side of the bag. The rising dough scent of his mother hung in the room like an echo and Martin couldn't tell how long ago she'd been there.

Now sweat collects in his armpits as he picks his way through dense trees, and without stopping, without breaking the motion of walking, Martin peels off his jacket and ties its sleeves at his waist. A cool breeze wraps itself around his body and he is suddenly cold, shivering and prickled with gooseflesh. He smells what he thinks is himself before placing it as part of the forest, the rich, rotten smell of wet dirt and crushed leaves.

He thought the clearing back at his trailer was quiet, but the woods are quieter still despite the crunch of his steps. He listens for rain on the canopy but it isn't there, and the absence of birdsong is audible—a cliché, a bit of nonsense, but a description no less true for that.

He's driven on by a restless desire in his legs and an impulse to follow. Never mind that the fox has slipped out of sight, some mysterious certainty of the creature's path pulls him behind it. Martin walks through what little remains of the morning, past a rusted old car so deep and so long in the forest a tree has grown up through its hood and pushed the engine apart. Fallen brown leaves lay all over what remains of the car, about the same shade as its rust. Years of wind and weather have piled dirt and branches against its doors, filled its wheel wells with mud and debris and—though Martin can't see all of this—a crowded nest of squirrels in the trunk and a flattened patch of ground on the far side of the car where a deer bedded down for the night to get out of the wind. The machine has become so much a part of the forest he has to slow down and look twice to be sure it is hiding in there at all.

He rests against a downed log, blanketed with bright green moss and half-rotted. On its side it is nearly as high as his waist, and younger trees have taken root in its surface, a row of them extending the length of the trunk. Mushrooms and ferns crowd its shadows and the moist, dark soil made rich as the tree comes apart, and though Martin can't see them, not yet, beetles scurry and worms curve under the log, in the earth—in the dark, loamy world this fallen tree brings to life. A nurse log, I've heard your kind call these, but out here in the woods we just call them lives. New lives emerging where old ones are lost, a space cut in the canopy so young trees might grow toward the sky—layers upon layers, time upon time.

Martin walks into the long afternoon until at last he reaches a crumbling wall of gray stones rising out of the brush. The wall becomes better preserved the longer he walks beside it, as if being raised while he watches. Near the top of a hill it seems to be whole, its stones woven tightly and not torn asunder—as other walls Martin's spotted have been—by tree roots pushed under and through over the long course of years.

Then it ends against the foundation of a burnt house, two feet of blackened stone half-buried in leaves. Nothing remains of the timbers the foundation must have at one time supported. There's a gap in the wall that was once a door, and Martin steps through to the single large room of the house. At one end a hearth stretches from corner to corner with a broad, soot-darkened fireplace in its center. A cast-iron arm still hangs on a hinge, withered by years of rust, a scarred kettle dangling from its hooked end. It strikes him as strange that the kettle and arm should still be here at all rather than rusted away into nothing, but Martin doesn't know much—nothing, really—about how quickly decay comes in the forest, and he knows little of rust, so he assumes the metal knows what it's doing. He's a man who puts buildings up and he's never paid very much mind to how they come down.

Exhausted once he stops moving, he first leans against the stones of the foundation then sinks to the thick carpet of leaves piled inside its walls. Shivering, he unties the jacket from his waist and pulls it on over his head. As he catches his breath, he wishes he'd taken a bottle or two of water from the plastic-wrapped case back in his trailer. A lump of thirst clogs his throat and swallowing makes it larger.

It's dim in the shell of the house, with the thick shade of trees overhead. Martin wishes he'd brought his phone, or worn his watch, and had some way of knowing what time it is; even if he knew how to read the hour from the sun, it wouldn't be much help out here in the trees. He walked for hours, but it only feels like a long time now that he's stopped. The day passed in a blur of rising and falling, valleys and hills, back and forth strokes of fox tail—when he could spot it—decisive as the hand of a clock, and finally this abandoned stone house. His calves quiver with cramps and he raises filthy pant legs to knead the sore muscles beneath. He has no idea where he is, either in relation to his trailer or to the town, and for a second he feels as if he's been led, as if something—the fox?—wanted to show him this house and drove his legs forward as metal is urged onto a magnet, but the idea evaporates quickly, replaced by the feeling he's foolish.

Still, there is something familiar; the ruin resonates. Its calm isolation echoes the house Martin imagines when he pictures the home he might have. This quiet is what he looks for when he paces through empty houses before their owners move in, listening to floorboards he's the only one walking, inhaling the sterile smell of a never-used shower. He thinks of empty houses as souls awaiting their birth, and life lingers in this burnt-out shell long after its walls came down. It still feels like occupied space.

One of his mother's boyfriends—the one with the dog—had three bedrooms and several acres and they stayed with him for a few months. It's the only actual house Martin has ever lived in, and the first night he lay awake feeling thin as a ghost, behind walls so thick he couldn't hear the rest of the rooms. The night was so dark on the other side of his window he waited for it to burst through the glass and swallow him whole.

23

Later he grew used to the silence, when his mother and her boyfriend went away for a week and left him alone with the dog, a Finnish Spitz named Aino. Sitting on the front steps of the house with Aino beside him, her spiral tail flicking the air as she napped, Martin knew there was traffic a mile away but he couldn't hear cars or see dust rising over the road. He spoke to the dog a few times that first day, but by the time his mother returned Martin marveled at how quiet he had become and how far time could stretch in a comfortable place. When that boyfriend was gone, after Martin's mother had steered the two of them away from his house and into their next short-term home, it was Aino he missed, and these three decades later he's promised himself that once he moves in, once one of these new homes is his, a dog will move into it, too.

The bones of this house bring him back to that limitless week, to having a house to himself and not trying to fill the whole space. He's built lofts that swallowed three stories of high-rise buildings, and mansions that could swallow those lofts. He began by carrying boards and sacks of cement when he was in high school, then moved up to hammering nails and framing walls. In time he came to handle the materials and tools less often himself—it wasn't long, really, before his employers recognized his talents for construction were in paper rather than wood, that his aptitude wasn't with saw blades but schemes—and spent his time arranging for larger and larger spaces to be walled in. Architects delivered the first two dimensions, the shapes and the lines of a house, then it was left up to Martin to turn those lines into boxes large enough to contain the lives that would happen inside.

Until this development here in the woods, he spent most of his time in his car, on the phone, driving from one job to another to make sure the people he paid to hang sheetrock and plaster ceilings were doing things how he wanted them done. Long before giving up an apartment so high in the city he couldn't hear any sound from below, in favor of his trailer amongst the trees, he raised a towering beach house for a man who lived all alone. Before the owner moved in Martin paced through the house with all its wide windows closed but the sound of the surf outside filling the halls. As he followed his echo across each hollow story, his heart sank into his legs and dragged behind him across the waxed floors. He'd made something dead, and it would stay dead no matter how many antiques and empty bedrooms it held. However grand the parties it hosted and rare the wine. He decided to build something different, more than a shell for one lonely soul; he decided to build a whole neighborhood and to stay long enough to see someone move in, to see himself become part of the lives to be lived in the houses he'd made.

He told his partner about the houses he wanted to build in these woods and was bombarded with the practical questions that he himself, for once, wasn't willing to ask. He and his partner only started working together because it made sense, not because they were friends or even knew each other away from the shared job sites they'd been on for years. Even now, five years later, they're still partners on the letterhead only—Martin knows his partner is married but has never met the man's wife; the partner knows Martin has never been married but not whether he wants to be. So what Martin does with his money, whether he risks all he has on a cluster of houses in some far away town without even a mall or decent restaurant to its name, what business is that of his business partner?

Martin announced he'd be living on-site for the duration of his pet project, and his partner asked why he couldn't stay in the city, rely on a foreman the way they usually do and make the occasional visit. But Martin said no, not this time, he would come to the woods. He would see this project from start to finish. He didn't mention his need to keep these houses from becoming more square feet of death, and his partner agreed to oversee the rest of their projects as long as Martin kept in touch on the phone and came to the office when there was something to sign. Their machines make the distance much shorter, or should, but Martin's phone has been unreliable on its best days. This forest needs a new cell tower, by Martin's measure, the way it needed stone walls before. And a bigger, better power grid to handle all those new houses and their new machines, because already the lights flicker in his trailer and he knows there are blackouts at night because the clock on his microwave is so often timeless and flashing when he wakes up.

On the ground inside the foundation, now that he isn't moving, Martin's hunger becomes so acidic it makes him feel sick and he fights the twitch in his throat that always comes before he throws up. With his back against the cold stones, he closes his eyes and breathes deeply, willing his stomach down.

Wind rushes through trees overhead. Blood thunders behind his ears. As he waits for his legs to stop aching enough to start walking, he tries to imagine a path that will lead him out of the woods but it's hard to retrace a route he wasn't paying attention to the first time. After a few minutes his spent body drifts into sleep.

There's a twitch in his knee and he jerks his eyes open, but the world doesn't get any lighter. He rubs his tongue against the roof of his mouth to scrape off the sour taste of sleep. It's so dark he can't see his own hand in front of his face, an expression he has, until now, always assumed hyperbolic. His legs aren't as sore as they were, or they're still asleep, and his stomach has given up thoughts of eating and seems satisfied to gnaw on itself. After waiting a few seconds for his eyes to adjust he accepts that they won't, that while he slept in this hollowed-out house night has fallen around him.

He wasn't afraid when he was simply lost, but waking in the dark brings his childhood fear rushing back and he curls his body against itself. Every leaf brushed by wind, each acorn or pine cone falling beyond the low walls, is some horrible beast closing in; each second he waits in the dark brings whatever moves through the woods closer to where he sits exposed. He pictures the forest floor seething with snakes and with rats, and the larger bodies of panthers and foxes out there somewhere, too. As much as his mind assures him that these visions are drawn more from movies than the truth of this place, the fear won't be shaken off.

And he isn't entirely wrong, because here we are.

Wind hisses and dips into the foundation. Where his clothes remain damp Martin shivers, and he zips the jacket up to his neck. Something is walking on the other side of the wall. Something shuffles through crackling scrub and creeps closer to where he huddles. It walks a slow circle around the stone square, and Martin follows the path with his ears. The footsteps are light but steady, punctuated with the occasional snuffle or snort, and he wonders if the animal knows he is there. He listens as it comes closer to where he thinks the door is.

Wherever he sleeps, in hotels and apartments and even the trailer he occupies now, Martin pushes his bed as tightly into a corner as he can wedge it. The more sides on which he's protected by walls, the more soundly he sleeps. Waking up with no roof overhead and only the stumps of lost walls at his sides has sent him into a panic that feels both familiar and long forgotten. It's primal, an instinct, and he feels his way along the foundation until he finds the higher stones of the hearth. At last his forehead strikes the rusty remains of the kettle on its hook with a loud, rolling clang. The pain in his head isn't as bad as the silence that follows the sound—everything in the forest has stopped what it's doing, everything knows just where he is now. With his fingers on the top edge of the opening so he won't bump his head again, Martin slides backward into the mouth of the fireplace. It's high enough for him to crouch with his legs pulled to his chest and his forehead bent close to his knees. He's still exposed to the forest, but only in one direction.

It's warmer out of the wind, but not by much. He hunches with his eyes open but there's nothing to see: no fireflies, no fire, no yellow, glistening eyes. He strains his ears for the footsteps, but either the creature was chased off by the sound of the kettle or his own breathing echoes so loudly in the hearth that he can't hear the animal moving.

Home from college once, on a rare visit, Martin finally asked his mother why they had moved so many times. "I wanted to find a place that felt right," she told him. They were in the cramped kitchen of her apartment—hers alone, for the first time since he had been born—and though there was hardly room for the two of them to work together they were rolling out dough for some foreign pastry she'd learned to make from a man who had come and gone without meeting her son. As she answered his question, Martin's mother looked up from her rolling pin, and he noticed that flour had settled into the creases and lines of her face. It made her look so much older than she actually was, every wrinkle made bright, and the white streaks in her hair looked as if they'd been floured, too.

He asked, as he had before with other words, "Did it feel like the right

27

place with my father?" His mother dusted her hands over the dough, rubbing one against the other so a white cloud rose then drifted down, and said she needed to look at the recipe to find out what to do next.

But don't mistake all that for Martin's story. It's where he comes from but not what he's worth. It's easy to fall into the trap of thinking origins are more important than outcomes, that a beginning determines the lifetime ahead, but I've lived long enough to know that how a life starts only matters so long as it does; it's the ending you need to aim for. Don't miss out on a meal for today while you're remembering what you once ate. No mouse was ever spared by an owl because it grew up in an unhappy hole.

He watches the dark before the fireplace until his eyelids grow heavy, and though the wind doesn't find him at the back of the hearth it swells inside the foundation as the sea swells in a shell, and the sound returns him to sleep despite anxious fears. The forest rustles and stirs with comings and goings on four legs and six legs and eight, and in the treetops sleeping birds twitter as bats squeak and wheel, aloft and prowling for insects. An opossum inches along a branch overhead, its eyes wide and bright, then scuttles away on silent feet.

There's no reason for us to wait here while he sleeps, so let's weave our way through the woods to his trailer where the door still stands open. It isn't as far away as he thinks; if he only knew how close he is to his home, that his wandering has traced a circular path almost back to where he began, then he might get there before us and claim the bed for himself. He could have followed the wall—lines so deliberately drawn always lead somewhere, whether it's stone walls or wires or roads. They aren't as meandering as stories and echoes—or dreams—shaped and reshaped and veering in all directions. Passed from teller to teller and place to place, as arbitrary as those new humming waves in these woods or the seeds that cling to fur and sock alike to plant themselves in new fields.

Martin could follow that wall, but in his mind he's lost in the forest so his body believes. Which is all the better for us—we may be wearing these nocturnal shapes, but we've been following Martin all day and I suspect you're as tired as that borrowed body. So we'll creep to his trailer, climb into his bed, and make his life our own for a while.

28

3

THE SQUARE SHOULDERS OF GIL'S BLACK-AND-WHITE CHECK-ered jacket plow through scrub pines near the top of a mountain. The hunter charges ahead without ducking low branches, without shoving saplings aside. It's as if he expects the forest to step out of his way and the forest seems to oblige. Martin hurries behind, dodging those branches as they whip back into place from Gil's passing. Again and again his clothes snare on brambles and twigs and he has to stop, pluck them free, and rush to catch up.

It's a dream, of course it's a dream, and what else would it be? Dreams bring you closer to the world the rest of us live in than anything else, and in this dream Gil has three rifles slung on his back and a fourth in hand at his side. The arsenal seems excessive to Martin, but as if Gil is reading his thoughts he calls back, "Different calibers, Marty. Never know what you'll run into or what size hole it'll need."

"What are we hunting for?"

"You tell me. It's your dream." Gil laughs, and adjusts the cap on his head, a fixture in waking life and dreams, too. There are smudged finger-prints all over the brim where he's gripped it over the years, as there are on the real thing.

A hawk circles above them without moving its wings, and Martin tries to watch as he walks. With his eyes on the bird, he stumbles over a half-buried point of dark granite.

"Look where you're going there, Marty," Gil scolds without turn-ing around.

Martin apologizes though he's not sure he needs to, then walks with his eyes on the trail for a mile or so. But when he looks up again there are more hawks, seven or eight of them now, hard to count as their paths cross and re-cross, wheeling in spirals high overhead.

"Have you noticed those hawks, Gil?" he asks.

"Don't mind 'em. They're after smaller meals than you."

Each time Martin squints up at the silver haze of the sky, the group of hawks—Flock? he tries to remember, or is it a murder, like crows?—has swung lower, and now he can see individual feathers in the dense mail of their chests. "They're flying pretty low," he says, but gets no reply.

Gil steams forward as the scrub thickens on either side of the trail. The forest still avoids him even as more and more branches strike Martin's chest, arms, and face. The back of Gil's neck is creased as an old leather boot and as wide as the head it supports.

Martin hurries, trying not to look up, trying to keep up with Gil, and all of a sudden there's a stabbing pain in his foot.

"Ow!" he hollers. "Shit!" Gil doesn't turn. For some reason Martin is barefoot, the boots and socks he's sure he was wearing a few steps ago gone, and a long, crimson thorn has punctured his sole. Cursing, he leans against the trunk of a tree. He plucks out the thorn and a bead of blood blooms. He wants to rest, to let the cut scab, but already he's losing sight of Gil out ahead so he walks, wincing with each tentative step.

It all seems familiar, he thinks, like he's been here before, though Martin isn't quite sure what "here" means. It might be the woods, or the moment, or perhaps the dream because it, too, is familiar—tidier than his usual dreams, too tightly tied to his life, because I've tied it there.

"Probably not," answers Gil, listening in again on Martin's head. Suddenly the checkered shoulders are still and Gil swings the gun up from his hip to level it at something ahead. The three barrels still slung on his back rattle together with the inertia of stopping.

"What is it?" Martin asks, stepping close behind his neighbor, who grunts, or maybe growls, in reply. Martin looks up the trail but doesn't see anything. Gil's hands are steady, liver-spotted stone on the gun.

Then a loud crack echoes out of the woods and movement catches Martin's eye on his left. He turns toward the trees and shouts, "Gil, over there!"

The green curtain shakes as a tall, dark shape passes behind thin trunks. Gil sets the rifle butt against his shoulder and squints along the barrel into the woods as Martin holds his breath, waiting.

"Scratch," Gil says, without looking away from the gun.

"Scratch what?"

The hunter hisses at him to be quiet.

There's another loud crack in the shadows, then a long shaft of pine with needles and branches still hanging from it hurtles through the air toward the men. Gil roars and squeezes a round off at nothing before the trunk crashes into his chest and knocks him down.

"Gil!" Martin shouts, but the other man doesn't answer. He's pinned beneath the log and isn't moving. His eyes are closed and the gun has been knocked from his hands. The other three weapons are trapped by the trunk and his body.

Martin turns toward the trees, not sure what to do, and the figure he saw in the shadows comes charging out of the woods. He barely sees the bottle-green eyes and the curve of white teeth before he pivots and runs up the trail the way he and Gil came. Each step on rough ground slashes his feet, but Martin runs as fast as he can without looking back.

The hawks are circling so low now that when they pass overhead the air displaced by their wings is as loud as a river.

A cramp burns in his side but he runs on, afraid the heat on his back is his pursuer's breath. He's sure the snarl behind him is getting louder the longer he runs, but he doesn't hear the thundering steps he expects there to be if he is being chased.

Then he trips on a tree root curving up from the ground, and his face and his chest slam hard against the packed earth of the trail. A strong hand—a strong paw—grips his arm and slings his body over, and Martin is face to face with a bear. Its lips are peeled back from pink gums, and its tongue squirms in the enormous dark space of its mouth as it roars. A sticky drop of saliva plops between Martin's eyes and he squeezes them closed, turning his head and puckering his face as he waits to be killed.

The bear isn't as big as he would have expected.

Then pain jerks him awake and he's stretched on his back in the burnt-out foundation. He's been dragged feet-first from his fireplace bed by a bear, a real bear, and now it rises to its full height and crashes down hard with its paws on his chest.

Martin lets out a sound that would be a yell if he could gather enough air to make one. His attempt to draw breath expands his chest enough to increase the pressure and weight of the paws.

The bear leans across his body so its hot belly swings against his thighs. The pressure on his ribs is immense, and pushes the last gasps from his lungs. His hands spring to his defense without being asked, wrapping themselves as far as they can around the bear's legs above each of the paws, wrenches too small for the job. He pushes and pulls, struggling to move the thick legs, but they will not be budged. The pressure on his chest doesn't increase but it doesn't lighten up, either, and Martin wheezes and rasps, his struggle for breath made all the worse by his panic.

He feels the bear's gaze on his face along with its hot breath, but he fights the urge to look. Some old memory, from a book he read as a child or some rerun he saw on TV, insists that the worst thing to do in a situation like this is to look a bear in the eyes. As if a situation like this happens often enough for there to be a wealth of advice.

He feels five sharp points of pain, and when he lowers his eyes without moving his head he sees that the claws of one paw have punctured the jacket, the T-shirt, his skin. The details of the holes are strangely acute, each frayed thread on his jacket individual and distinct and each curved claw glazed with its own unique pattern of cracks and chips. The other paw still presses his ribs.

Martin studies the claws for a long time, a moment so slow he starts to think he has already died and his spirit has drifted away from his body, that he's watching all this from somewhere beyond himself. His head swims and he becomes dizzy despite lying flat on the ground. The treetops bordering his field of vision sway like the waves of a rough, green sea he is sinking under.

Then the bear grunts, and without increasing the weight on Martin's chest it leans closer, filling his eyes with its body. Black fur streaked with copper surrounds him, and the bear smells of old meat and wet dog. Its cold black nose sniffs a circle around his head. He tries to lie still but can't stop his body from shaking. The bear snorts beside his face and the air is so hot he feels it deep in his ear.

This is it, Martin thinks. This is the way I die.

No sooner does the thought cross his mind than the bear moves, draws its paws away from his body in a swift, sweeping motion that tears five bloody tracks through two layers of cloth and the skin underneath.

Now he does scream, loudly and at a high pitch. He sustains the harsh note until the bear rears up then slams a forefoot to the dirt beside each of his ears, shaking the scream from his throat. The back of his head bounces against the ground with the force of the impact.

The bear turns murky eyes onto Martin's blue ones, and that hot breath makes him gag. He tries to stop his body from shaking, afraid it makes him look appetizing the way a lively fly lures a fish. He tries to look away from that wild gaze, the orange and yellow and brown of a fire, but the flame holds his eyes.

Then at last the bear's body relaxes and the creature steps forward. It slides across Martin's body so its hot, heavy fat slaps his face as it passes. The chaff and dust of dirty fur fill his nose, and he fights back a strong urge to sneeze. When the whole broad, black body has passed over his face, the bright light of morning rushes into his eyes and the sneeze bursts out before he can stop it.

The bear rises onto hind legs and climbs over the wall of the house. There's a thud from outside the foundation, then Martin listens as his attacker lumbers away. He hears the thumps of the animal's first few steps before the forest falls quiet again and there is only the pounding of his own pulse.

Then birdsong sneaks back in, leaves rustle, trunks creak and boughs crack. The world carries on as if none of that happened. As if it was no more than a dream or a story.

The cuts in his chest sting and burn. His head pounds. His peripheral vision is laced with black worms, from dehydration, or the rush of breath back into his vacant lungs, or a combination of both. Martin lies on the ground with his eyes closed, fighting to suppress his sick stomach, then gives up and rolls onto his side to spill a yellow stew on the ground. Again and again he retches, each spasm lighting a fire on his chest, and his body goes on heaving after nothing more emerges from his empty gut.

For a long time he lies still on his side, upright as the stone walls around him. The chills that follow vomiting come quickly as his bloodless face tingles and stings. Cool ground-level air makes his eyes water. When the retching subsides, his nostrils clog, and they whistle as he breathes through them.

He waits in resigned expectation for the bear to return. Having convinced himself he was seconds away from his death, that the beast's intent was to kill him, the heavy mantle of that resignation is hard to shake off even after his attacker is gone, phantom pain from a lost limb. His chest aches from the torn skin on the surface all the way down to his heaving lungs. Gingerly, Martin feels his way up one side of his ribcage and down the other, as if he would know a broken bone when he found it. The pain stretches from top to bottom and side to side, but apart from the center-left of his chest where the claws broke the skin—where the pain is different, if no more intense—there isn't any one spot that hurts more or less than the rest. Under the circumstances, he takes that as a good sign.

The bear does not come back, and in time Martin's breathing returns to something near normal as the pain in his chest and back becomes familiar enough he can once again feel the more mundane aches of hunger and thirst. And a different kind of pain, too: the awareness that had he died here, had his body been left by the bear or dragged off to be eaten—if that's what bears do—it would have been a long time before anyone in the world outside these woods knew what had happened to him. A very long time. That gloomy thought buoys Martin up, in its way, and fills him with a desire to get to his feet and find a route out of the forest. To get himself back to his trailer and his unbuilt homes, where he will see and be seen by other people.

He hasn't any idea what time it is, or how long it will be until his employees arrive at the construction site to start work. He only knows it's early enough for the angle of sun to be low, curling between narrow trunks instead of raining down through the leaves, but late enough for light to have risen over the mountains to reach into these woods.

On shaky limbs, Martin lifts himself onto his hands and knees. The motion makes him keenly aware of the soreness his body has already begun taking for granted, his body's new normal for now, and he pauses in that position a long time before forcing himself to move on.

At last he rises and balances with one hand on the foundation wall. His stomach grumbles and growls, filling his mouth with rotten air, as hot and dry coming out as the bear's breath was going in. He steps through what once was a door and staggers into the woods, then turns in slow circles as he considers all the directions he has to choose from. Which way to walk, which way did he come, which way is it back to the road? He knows the rising sun is in the east, so the stone wall heads away to the south, but neither of those details is helpful because he's not sure where he is in relation to where he began.

He wishes for the straight lines of overhead wires, something he knew he could follow and where it could lead. He wishes he'd brought his phone with its online maps and GPS; even the robotic voice that reads him directions would be a comfort right now. But he knows the phone would be a useless black lump—he can't connect when he's in town, or on the wide open space of the building site at the edge of the woods, so he'd never get a signal out here.

Not the kind he's after, at least. Not the kind of signal that might make his phone work. The forest is full of the signals of stories and dreams, humming and buzzing and bouncing off trees, passed from one head to another, though never along the straight trajectories of power lines. They're a wireless mesh for a wireless world, and that's why they're becoming so tangled these days with your own buzz and hum, the dreams of a bear warped by and also warping a phone call about what? About dinner or money or nothing at all, when it pushes its way through the woods but doesn't get through. So Martin has taken to leaving his phone in the car, after years in which the device was rarely out of his pocket or hand, because all those other voices spilling out of the trees mean he has to drive around town until he finds a spot where his phone can connect.

His stomach turns over again. He's so hungry his knees actually shake, which he thought only happened in cartoons, so he pulls his leather belt tighter in hopes that other cartoon truth will hold, too. Then he walks, not beside the stone wall he followed to get here but toward the sun, stumbling along on what may or may not be a trail.

He walks with one hand up under his shirt, its palm spread over the gouges made by the bear's claws. Gently he tests the cuts with his fingers and they don't feel deep—they're painful, they're bleeding, but as much as he winces at the attempt he can't push a fingertip in very far. Already the blood seems to be slowing. The pain in his muscles and bones is far worse than the cuts. His chest is darkening purple, and even the ordinary expansion of each breath he draws strains against his sore ribs.

He steels himself for a long walk on an empty stomach and, even worse, without water, now that his tongue is too thick for his mouth.

How long will it be before anyone sets out to find him, or even realizes he's gone? The crew should arrive on the site around eight o'clock, and they might notice if he doesn't emerge from his trailer. But they might think he's off to the city on business if they don't spot his car parked across the street beside Gil's, or they might think he's working inside. The crew he's hired know what to do, they've got their orders and they've got a good leader in Alison to make sure it gets done, so there's no reason they'd need him this morning. Perhaps the trailer door he left open will invite someone to look; perhaps Alison will poke her head through with something to tell him and see he isn't there and that will be enough to draw her concern.

He can already tell the day will be hot. He's sweating first thing in the morning, still sticky from yesterday's walk, and gnats swarm the back of his neck. The mosquitoes go on biting in these first hours after sunrise, getting in their last nips before they retire for the day, and though he feels every jab, he's too tired to smack them away

Something Gil told him over beers on the porch floats up through the murk of his mind. Martin missed most of the story, because by this point in the evening his neighbor's insistence they match each other drink for drink had him hanging onto the sides of his chair. Gil had been talking about the war, *his* war, the way he has several times since Martin began spending long nights on the porch over drinks. It's embarrassing, but he doesn't know which war Gil was actually in; he must have missed that in the first story or else it was never revealed, and now it's too late to ask. The details always seem interchangeable from one place to another, Korea or Vietnam or even Europe, and without knowing how old his neighbor actually is, he can't even guess. There was a swamp in the story, and soldiers holding painfully still while black flies and mosquitoes and other insects nobody could name chewed their skin. He thinks they were waiting to spring an ambush, but isn't sure if that's what Gil actually said or if his memory is filling in blanks. Gil's point in telling the story hadn't been clear—was he trying to say something about being steadfast, refusing to bend despite bodily pain, or was it just that the world can be dangerous in miniature, too? So often Gil's war stories come so late at night, or else so deep in the very small hours of morning after a long night of drink, that something never quite comes across.

Martin has only been walking for a short time when he sees several thin, flat stones standing over the brush at the side of his makeshift trail. He draws closer, and discovers a small plateau, squared into a short drop-off on three sides but approachable up a shallow slope on the other. And he finds that those stones aren't just any stones but tombstones laid out in five rows. The stones nearest the slope are worn smooth, whatever names or dates they once held wiped away, but each following row seems slightly newer though no more legible than the first, except for the final row on which the words are at least visible where moss has grown into the etched shapes of the letters, whatever those letters might be.

On another morning, a morning on which he hadn't been attacked by a bear, he might stop and study these stones. He might spend more time thinking about how they've come to be here, deep in the forest—as far as he knows—and far from any road. He might make a connection between these grave markers, these generations of death and stories erased along with their names, and the abandoned home he discovered. He might ask how the oldest stones came to be at the front, and where the next generation of dead might have gone.

But today, on this morning, an overgrown cemetery lost in the woods is one more strange thing on a very strange day, and wonder is no match for pain, so Martin urges himself to keep walking in the direction he thinks will lead home.

Before long the canopy thins and the trees spread apart. The ground levels off and the trail becomes more apparent, then all at once he breaks through the edge of the forest and finds himself back on the site. It's the opposite end of the clearing from where he entered the woods, behind his trailer and close to the road. He still doesn't know the hour but is glad to see the trucks and tools lying idle the way he left them, glad there's no one to see him emerge in this state, stumbling toward the road. The black band of asphalt is several inches higher than the muddy ground beside it, as if pavement came as an afterthought to this part of the world and was only laid down a few hours ago.

All that walking to go in a circle—he might never have entered the forest at all, if not for the proof bleeding under what's left of his shirt. The wounds across his bruised chest have begun to scab with a crust that is sticky against his fingertips. Martin walks toward his car, toward his GPS-equipped phone already waiting in its dashboard mount, and he hopes it will find enough bandwidth to guide him to the nearest emergency room. He hopes because he doesn't yet realize the purest signal of his whole life has just been received, transmitting the first true story he's ever been told.

4

AS MARTIN STUMBLES TOWARD HIS CAR GIL CALLS FROM THE porch, "What's got you out and about so early?"

Martin looks up at his neighbor's wrinkled red face looming over the railing. He doesn't answer the greeting, too shocked at this first real proof he remains in the world of the living despite the attack, as if the remembered weight on his chest pins his tongue, too.

Martin wobbles on his feet and falls to his knees near the far edge of the road, and Gil rushes to wrap an arm around his shoulders and help him sit on the lowest of the porch's three steps. He squints at the torn fabric and dried blood on the younger man's chest and asks, "The hell happened to you?"

Martin stretches his legs across dry, brown grass and his body falls back onto the steps. He breathes, nothing else, for a long time.

"A bear," he answers at last. The word sounds absurd, meaningless— the idea he was attacked by a bear doesn't seem possible now that he's back among humans. It's as absurd as the notion that announcing the name of his attacker will describe what actually happened.

Gil raises an eyebrow. "A bear did this?" He pulls apart the torn flaps of the jacket, exposing the cuts, and exhales with a sharp whistle. "Christ, it was a bear. Where?"

Martin doesn't say more as Gil probes the cuts with rough, steady fingers, spreading the gashes open enough for them to start bleeding again, but slightly. "Not too deep," he says. "You're lucky. Bear could've killed you if he'd wanted to. But we'll have you patched up in no time."

Before Martin can ask where the hospital is, Gil has rushed into the house and left him staring at the plank ceiling over the porch, struggling to keep his eyes open. He hadn't been thinking about the cuts, overshadowed as they were by the bruises and aches, but now that they're open again they sting worse than before. Gil's ministrations have broken the first layers of scabbing, and with each rise and fall of Martin's chest the remaining crust pulls at fine hairs near the wounds.

Gil returns with a rusty red box marked with a white cross, a bowl of hot water, and bottle of supermarket-brand whiskey. Martin smells him coming before he appears, the burnt meat and cigarettes of an old man who has lived alone for a long time. He doesn't know if Gil has ever been married, if he has grown children in town or someplace else or if he has any family at all. All he knows is that this is the house Gil grew up in and he's alone in it now, rambling through its rooms and alcoves and barn by himself. He tries to imagine his neighbor, stubborn and strange as he is, sharing a space with anyone else, and he struggles to see it.

"Show me that scrape. Take your shirt off."

Martin sits up. "Shouldn't we go to the hospital?"

"No need. I've dressed worse than this in the woods. Besides, Marty, those cuts're ugly, not deep. They'll look better when we get 'em cleaned up."

Martin lifts his jacket and shirt together, but when he tries to drag them over his head he winces and groans from the pain in his shoulders and back. He has to let the other man pull them the rest of the way. When the bruises are uncovered Gil asks, "Hell, what'd he do, stand on you?"

"Pretty much." Martin tries to force a small laugh but the pain is too much.

"You look like a damn eggplant. Lemme check your ribs." Gil feels up one side of Martin's chest then down the other with firm but reassuring pressure. He seems to know what he's doing. After repeating the procedure on Martin's back, he says, "Nothing broken, you lucky bastard. Claws'd gone deeper you'd be in trouble. Wouldn't have made it back here, never mind a hospital. That bear had weighed more, he would've crushed your lungs. Or your heart. But he wasn't lookin' to kill you, so you'll be okay."

"I really think I need a doctor. What if it's infected?"

Gil steadies Martin's body with a tight grip on one shoulder as he peers at the wounds from close up. "You don't need a doctor."

"But . . ."

"Hey," Gil snaps, "how many bear attacks have you seen? How many claw wounds have you dressed? 'Cause I've seen a few and I'm saying you don't need to go anywhere."

Shocked by the sudden insistence, by the change in Gil's voice, Martin closes his eyes as damp, early air prickles his bare chest and arms. It feels colder on the exposed cuts than anywhere else, as if the wind is creeping inside his body through those crevasses, brushing against tender parts of himself that hide under his skin and away from the elements.

"Right. So let me take care of this."

Martin knows a hospital is where you go when you're injured, for car accidents and burns and attacks by a bear. He knows, though he's never made use of the knowledge in a life of good health and near misses. But he doesn't have the energy to argue right now and lying across the steps of Gil's porch is the most comfortable place he's ever been as far as he remembers right now, so he's easily dissuaded from getting up.

Gil unscrews the cap from the whiskey and holds out the bottle. "Drink."

"Not yet . . . maybe water?"

"Drink. It'll calm you down. Dull the pain." Gil presses the lip of the bottle against Martin's mouth until he gives in and takes a sip. The whiskey burns in his throat and empty stomach, and he thinks he'll throw up again.

"There. That wasn't so bad." Gil takes the whiskey back and draws a long drink himself. He wipes his mouth with the back of one hand and sets down the bottle, leaving it open. "I've seen fellas get bullets pulled out with nothing more than a drink, so it'll do for your scratches."

He slides drugstore glasses from a shirt pocket and fits them onto his red, swollen nose. A wad of grayed tape where the rubber pads should be balances them on the bridge. Gil leans close to Martin, his face almost touching the parallel cuts, and says, "Well."

He opens the first aid kit and pulls out a brown plastic bottle of strong-smelling soap, then cleans the cuts with a hot cloth. His scrubbing is so vigorous that pain flares across Martin's bruised body and he fights an urge to cry out. Gil washes and rinses the wounds several times before drying them at last with a second white towel. Then he fishes a creased metal tube of unlabeled ointment out of the box.

"You'll live," he says. "I've had worse in the kitchen."

Martin doesn't believe this, but the rasp of calloused fingertips over his skin is comforting in a strange way. His mind flashes to an afternoon spent with his mother's father when he was young, not long before his grandfather died. Martin had been in kindergarten, or it was earlier, maybe, but he remembers riding high on a shoulder as they walked down the street. The thin white hair on his grandfather's head was combed across the chapped, red scalp below. Gil has his grandfather's eyebrows, snowdrifts piled in wind.

"What happened?" Gil asks as he squeezes some ointment onto a cotton swab with a long wooden stem. "Where'd you run into a bear?"

"I don't . . . in the woods, there was an old house. A foundation. Somewhere that way." Martin waves his arm in the vague direction of where he emerged from the woods. He feels the strain of even that minor movement in every one of his ribs.

"The Pelletier homestead. Your land used to be theirs."

Martin winces as Gil digs the head of the swab into his chest.

"Hang in there. You want those cuts to be clean. What were you doing out there so early, anyway?"

Martin says he got lost on his walk and slept in the foundation, and Gil laughs. "I'll make a hunter of you yet—already tangling with bears and sleeping rough. And you call yourself a city boy."

Gil drops the swab on the porch and rattles his fingers in the first aid kit. "Saw your door open last night. Figured you were hot in that sardine can and wanted the breeze. Wondered why you didn't come over." His hand emerges with a thick roll of gauze bound by a red elastic, and a small pair of surgical scissors.

"Shouldn't I get stitches?" Martin asks as Gil unrolls the bandage.

"Never sew a claw wound. Traps the germs in the cut and you'll get an infection. You want to get some air in it. Anyway, I told you, they aren't deep." He spools gauze across the slashes on Martin's chest, then around his back and across them again.

"Why is that house in the woods, anyway?"

"Pelletiers had a farm there, long before my time. Used to be clear ground but the woods've grown back since they pulled out. Lots of folks gave up harvesting rocks for mill jobs back then. All those stone walls in the woods used to be around pastures. Folks talk about the woods getting smaller, but that's not the case here. It's been growing back since before I was born."

The cold steel of scissors against Martin's chest makes him twitch. Gil clamps a hand on his shoulder and tells him, "Hold still." Gauze sticks to the reopened wounds, and dark red lines with yellow edges well up through each white strip. Gil wraps until he's covered all five cuts and gone over them tightly a couple of times.

I remember the family Gil's talking about, the Pelletiers, and so many families the same—they came here and pulled pastures from under the forest, and laid their stone walls around them. Their pigs broke loose constantly, fattening themselves on acorns and beech same as the dogs of today's town gorge themselves on the birds that fall bloody and burnt beneath the high power lines. But those families, those settlers, were never quite settled. They were always talking about where they'd come from, Ireland and England and sometimes Quebec, or they talked about where they were going, where the ground might be softer, the soil more rich. Neither one sounded real to me, only the wishful thoughts of homesick farmers suspended between one dream and another. The dreams of an animal too long in hibernation.

"Wish I was surprised you met a bear so close to the road. They used to stay pretty deep in the woods. Used to know they aren't living in Yellowstone and nobody's going to feed them. Been showing more of themselves. Getting into trashcans downtown."

He tests the tension of the bandages with a finger before repacking his tools in the box. "Guess they've decided the Pelletier place has been abandoned long enough. It's part of the forest again. Bear's probably pissed you were sleeping in his house, Goldilocks. You ruined his morning."

"But the bear attacked *me*."

"What'd y'do, sneak up on him? Spook him?"

"No, nothing! I was sleeping in the fireplace, and it pulled me out. It jumped right on me."

"You sure that's how it happened?" Gil's eyes are tight, he's trying to get the story to focus. Martin nods.

"Damn." Gil stands, then pulls off his glasses and pinches the bridge of his nose so the bulbous tip glows an even rosier shade of red. "Damn," he says again.

Martin looks up with curious eyes, but remains seated on the edge of the porch. "What? Why does it matter?" He reaches for his ruined shirt but in such rough shape it's not worth putting on, so he pulls what's left of his jacket over bare skin. Raising his arms into the sleeves strains his wounds and his ribs, but he tries not to let it show on his face. The holes torn by the bear flap over his chest, revealing the blood-streaked gauze underneath.

"Well, if the bear attacked without being provoked, could be he's sick. Or felt threatened. Maybe you were too close to her cubs or . . . was it a male or a female?"

"I don't know. How do you tell?"

"Do I need to explain it? You really do need to spend more time with that Evans girl."

Martin looks away, his face warm. "Can you tell from the mouth? Or the teeth?"

"Male's bigger, but any bear'd look big on top of you, I suppose." Gil pulls a crumpled pack of cigarettes from the pocket of his green pants. "Used to be bears knew enough to avoid trouble, which is more than I can say for some folks." His expression lets Martin know some folks is him. "Now we're not supposed to shoot 'em unless they're a threat. They learned to be afraid of us, now they're learning they don't have to be. I told you, animals're getting strange around here. Showing up where they never did."

"Like a mountain lion?"

Gil gives Martin a look, as insulted as it is annoyed. "Mountain lions don't live around here."

"But Elmer said . . . "

"Elmer sees all kinds of things. Hell, he might've seen a big cat, but it'd just be passing through. A ranger found some markings a while ago, but no sign of 'em staying. No, I don't mean mountain lions. I mean bears in a dumpster. Went to buy tires a few weeks ago and there were sparrows waiting outside the door. They aren't big enough to set off the door's electric eye but they live in the rafters. Strange stuff. Who taught birds about automatic doors, Marty? You tell me that."

Whatever ointment Gil put on the swab, it seems to be easing the sting in Martin's chest, or else it's the whiskey. He reaches for the bottle and takes a long drink.

"Of course, could be it wasn't a bear you saw at all." Gil smirks on the side of his mouth that isn't holding a cigarette. "Coulda been Scratch. You were in his neck of the woods, after all."

The name is familiar somehow—Martin tries to remember where he's heard it before, but the answer won't come. "Who's Scratch?"

"The bearman of the north woods?" Gil laughs, then drops the stump of his cigarette onto the porch and grinds it out with a bare, calloused heel. He slips another cigarette into his mouth but doesn't light it, then reaches for his coffee cup from the porch railing and sips. He pulls a face and mutters about it being cold then pours in some of the whiskey before drinking again.

"Scratch is nothing but an old legend from the Indians around here. The story's lasted longer than they did. Supposed to be a bear that was cursed, maybe a man that was cursed. I've heard it both ways. Whichever it is wanders the woods stuck in a body that won't die or get old."

"People believe that?"

"Doesn't matter. Scratch has been blamed for so much that he's real enough. Indians said he stole their babies. Settlers blamed him for stealing women, sheep, whatever went missing. Grabs 'em, eats 'em, and tosses the bones in his pile. Loggers used to say he snuck into camp at night to rust up their saw blades and grind down their gears."

"He has a pile of bones?"

"Who doesn't? Every so often folks find a gnawed sheep's leg or a dog that crawled off to die. Tear ass into town hollering they've found Scratch's bones." He takes a sip of his coffee. "Made a good story for me to tell the weekend warriors, anyway. Take 'em hunting and give 'em their money's worth in scares, too. All part of the package. Used to have a couple of caves I kept stocked with bones."

"Have you seen him?" Martin asks, then tries to backtrack with, "Do you believe it?" instead, but the hunter is already talking.

"Me?" Gil grins and pulls a plastic lighter out of his pocket. It takes three scrapes of the wheel for it to catch, then he ignites the cigarette that hangs from his lip. "Not so far as I know. Seen plenty of bears, but I can't say any of 'em was Scratch. Besides, the Indians thought he could change shape, look like a bird or a wolf, whatever he wanted."

He pulls on his cigarette so the end flares. It occurs to Martin that as much as Gil smokes, he never seems to run out of cigarettes. He imagines a closet full of unopened cartons stashed somewhere in the house.

"Maybe I have seen him," Gil says. "Who knows? Older folks in town— even older than me, if you can imagine—say they have, out in the woods, a bear that walks funny. Staggers like he can't find his legs. Or got caught in a trap."

A pair of gray squirrels approach the foot of the stairs, a few feet away from the men. "Will you look at that," Gil says. "Even the squirrels are getting brave." He stands and waves his arms with a bark, scaring the squirrels off into the yard.

Scratch isn't a bad thing to be called. I've had other names, in other languages I don't hear in these woods anymore, but this one's as good as any other. I've been here longer than I've had a name, and I was nameless for a far longer time than I wasn't. But it's always scared people more when they have a word for the thing they're afraid of, so the names have stuck to this place.

They never get the details right, though, what I do and how I do it. Never the why of it all. I didn't begin as one of your own who was cursed—I was in these woods without form before the first warm-blooded body appeared. I was here before your kind arrived, before *any* kind arrived, because you needed me here to become what you are. You needed a reason to raise up the walls you hoped would keep me out, and to invent the electric lights and alarms that allow you to sleep through the night. Without me to spur your inventions, what would your kind have become? What would your languages be without the need to give your fear names?

Martin doesn't know me yet, not exactly, but he's come across me in his dreams during these recent nights. He knows that since he came to these woods, to the hole in the forest where his trailer stands, his dreams have carried over into waking life more often—and more completely—than ever before. Dreams led him into the woods on his walk, and dreams led the bear to his fireplace bed. Dreams are where I have the most reach, the most power. It's hard to touch waking lives, in those hours you're convinced you understand more of the world. But the more your kind come to insist things beyond what you know to be real cannot be, the more willing your dream selves become to believe. The more eager they are to listen, and to remember the other things you used to know.

I pushed Martin toward the bear and the bear toward Martin until their paths crossed. So much depends upon their meeting that it couldn't be left to chance. I wasn't entirely sure what would happen when they came together—I can set events into motion, not control how they occur—but so far it's worked out. Martin is on the path I was pushing him toward. The bear let him live, but went back to the woods, and his confidence in knowing how the world works has been shaken enough for my needs.

5

BACK IN HIS TRAILER, MARTIN WRAPS A LAYER OF CLING film around the bandages on his chest before squeezing into the small plastic shell of the shower. He doesn't want to get the gauze or the wounds wet, but his body is sticky with dried sweat and dirt, pungent from yesterday's walk and a night in the woods.

The water arrives cold, and he stands back as far as he can until it warms up. Then the spray is too hot, and where his skin is bruised it feels even hotter. It rattles against the plastic over his wounds the way rain does on the trailer's thin windows.

He faces the spray with his forehead against the wall as hot water rolls down the back of his neck and his shoulders, uncoiling muscles one at a time, until his body feels like his body again. He nods off in the steam for a second, then wakes with a jerk as a few trickles creep under the top edge of his plastic wrap and make their way toward the gauze, so he presses the film tighter against his skin.

If it weren't for the bandages and bruises all over his body, he might think the bear had been an uncomfortable dream. That he spent last night the same as any other, sleeping in his own bed, while his imagination wandered the woods. Even though it has only been a couple of hours since he left the forest, and less than a day since he set out on his walk, it seems a lifetime ago. He's stung by the shame of getting lost, but it's more the vicarious embarrassment of watching someone else make mistakes than something that happened to him.

As he winces his way through getting dressed in the main room of the trailer, Martin notices strands of brown fur scattered over his bed. The long shape of a body stretches out on his blankets, and one of his pillows looks kneaded. He lays his hand in the egg-shaped dent on his mattress, annoyed now that he left the door open. The sheets seem warm; either they're reflecting the heat of his hand or else whatever slept there last night hasn't been gone very long.

He leans close to the sheets and breathes in the smell of his guest. He's shocked at how much it smells like the bear, the bear's breath, but also by the full picture the scent plants in his mind—a flickering image of not one but two creatures curled on his bed. He recoils from the unexpected acuity of his own senses. When the shock has subsided, Martin remembers he hasn't eaten in nearly a day, with nothing but Gil's whiskey to drink, and takes comfort in dismissing that sensory overreaction as a result of his deprivations—his imagination running away with the smell, turning it into more than it is. He looks around the trailer, red-faced, as if there might be someone watching.

He doesn't know how nearly he missed us, slipping out before he slipped in. Or that we haven't gone far, watching through the window from under the bushes as the day becomes brighter and the final droplets of last night's dew burn away.

It isn't Martin we're hiding from, though. It's one thing to be spotted by him, as at sea in the woods as he would be at sea, but another to be seen by the men who will build his houses for him, men who have lived near these woods their whole lives. Men who hang guns in their trucks and pull them down as casually as one cigarette follows another into their mouths. Like Gil, they are less patient with the novelty of animals coming up close. None of them would have been lured so easily as Martin was by the tail of a fox. They could be led, too, each in his own way, but Martin is the man for my story.

He lifts his steel watch from a shelf by the bed, and as he buckles it onto his wrist his fingers find the sharp burr to blame for that hole in the sleeve of a jacket ruined now altogether. He's shocked that despite his already full morning, despite being tired enough for the day to be over, it is only a few minutes past seven o'clock. He opens both kitchenette cabinets and the tiny white fridge tucked into the wall, looking for something to eat. But his stomach has been empty for so many hours it threatens to reject any offer of food, so he plugs in the electric kettle and decides to make do with instant coffee from crystals, and a spoonful of powdered creamer.

When his phone, retrieved from the car, rings with the electronic chirp of a bird underwater, Martin splashes hot coffee all over his hand. He barely avoids dropping the mug and, cursing, sets it down on the counter. The phone rings again, and he walks to the end of the trailer where it rattles and dances across the surface of his drafting table. As he shakes the burnt hand to lessen the pain, he answers the phone with the other.

The connection is crackling and weak, far from the nearest cell tower with tall hills between, and though it's good for what he usually gets in the trailer he may as well be speaking into a tin can on the end of a string. The number on the screen tells him it's his partner calling from their office back in the city. They speak every couple of days to touch base, but a signal is so hard to come by they communicate mostly by voicemail, always a few hours out of step with each other. He's hardly on the phone at all these days, a change from his usual routine of calling suppliers, subcontractors, and building inspectors, sucking up daily to bureaucrats and their factotums.

At first the difficulty of keeping in touch made him feel isolated, as if these woods were an unmapped desert island and everything worth being a part of was happening on the other side of the ocean. But lately he's felt the opposite, after settling a bit into his trailer home. Some mornings he has awoken concerned with what might be happening in this small town instead of the city he left behind. His first days here he spent constantly driving closer to town where his phone's signal is stronger, but now he waits to be called and it takes him hours sometimes, the best part of a day, to move to a place from which he can call back.

He doesn't even bother saying hello before setting the phone down again; his partner on the other end of the line won't be able to hear Martin's voice any better than Martin hears his. He'll check the message and leave one of his own when he comes within range of a signal.

As he sips his coffee, a car rattles off the road onto the rough ground of the site. He spreads the slats of the plastic blinds in his window so he can see through, and watches Alison Evans' battered red SUV pull toward his trailer. He's never worked with a forewoman before—he's never even met a woman who wanted to be one—but so far Alison is working out well, keeping the project on track, as far she's able. The biggest delays have come from the weather, though after watching her work Martin wouldn't be surprised to see her whip the elements into line, too.

She climbs from her car with a scarred yellow hardhat, and walks toward the trailer with the graceful lope of a cowgirl. Her hair is spiky and short, blonde laced with gray, and she reminds Martin of female characters he's seen in science fiction movies, blasting through alien hordes with oversized guns in their arms. He sets down his coffee cup and steps out of the trailer to meet her.

"Good morning," he says.

She nods. "Mr. Blaskett."

"Alison. Please. Just call me Martin."

"I forgot." She smiles, brightening her face so Martin pictures ice struck by sunlight and the thin web of wrinkles beside each of her eyes expanding cracks in its surface.

"Good weekend?" He crosses his arms across his chest but the stance feels both unfriendly and painful so he slides his hands into back pockets. That position is uncomfortable, too, it feels like a pose, so he lets his hands hang at his sides with nothing to do.

"Not bad," she says. "Brought Jake, Jr. up to the lake. Painted the bathroom. Nothing special." She doesn't ask about his own weekend, but looks at him as if she's waiting to hear.

"I went for a hike yesterday, out that way." He points toward where he entered the woods, and hopes he looks like he knows where he's pointing. Martin doesn't mention how easily he became lost in the forest. He tries to sound casual as he adds, "I ran into a bear."

"Yeah?" Alison leans closer.

"It attacked me, actually." He traces a finger through the air in front of his chest. "I've got cuts here, and bruises all over my ribs." Martin grabs the front of his shirt, as if he's going to lift it and show her the bruises, then suddenly stops, embarrassed. He's afraid his attempt at nonchalance has come across as lunacy, or macho bragging.

"Oh my God! Are you okay?"

"Gil thinks so."

"Lucky it didn't kill you," she says. "Bear attack, that's something."

The sound of approaching engines grows louder, and they turn toward the road at the edge of the site.

"Not a lot of folks get attacked by a bear. And live, I mean. Lots of folks get attacked."

"Really?"

"Maybe you should go to the hospital."

"I thought so, too, but Gil patched me up. He said the cuts aren't deep." Gil's explanations made sense at the time, but now, as he repeats them out loud, Martin begins second-guessing how easily he was persuaded.

"Well, he would know."

He's about to ask Alison about her son or some other part of her life beyond this project, anything to turn the conversation away from himself and to find out more about her. But the half-formed question on the tip of his tongue is interrupted by the rumble of vehicles bumping onto the shoulder between the site and the road.

Members of the crew begin arriving in heavy trucks with doors that don't match. The bulldozer operator rumbles up on the motorcycle he assembled himself from spare parts, or so Martin has heard. The crew is still small at the moment, just enough men run an excavator, a bulldozer, and a dump truck; this is their first day on the site, replacing the tree crew who finished on Friday.

The men park in the mud along the edge of the road, and Alison walks toward them, leaving Martin behind by the trailer. He watches as she speaks and gestures to the crew, giving instructions or telling a story, but he can't make out what she's saying over the chaos of further arrivals.

A shiny silver food truck parks on the soft shoulder, and its wall swings open in a burst of white steam. The crew crowds around to buy coffee, cigarettes, and pastries with no particular flavor. Construction on this scale doesn't take place in these parts too often, so there isn't much need for such a truck, but when one of the local farmers heard Martin's plans in town meeting he took out a loan and bought it. He's hoping this development will lead to more building in the near future, and his glistening steel gamble will pay for itself the way his farm hasn't in so many years, the way his ancestors supplemented their farming with maple syrup and logging and furs, the way some of his neighbors craft handmade authentic antiques in their barns after dark and the way their grandfathers did, too.

The men mill around in the mud, smoking over foam cups of coffee. They greet Martin with nods and grunts and the occasional word, polite but impersonal. He tells the first few good morning, then tilts his head to the rest, suddenly exhausted and struggling to keep his eyes open. He was flush with adrenaline when he walked out of the woods but he's coming down fast and all of his aches are turning to throbs and his clarity is becoming a cloud. The cuts sting again, Gil's ointment and whiskey both wearing off, and he absentmindedly holds the buttons of his shirt away from his chest as if it's the pressure of the fabric causing him pain. The skin he kept dry in the shower didn't get washed, and now that the rest of his body is clean the itching in that area has grown even worse.

He feels every bruise as a weight on his body, as a tightness under his ribs, and he stretches his arms up behind his head to expand his lungs and relieve the pressure. He doesn't feel like himself; he's aware of muscles he doesn't recall being aware of before, only noticing them now because they're so sore. His head swirls with the flotsam and jetsam of exhaustion, images and phrases rising to the surface of his mind without order or purpose, as if they aren't coming from Martin at all but are bubbling up from somewhere else.

His struggle may sound familiar, his mind and his body at odds for control. That's probably about how you're feeling right now in your borrowed coyote, pestering you with its canine urges and heightened senses. Wearing a new body is always a change. It takes time to get the sense of your shape.

A long time ago, before even the oldest tree rings in this forest had formed and the great-grandparents of today's oldest trunks hadn't grown, I had no shape at all. I hadn't yet learned I could take one as I drifted across the still unseeded ground.

Drifted isn't quite right—that sounds as if I was moving and I never moved, I never came and never went, because without a body to limit my range I was everywhere in these woods all at once. I occupied no space so I wasn't limited by the size I took up in the world. I watched the first saplings grow, and the first humming insects rattle their wings before lifting off into the air, and I wondered how it must feel to be one of them. So I squeezed myself into the hard-shelled shape of a beetle and suddenly the world became smaller. After knowing everything there was to know in these woods, the grand scope of time and the intricacies of how each life and death fit together with every other from one year to the next, I became a finite, miniscule part. And I was shocked at how complicated the world can appear from that angle—I'd expected the opposite, that the confines of a limited life would be boring, constrictive, but the forest was as rich through the eyes of a beetle as it had ever been when I could see the whole world at once.

I didn't stay in that first insect body for long; the compression of my consciousness was too shocking. But over time, across what you might measure out in millennia, I became more adept. I wasn't as startled by how the world shifted from species to species. I grew used to having a body, any body, and it's been ages now since I spent very much time in the shapelessness of myself.

I knew, before, what all the animals and trees in these woods were thinking, but I knew it the way you know the sky is up there and the ground is down here; I took all those momentary lives and flickering thoughts for granted, but when I put myself into that beetle—and the oak trees and foxes that followed—each individual life in the forest became a story I needed to know. And I needed to know each of them in their own voice. I've had a long time to listen to the stories of creatures you may not know ever existed. And that collection is the closest thing I have to a tale of my own—all those borrowed shapes and borrowed stories, one after the other, lives piled upon lives, almost add up to a shape that is mine.

6

MARTIN MET ALISON OVER BREAKFAST, AT CLAUDIA'S CAFÉ
near the town square. It was a few months ago, when he was in
town to grease some permits through the appropriate hands and
take another walk over the site before tying up any loose ends in
the city and moving into his trailer. More urgently, he'd just learned the
man hired to be his foreman, on the recommendation of a contractor he'd
worked with before, would now be in jail for the next couple of years. He
had to find someone else as soon as he could because there wasn't much
time before tree felling was set to begin.

He had passed by Claudia's without stopping on previous visits, in his
car and on foot as he crossed the square, but this time he went in. He took
the corner booth by the windows, its table still sticky with residue from an
earlier diner, and he spread sheets of construction plans over a strawberry
smudge while awaiting his order of eggs Benedict, hold the Canadian bacon. Despite his aversion to eating meat, Martin has never given up eggs;
it's a slippery boundary he's drawn for himself, but one he observes as if
it were fixed.

Before his meal arrived at the table, he daydreamed about the future
homes of his development, how he would landscape the yards with Japanese maples and single mimosas where acres of oak, ash, and birch cur-
rently stood. He made notes in the margins of the bright white plans un-
rolled on the table before him. Then a woman with graying blonde hair,
spiked as the stubble of a cornfield in winter, warm in that same cold way,
sat down across the table from him. She looked to be about his own age, in
her late thirties, and her tanned face was weathered in a way she wore well.

"Hello?" he asked, jarred from his stroll through imaginary houses and
across unseeded lawns.

"You're building on Fisher Trail," she said, and there wasn't any hint of
it being a question.

He confirmed that yes, he was planning to build there, and he rolled the top edge of the plans toward himself with the fingertips of both hands.

"Scott Robbins was going to be your foreman. And now he can't."

Martin leaned back against the vinyl cushion of his seat and slid the sheets of paper toward himself. "I guess word went around fast."

"It's a small town. Have you got a new foreman yet?" The window to her right flared with the changing angle of the sun coming over the hills, and she squinted the eye on that side so Martin thought of a pirate.

"No . . . well, no."

She introduced herself as Alison Evans, and reached a ropy forearm across the sticky table and said she wanted to run his project for him. Her hand hung between them for a second before Martin took it and felt its rough calluses against the smooth skin of his own palm, unsure if that handshake was an introduction or an agreement or both. They sat without speaking, Martin pinned in his seat by her insistent, expectant blue eyes.

Before he had answered her question, Claudia—the restaurant's only waitress—brought his plate over and set it down at the far edge of the table where it wasn't on top of the plans. Two hazy poached eggs swam in a bright sea of Hollandaise sauce, and he could see the reflected motion of the ceiling fan in its yellow surface.

He made a common mistake that morning, assuming Claudia the waitress is the woman the café is named for. It's a coincidence, or at least a fluke: the owner's name is Bruce Barlow, the brick house of a man in a dainty white apron perpetually hunched over the grill in the kitchen. The original Claudia had been his grandmother, and the establishment's founder, so when Claudia the waitress applied for the job, he thought it was too good to pass up.

Claudia the waitress smiled so her glasses rose high on her red face. "Hittin' him up for a job already, Alison?"

"Do what I have to."

"That's the truth. How's your boy?"

"Excited for his birthday."

"What's he now, nine?"

"Ten."

Claudia turned back to Martin and asked, "Get you anything else, hon? Ketchup?"

"No, thank you, I'm fine." He rolled the plans and slipped a rubber band over the end before standing them against the back of his seat. Claudia went on to the next table and Martin pulled his plate close. He salted his eggs without tasting them.

"So?" Alison asked. Her elbows stood on the table, and her hands wound together above the speckled pink surface. "What'll I need to do to get this job?"

Martin looked up as he lifted the first bite of egg and English muffin into his mouth. He chewed as slowly as he could, an excuse to think before giving an answer. He noticed Alison's fingers without a ring or a line where one had been lately, and thought of the son his waitress had mentioned. "Are you . . . have you got experience?" he asked.

"Much as anyone around here. More than Scott Robbins." She smiled, and her face grew in all directions. "And I don't drink as much, either, so I won't be going to jail."

"Look, I'm not from here. But you probably know that. So I need someone who knows the area, someone who can get a crew together and keep them on target. Someone they'll listen to."

"I've worked with everyone around here you'll need for your houses." She leaned closer, eyes tight. Her arms angled into each other on the table as if wrestling themselves, or waiting for Martin's own hand to enter the fray.

"I've never had a woman in charge before."

"Hell, I've never been in charge before. But it's like I said: I've worked with everyone, and I've been on every job in three towns for years. I figure it's time. I'm licensed. I've had a license for years, for whenever the chance came to use it." She knotted her fingers more tightly then relaxed them a bit. "My son's getting older."

"Don't take it the wrong way, but do you think it'll be a problem? You being a woman, you know, running the crew?" Even as he asked he knew it was naive—the unwavering stare of Alison's eyes was enough to tell him she could keep anybody in line.

"Ask around. I won't have any trouble."

Martin did ask, and her reputation was solid—well-liked, local, from an old family, and she'd learned the building trade from her father who'd raised many of the more recent homes in this town and some others nearby. Later, after Alison had already begun working for him, Martin learned from Gil about an incident three summers ago in a bar one town over, a place called The Antlers. A welder drinking with some of his friends suggested a little too loudly that Alison give up construction and bake him some cookies instead. He lost three teeth and Alison gained a grudging respect, overwriting whatever stories might have been told about her with one of her own.

He still doesn't know much more about her than that, as often as he's tried to engage in the small talk at which neither of them is adept. He knows her son, Jake, Jr., is the biggest thing in her life, but he doesn't know where or who Jake, Sr. is. He knows she's getting work done for him, has the ground cleared for digging almost on schedule, and that the rain delays can't be blamed on her. And he knows that apart from Gil she's the person in town he's talked to the most.

Now Martin watches from the steps of his trailer as Alison sets the crew to work for the day, preparing to dig the first foundations. She moves among the men the way Gil walked in Martin's dream, pushing the world out of her way without trying. He watches her stir sugar into a foam cup beside the quilted steel wall of the food truck, lit up orange with sun coming over the forest, then he ducks back into his trailer and pulls the door closed. He rolls a tall stool to the drafting table-cum-dining room at one end of the trailer and hunches over plans held flat by a square of tape at each corner. With an index finger he traces the lines of the first house they're going to build, on the lot where ground is about to be broken. Then he pulls another tight tube of paper from the rack on his wall and spreads it over the first.

It's a map of the area around the site, the town and the roads and the woods, at a larger scale than the house plans. He's been using this to think about where a cell tower might best be placed, to serve the houses of his development and the rest of the town; he'd thought near the highest point of the forest would make sense, but he's waiting for the specialists he's hired to figure it out. Not that they'll make sense of it, either, because whatever tools they haul into these woods, whatever measurements are made and tests taken won't tell them it's more than radio waves and electricity that run through the trees. The stories and voices and dreams carry signals as strong as any antennae might bring so they're all erasing and overriding each other so nothing gets through any more.

Nothing but me, and the story I'm telling.

Martin's map shows the irregular shape he has cleared from the forest and the sure, straight lines of foundations to come. It shows the road there is now, between his land and Gil's, and it shows the road and branching driveways he'll pave to the door of each house. It even shows where, at the edge of the road, the draftsman assumed Martin would want a sign to announce the development's name, but there isn't going to be any sign. And there won't be a name for these houses, either, apart from the names of each family in them. He doesn't want to make more of them being new than he must, as if they grew from this ground over time same as the trees and the ad hoc architecture of Gil's own family home on the other side of the road.

Martin follows lines with his finger as he tries to determine where he entered the woods yesterday. He thought the ridge he followed led north but on paper it arcs in a west to east frown. There's no trace on the page of the stone wall he followed or the foundation where he spent the night. Yesterday, he trusted this map: it showed him the forest, the work site, the town, but after his night in the woods, after the fox and the bear and the blood, the map shows so little and seems so ordinary.

He estimates—guesses, really—where he came out of the forest this morning based on how he remembers approaching the road. He pencils in the box of his trailer to help, as rectangular as the foundations are shown but the lines have less weight in lead rather than ink, drawn in by his hand and not by a machine. Then he works backward, thinking of where the sun was as he walked away from the attack, how the land rose and fell, and he decides where the foundation must be then sketches it, too. Then the stone wall, which is more speculation than measurement, as he tries to reconstruct his route through yesterday's long afternoon all the way back to where he entered the woods from the site.

He marks, more or less (and it is mostly less), where he might have found the fragments of china, and where he thinks the rusted car was. He's not sure why these things matter, if they're only his overtired mind latching on, but it seems important right now to mark these things down, so in the foundation he thickens one wall where the fireplace is and marks an X where the bear attack came.

An X, and he thinks of crossed bones, of how much worse it could have been, and the tiredness that ebbed as he manically mapped comes washing back over his body.

Martin yawns over the paper; his night of restless, uncomfortable sleep and rude awakening at the claws of a bear are catching up with him at last. He yawns again, and a tiny birdcall of a moan leaks from his lungs as his bandaged chest expands against the edge of the desk. He folds his arms on top of the paper, letting the untaped top sheet curl at the edges until it bumps into him on each side, then he lowers his head to the cradle of an elbow and in seconds he is asleep, mouth open and drooling onto the map.

Outside the trailer the crew goes on working, checking and re-checking measured marks on the ground and waiting for the excavator operator to arrive on the site. Alison unrolls a sheet of plans identical to the ones on Martin's desk across the hood of her car, and pins it flat with both hands. Her eyes trace the lines that will grow into walls and double-glazed windows meant to keep the forest at bay—to stand fast between the bodies inside these eventual houses and the bodies we're wearing right now.

Let's move before the digging begins—those yellow machines will be roaring and rumbling and shaking the ground before long, and as long as I've been watching the behavior of humans your machines still make me nervous. We'll stake out a space beneath Martin's trailer from which we can see without being seen.

I can see you growing more comfortable in that borrowed body. You don't seem to be battling your legs when we walk. You may yet find yourself rolling in clover or going nose-deep in mud, giving in to the urges that come with your form, and there's no reason to fight it. No reason you shouldn't enjoy this respite from your own shape—it won't last very long, in the grand scheme of it all, and when you've gone back to looking more like yourself you might cling to the vague memory of being a coyote as if it was only a dream you once had, a dream like the one Martin is having right now.

7

HIS BODY DOESN'T FEEL LIKE HIS OWN.

It doesn't move when he says to, not right away: the brain tells the left leg to lift for a step and it happens a split-second later, an actor out of synch with his lines. There's too long a delay between command and response for him to feel in control.

He glances down at himself and finds his body unchanged except that his wounds and their bandages—and his clothes—are all gone. He lifts his hands to his face and they look the same as they always do yet he knows they aren't his, that this isn't him, not exactly.

His legs decide to run and he crashes along behind them, through branches and brambles and brush. He feels his skin scratching but without the pain he knows should be there.

This strange other Martin thunders along, leaping fallen trees in his path and knocking saplings aside with stiff arms. He rumbles and runs, out of breath but not slowing, his body leading his mind.

He's filled with a strange sense of power. This body is stronger than his; it takes up more space in the world despite being the same size exactly.

Some tickling memory at the back of his mind reminds him he took his clothes off, left them somewhere, that he won't ever need them again.

And he runs.

And he rumbles.

In this body not quite his own he bursts into a clearing, a pool of swaying sunlit grass ringed by pine trees as slim and as straight as tall needles. At the center of the clearing a patch of brown shows through the green, a ragged dirt circle flattened and worn smooth by feet.

He approaches slowly, swinging his eyes from side to side, hunched close to the ground.

As he nears the dirt circle, another naked man slides out of the woods on the opposite side of the clearing. He's older but more muscled than

Martin, and his wrinkled body is peeling and red from the sun. His face is familiar but Martin can't make sense of why.

A breeze cuts through the forest and a thick mane of white hair billows around the stranger's head.

Without a word or a nod to each other the two men move into the ring, walking sideways in circles, wrestlers sizing up their opponent. They circle and spin, around and around past the point where each of them started and past it again.

The older man sniffs and he snarls, squinting at Martin with dark, beady eyes. In fast, fluid motion he drops to all fours and tears for the trees in a blur of beige skin.

For a second his body stretches with those first quadruped steps, growing longer and leaner as he speeds up. As he runs his shape loses all definition and his edges ripple like fur on a fast-moving cat.

Then he's gone, away into the trees, and Martin is Martin again, standing in a circle of dirt in a clearing somewhere deep in the woods, naked and lost, awash in a wave of curious guilt.

He backs away from the exposed space of the clearing, out of the sunlight and into the forest. A metallic thump echoes from the far distance and he covers himself with his hands as much as he can. The sound and its echo come again, and again, then the thump isn't out in the woods anymore, and neither is Martin, and he sits up from his desk with a start as someone bangs on the door of the trailer.

"Mr. Blaskett," Alison calls through the thin wall. "Mr. Blaskett, are you in there?"

"Hang on," he calls back. "I'm coming." He rubs his eyes and wipes a crust of drool from his cheek before he opens the door.

"What is it?" he asks. "What's wrong?"

Alison hangs her hat from one hand and runs the other through her silver-laced hair. One side of her mouth curls into a shallow frown. "We found something," she says. "In the first hole."

"Found what?"

"Bones, Mr. Blaskett. We just started digging, and the ground's full of bones."

The curtain of his dream hangs between his mind and the world, and as he steps down from the trailer and walks to where the crew began digging, his body feels out of sorts, still asleep or not paying attention to him.

He walks to where the dump truck stands by and the excavator is idle. There's a single long trench scraped through the edge of the marked off rectangle where the machine took its first stroke, and Martin stands at the top of the hole and peers into the ground. Thin white roots trail like veins through dark mud, and the stumps and shafts of brown bones stab the air in all directions. Long bones and short ones, intact bones and shattered nubs. Skulls with empty eyes peering up at the workers. A tangle of tibias and femurs and ribs and the roots around them a big ball of twine woven tight.

"What the fuck," Martin says to no one in particular.

"No shit," answers the dump truck driver, his tough pose betrayed by the shake of his cigarette.

"Are they . . . " Martin begins, but he doesn't finish the question.

"Human?" Alison asks.

Some of the crew stand over the hole inspecting the bones, but most of them have wandered off toward the road and are smoking or sitting on piles of equipment, on their plastic lunch coolers or the hoods of their trucks. They mumble to each other and sometimes look Martin's way with a tip of the head or a frown. A man with a long red beard, whose name Martin doesn't know because Alison hired most of the crew, stands up and gestures with two chopping hands to the others. Whatever point he's making with such insistence can't be understood across the distance, but his voice gets louder and louder as Martin makes out "we all know what," and "bullshit," but the other men turn their faces away and go back to their mumbles.

"Anyone?" Martin asks. "Are they?"

"How can you tell?" asks the driver.

"I don't know. I'll need to talk to someone."

"Should we dig somewhere else?" Alison asks.

"No, let's wait while we figure this out."

Martin returns to his trailer, scratching his head. It's not the bones that confuse him—bones turn up all the time, it's part of digging, it's part of the passage of time and the laying of ground—but the number of them in one place. Maybe he's building over a graveyard—another small cemetery like the one he found in the woods—and wasn't told when he put in his bid on the land. He thinks back to what Gil said about Scratch and his bones and wonders if this is one of the spots where hunters pay to be spooked before doubting they pay to dig holes.

He sits on the steps of the trailer and takes out his phone, scrolling through a long list of numbers until he finds the one for town hall. He isn't sure who he needs to talk to about this, to find out whether or not he can keep digging, but he figures local bureaucracy is the place to begin. As his phone dials, Martin crosses his mental fingers in hopes this won't mean more delays, and that the bones won't turn out to be sacred and tribal or an archaeological treasure of one kind or another. He hopes they're plain old dead animals or people of no interest to anyone else.

When his phone bleats in his ear, he remembers the poor coverage here on the site and hangs up almost relieved—he's made an effort to enter the proper channels and has failed through no fault of his own. He can always call someone later, when he's in town. In the meantime, however, he doesn't know any better what to do with the bones.

He starts back toward Alison and the few men still clustered around the top of the hole, speaking in a murmur of voices broken by occasional laughter. Their heads dip low in front of their bodies, and all Martin can see are their backs and hunched shoulders. It reminds him of the graveside crowd at a funeral and he's struck that the connection is more apt than he meant it to be.

He looks toward the road and sees Gil kneeling down on his porch. He's at work on some project but Martin can't make out what it is from this distance. "Gil," he says out loud, to himself, but his voice carries and some of the crew turn his way. If anyone will know what kind of bones his men have uncovered, it's Gil; he'll know whether work can go on, or will have to shut down while some state agency sorts it all out or shuts down construction without sorting anything out, which is equally likely. He hasn't pegged Gil as someone particularly concerned with protocol and bureaucracy, so expects he's got a better chance of staying on schedule if he asks his neighbor to have a look before calling anyone else. Before asking someone official.

As he crosses the road, he can see Gil is painting a chair that stands upside-down over newspaper sheets. The creamy white of raw wood still shows on the sections that haven't been slathered in red.

"How's your chest?" he asks as Martin approaches.

"Okay. Stings a little." He ascends the three steps to the porch, and doesn't mention that the brief climb makes every inch of his body ache.

"Stinging's not bad, considering. What are you all looking at over there? Lotta fellas getting paid to stand around."

Martin sighs. "We started digging and the ground's full of bones."

Gil raises his eyes and lowers the paintbrush. "What sort of bones?"

"I don't know. I was hoping you could tell me. Most of them are so broken up and worn down they could even be pieces of wood."

"Lemme get a look." Gil lays his brush across the open top of the paint can so it drips red onto the paper below, then he rises from his crouch beside the chair. Martin leads him across the street to where most of the crew greet him by name, and the rest ask each other in whispers who this guy is and why he's here and they mostly get shushed. The crowd parts at the top of the hole, spreading to either side so Gil can get close.

"Hey, Gil," Alison says. "How you been?"

"These boys listenin' to you? Need me to set 'em all straight?"

"Nah, they're fine." She looks over her shoulder at the crew, most of whom are looking away or talking to one another.

"Let's get a look," Gil says, then pokes a cigarette into his mouth. He lights it and looks into the ground without speaking for a long time. A barrel-chested crow lands on the cab of the nearby excavator, and hops from one foot to the other then back to the first before settling down to watch the humans and their strange fascination.

"Lotta bones," Gil says at last. "Saw a village like this once. Bombs shook all their skeletons out of the ground. Old bones mixed up with new ones, all those people running away."

He falls quiet again, and his eyes are far off as he smokes. Martin waits for him to speak, and the longer he waits the more uncomfortable the moment becomes, the further away Gil seems to be. Alison scuffs the toe of one boot in the dirt at the lip of the hole. Martin tries to form a question in his mouth, but all he gets is an ambiguous hum. The men in the crew have begun wandering off, out toward the road where they started the day, smoking and drinking coffee from insulated bottles.

"But you aren't digging in a graveyard." Gil kneels, and leans far forward over his knees to peer into the trench. "Hell, Marty. That's all animals, and not even big ones. See, you've got a skunk's skull, and a deer leg there, couple of sheep. Haven't been sheep around here since I was a kid. These're old bones."

He smokes and scratches his head through his cap. "That's only the ones on top. Can't tell what's at the bottom but no reason to suppose it's anything different."

"That's a relief," says Alison. "Thought I was in a horror movie for a minute there."

Martin crouches close to the hole and inspects the jumble of brown and white bones. "But why are they all in one place?"

"I told you, Pelletiers had a big farm out here. Cows, sheep . . . pigs, I suppose. Could be from their slaughtering. Could be there was a mud pit they all fell into over time." He smokes, and then smiles as he adds, "Or maybe it's Scratch's dinner bones." Gil raises his arms over his head and screws up his face, booming out a monstrous groan in Alison's direction. He takes a stiff-legged step toward her, but the sound catches in his throat and sets him coughing, bent double over the hole so he drops his cigarette onto the bones.

"Shit," he says when the coughing has passed, then lights a fresh cigarette, and again Martin imagines a closet, a room, filled with his unopened cartons.

"I'll get the crew back to work," Alison says. As she walks away she slides a finger into each corner of her mouth and whistles.

"Think I need to call the police about this?" Martin asks Gil.

"Hell, Marty, you bother Sheriff Lindon with this and he'll throw you in jail for wasting his time. Besides, it's Monday morning, and look at this weather. He'll be fishing 'til lunch."

A few minutes later, Gil has returned to his porch and to painting his chair. Alison has the crew back at work expanding the hole, and the rectangle of the development's first foundation has begun to take shape. The first bites of the excavator's rust-tartared teeth crack the bones where they lie, then each successive stroke disperses them in smaller and smaller fragments throughout the soil of the lot, breaking up like an echo until there are few pieces large enough to be recognized as anything that once was alive. At least not without climbing down from the yellow machines and looking more closely, which no one is willing to do.

The rest of the workday goes by without much excitement, men, woman, and machines all doing what they're expected to do, and staying more or less on schedule despite the morning's setback. Martin spends most of the day inside his trailer, fighting a strong urge to sleep as he fills out forms and makes a list of supplies to order the next time he's in range of a signal.

Eventually Alison calls through the open door of the trailer that she'll be leaving, and Martin steps outside to watch the crew disperse in their varied directions. Alison gathers her tools and hoists them into the back of her car, then tosses her hardhat onto the seat. For a moment she leans against the closed door, looking into the mountains or waiting for something, and Martin tries to think of a reason to keep her from leaving—some issue they need to discuss, some labor problem, but there aren't any because she does a good job. He considers simply asking if she'd like to get something to eat, to sit over a beer and talk for a while, but before he can cross the mud to within speaking range she is inside her truck and waving as she drives off. Then he's alone with the idle bulldozer and dump truck, their engines rattling as they cool off, and he remembers there isn't any real food in his trailer to offer.

8

LATER, MARTIN CROSSES THE STREET TO THANK GIL FOR HIS help and ends up as he so often has lately, drinking beer in a rickety cane chair that seems to belong at a dining room table instead of outside on a porch. He watches his neighbor cooking cheese sandwiches on a sheet of blackened metal set over the gas flame of his grill.

"Tomato?" Gil asks.

Martin nods, then rests his crossed ankles on the rail of the porch the way he's seen Gil do. But the older man is a few inches taller, or else his chair is, because the angle of Martin's legs is too steep to be comfortable as the blood rushes away from his feet.

Gil hands over a steaming sandwich on a camp plate with chipped red enamel. "Another beer?" he asks, then opens one and hands it over before getting an answer. Martin hurries to drain what's left in the can he's already holding. If he was in his trailer, his options would be limited to instant noodles or soup from a powder, so grilled cheese and beer is at least a step up.

Two large crows hop through the high grass of Gil's yard near the road, pecking at bugs in the dirt. One threads too close to the other and the larger bird shrieks a warning until the interloper moves off its turf.

"Thought about your bones," Gil says. "Figure there must've been a sinkhole there once. Animals fell in over the years and got stuck."

"I'm glad they were just animals. Still pretty creepy, though."

"Bones aren't so bad. Especially without any meat on 'em. The fresh ones get your neck hairs up. They take getting used to." Gil drains most of his beer in a single long slurp. "People are harder to take." He crunches the can in his fist so the top and bottom rims curl together, then pitches it toward a brown paper bag standing open at the end of the porch. The can misses the bag, bouncing under the railing and down to the yard.

"I've only ever seen them at funerals," Martin replies. "Bodies, I mean, not bones." He thinks of his mother stretched in her coffin almost ten years ago, with too much rouge on her sunken cheeks and pink pow-der filling hollows honed by disease. He arranged a funeral in the city she'd spent most of her life swirling around, from one home to another, at an upscale parlor near the furnished rooms he was living in then. But when it came time to bury her he couldn't decide on a place and she hadn't left any instructions. So he had her cremated after the service and spilled her ashes at the side of a bridge where they'd fished sometimes when he was young.

His mother had always been drawn to rivers. She'd always been hap-piest when she had a view of one from her windows; it's something she told Martin later, when he was grown, but when he looked back at all their homes together over the years he could see she was right.

"The water never stops moving," she'd said once when they were fish-ing, legs dangling over the river. "It runs down the mountains and past all the farms and right through the city before it gets to the ocean. It only stays in one place when we catch a fish and pull him out of the water to keep."

Martin watched a fish he'd caught flopping beside him on the hot ce-ment of the bridge, skittering a wet tail against his thin hip. What kind was it, he wonders now, but all he remembers is its upturned eye spread wide with what he took to be panic, though he later learned fish can't close their eyes. "I think this one wants to keep swimming," he told his mother, and she laughed and let him toss the fish back.

"We'll find something else for supper," she said. "We'll let that one keep moving. It's nice to be able to change your plans when you want to, isn't it Martin?" She leaned way over the side of the bridge to drop the fish, and as it fell she said, "Okay, fish, there's your second chance. What are you going to do with it? Which way will you swim now?"

Gil says, "You get used to bones," but he doesn't seem to be speaking to Martin as much as himself. "Bones are dead. The stuff between is what spooks you."

"Between what?"

"Well." Gil finishes his beer, and this can finds the open mouth of the bag easily. He pulls yet another drink from the cooler of melted ice by his chair, pops it open, and drains most of the can before speaking again. "Say you shoot a buck, and you think it's a clean shot. But when you get close it's kicking and moaning."

Martin turns his face away, not sure he wants to hear this, but he can't avoid listening without leaving the porch.

"It should be dead, it's shot through the heart. But the damn thing won't die. It's flopping around, trying to get up. Blood all over the ground. Try to help and you're likely as not to get kicked. Break your neck. Moving too much to shoot it again, not without making things worse, so you wait. Watch it die." Gil takes a drink. "Awful noise, an animal dying. Even the ones you think don't make sounds always find one way or another. Even a rabbit'll put you on edge. Gets you like howling wolves." He takes a long drink, and stares out into the yard, toward the hills across the street and beyond the building site, where the sun is approaching the peaks.

"Always go for the clean shot, Marty. Stay in control. You get panicked, you get jumpy, you'll have a half-dead buck and a kick in the head. No good all around."

Martin tries to shake the gruesome scene Gil has painted, but it's lodged in his mind's eye. "But, see," he says, "I can't help thinking that if the deer hadn't been shot in the first place . . . "

"It would get sick from being crowded," Gil snaps, "or it would eat your garden or get killed by a wolf. They die, Marty. Everything does. Can't be helped so you make the most of it."

Martin plunks tinny notes from the pull-tab on his beer can with both thumbs.

"Hell, say that bear'd killed you. Would you be complaining in heaven? Saying it wasn't right? Bear shoulda left you alone 'cause you don't eat meat?"

"No, but . . . "

"No nothing. That's how it works." Gil waves an arm toward his outbuildings and yard or perhaps toward the woods beyond them. "Can't have it both ways."

An uncomfortable silence falls between them—uncomfortable for Martin, at least—as they finish their beers and look toward distant hills slipping into shadow as the sun dips into late afternoon. Then a phone rings, and the two men jump at the sound. Gil gathers their empty plates and heads into the house. Behind him, through the screen door, Martin hears one side of a conversation but he can't make out the words. He watches a third crow join the others down in the yard, their beaks bowing in and out of the grass.

Gil's back on the porch a few minutes later. "Takin' a ride, Marty. Sheriff says Elmer Tully's gone missing."

"Did something happen to him?"

"To Elmer? I'll bet what happened is he got drinking and took a walk. Curled up under a tree with a headache. He's waiting for someone to bring him an aspirin."

"But the sheriff is concerned?"

"Way he tells it, Elmer's back door is all busted like something came in. Sounds like Elmer being Elmer to me, but I said I'd look." Gil starts down the steps toward his truck, pulling his cap down tight on his head. Then he turns back and asks, "You coming? Or you gonna sit there and drink all my beer?"

As Martin empties his can and carries it to the bag, he hears Gil laughing to himself in the cab of the truck.

Gil isn't rushing to Elmer's rescue because he's especially fond of the man. Neither is the sheriff, for that matter: it's duty, for both of them. Elmer may be the town drunk, a troublemaker more often than not, passing out on the town square and shouting obscenities at public events when he isn't muttering to himself or wandering catatonic; he may be all those things, but he's also part of the town, as much as the sheriff is, or Gil. As much as he can be a burden, he's one with whom folks are familiar so they're willing to accommodate his peculiarities more than they might be for an outsider.

Better the eyes that glare by the light of your fire than those that gleam in the dark.

So Gil's truck rattles along the dirt track from the main road toward Elmer's farm, and the two men bounce around on its bench seat. The track runs through a swathe of thick weeds meant at one time as a vineyard, according to Gil, and when Martin asks if you can even grow decent grapes this far north his neighbor shrugs. There's a crumbling white house at the top of the drive; its roof pitches sideways, lower at one end than the other as if it's sliding off the walls. Rusted steel drums and old washing machines litter the overgrown yard, and an enormous red pickup truck stands under a carport and gives the appearance it hasn't moved in a long time. Three iron bathtubs with clawed feet stand end-to-end by a collapsing gray fence, filled to their brims with rainwater and leaves.

The sheriff's car is in front of the house with a second cruiser behind it. "Let's see what's what," Gil says, and he and Martin climb out of the truck. A few seconds after their doors slam closed, Sheriff Lindon emerges from behind the house. His legs look too skinny beneath the brown pants of his uniform to support the barrel of torso balanced on top, and when he walks his body sways with each step as if battling its own inertia.

"Gil," the sheriff says with a nod. He glances in Martin's direction, but doesn't acknowledge his presence.

"Lindon," Gil answers. He's always called Sheriff or Lindon, and Martin doesn't know if that's a first or last name. He hangs back a few feet away as the other men step toward each other, both smoking.

"Well?" Gil asks.

"Somebody broke the back door pretty good. Cracked the jamb and popped the screen from its frame." The sheriff's voice is so rough that it makes Martin thirsty from listening, and he swallows twice to sooth his own throat.

"Seen Elmer?" Gil asks.

"Nope. That's why I called you." Lindon squints in Martin's direction then takes the last puff of his cigarette before flicking the butt hard at the dirt of the drive. He scratches at one of his bushy, salt-and-pepper sideburns with the fingertips of one hand. "Come out back, Gil. I've got something to show you."

Martin follows the other men around the side of the house, where an electrical line coming up from the street sags close to the ground. The gray steel junction box it's attached to has pulled away from the wall far enough that a hand could slide in behind it.

A white aluminum storm door is propped against the back stoop, twisted and sharp where the metal has split, and black shreds of screen flutter all over the ground. The door frame itself, unpainted wood gone gray with age, is gouged with sets of parallel lines. They could be the scratches on Martin's chest only deeper, deep enough that if the wood was his skin he'd be dead.

He touches a hand to his shirt, and feels the dull pain of the cuts under layers of cotton and gauze and the sharper pain of his bruises where he's pressed them.

"The hell?" Gil mutters as he climbs two cement steps to the doorway and crouches with his eye near the scarred wood. Martin tries to get a look at the damage without bumping into the sheriff.

Lindon sighs, then fishes around in his shirt pocket for a loose cigarette. "You know what folks'll say happened." Gil nods without bending away from the door frame. "We'll wanna nip that in the bud."

"What?" Martin asks, but no reply comes. "What will they say?"

"Those scratches go right down the hallway," Sheriff Lindon tells Gil. "Bedroom's a mess. Blankets torn up on the floor and pillow foam everywhere." He steps up beside Gil and looks into the house as he smokes. "Seems it oughta be bloody with all that damage, but there isn't a drop."

"If something got Elmer in bed," Gil says, "it'd be bloody. Can't see how it wouldn't."

"Sure."

Still on the ground at the bottom of the steps, with no room beside the other two men for him to squeeze up for a look through the door, Martin asks, "Did something attack him?"

The sheriff pivots his head for a quick look at the interloper, then turns back to Gil and keeps talking. He gestures lazily toward the yard behind the house and says, "Found some of his clothes in the yard here. Ripped all to hell, too. Gorman's using them for scent with the dog."

Gil runs his fingers and eyes around the sides of the doorframe. Then he stands up and lights a cigarette. "Nothing broke in, Lindon."

"The fuck're you talking about? Something did this."

"Take a look at these scratches." Gil points at the gouges nearest the doorknob with the glowing tip of his cigarette. "Door's pushed from the inside."

"Now what're you . . . " the sheriff sputters, then leans close to look where Gil's pointing. "Son of a bitch, you're right. What the hell happened?"

Gil doesn't answer but steps from the stoop to the yard. He shades his eyes with both hands wrapped around the brim of his cap. Martin follows his gaze down the slope of Elmer's farm toward the woods on the other side of a cornfield. "Look at that crush in the corn," Gil says, pointing. "That's where it went."

"Goddamnit." The sheriff pulls the radio from his belt and tells someone somewhere what's going on.

Gil turns and walks back toward his truck. He calls over his shoulder, "Guess I'll go see." Martin and Lindon follow him around the side of the house. He reaches into the cab and pulls a rifle from the rack in the window. Then he pops open the rusted cargo box in the bed of the truck and digs around in a rattle of tools before emerging with a cardboard box of ammunition; the box and its bullets are taller than Martin expected, but all he knows about guns would fit inside either one. After stuffing the box into his pocket, Gil digs out another and loads the gun, adjusts his cap, and asks, "Who's coming?"

Lindon says, "I'll stay here and see what turns up." He nods toward the deputy's car parked in back of his own. "Gorman's still looking down by the road."

Gil claps a hand to Martin's shoulder and pushes him toward the corn. "Come on, Marty. Help me out here."

As they start walking, Gil loosens his grip.

They crunch into the cornfield, rustling through tall, late-summer stalks. Martin isn't sure, but he thinks all the other cornfields he's noticed in town have already been cut, while Elmer's still stands so high.

Gil walks in front, bent toward the ground with the rifle across his body. Martin wishes, despite himself, he was armed, too. He's never fired a gun, or held one at all, but right now his hands feel too empty. He walks with his arms bent in front of his body, trying to keep the dry, sharp-edged plants from his face.

Gil stops and kneels down, touching the trampled husks and soil on the ground. "Went through here," he says over a shoulder.

"What do you think it was?"

"Probably Elmer. Got drunk and smashed up his house. Not the first time he's lost himself."

They press forward into the corn, startling four fat, black crows. The birds burst into the air screeching and cursing. Martin tries to imagine a human being—even one who drinks to the point of violence—doing the damage he saw at the house, but doesn't see how it could happen. "Could a person have done all that? Even drunk?"

"Folks do all kinds of things. Saw their own arms off to get out of a trap." Gil's voice is flat and direct in a tone that leaves no room for questions, though his analogy doesn't make much sense to Martin. Gil crouches and pushes apart some plants where they're pressed to the ground, then pulls something out from between the stalks and holds it up to his eyes. "Lookit."

Martin moves closer to look at a small tuft of yellow fur, pinched between Gil's oil-stained fingers. "What'd that come from?"

"Well, it wasn't your bear," Gil laughs. He rolls the tuft between the pads of his fingers and it tightens into a braid. "Color's too light to be any of the usual animals around here. Maybe that cat Elmer ran into." He points out some vague indentations in the dirt where they show through the crushed corn. "Footprints say so." Gil rises from his crouch and moves deeper into the field.

"Jesus," Martin mutters as he stands up. He looks around but all he can see is the corn rising over his head. When a breeze blows it rattles as if the field is full of snakes. "I thought you said a mountain lion wouldn't stay around here."

Gil stops walking and snaps his head around to look right at Martin. There's a new edge to his voice when he asks, "When did you get to be such an expert? If the cat's still here, it's still here. That's what the gun's for."

Martin keeps to himself any questions about endangered species and the legalities of shooting them, especially if you go looking to do it. He's too new in town to start crossing people who have been around as long as Gil has, not if he wants to get his houses built. And his neighbor has spent more time around animals, and more time in the woods, than he ever has. Far more. Besides, the snarl that has come into the older man's voice makes Martin less than eager to ask any questions.

They stand facing each other for a few seconds longer, then Gil's expression softens back to its usual red, wrinkled calm. But doubts must still hang on Martin's face because Gil finally tells him, "Well shit, Marty, we won't shoot it if it isn't a threat. Come on now."

They carry on through the corn without speaking until at last the field ends and they emerge at the edge of the forest. As his body sweats and strains, the pain increases in Martin's ribs. His bruised muscles ache and his back feels tight. In time, Gil points his rifle at a gap in the scrub and says, "In here."

The woods feel familiar to Martin within a few steps. These aren't the same acres he crossed yesterday, but they are filled with the same plants and sounds. They're drenched in the same sticky-sweet, rotten smell. The air under the trees is as hot and humid as a greenhouse, and sweat runs down Martin's neck to his chest and soaks into the gauze of his bandages, making the wounds sting again.

Stumbling along behind Gil, he asks, "What if it wasn't Elmer who messed up his house? What if something really did take him?"

"Elmer's too big to be taken by much," Gil answers without turning around. "Figure he left the door open and something locked itself in. Had to claw its way out. Maybe even this cat you're so fond of."

"Does that happen?"

"As often as Elmer gets drunk. Animals're always looking for a door to walk in. They're curious. Lazy, if you give 'em a chance. A few weeks ago I found a raccoon behind my couch sleeping away. Elmer says he caught a deer eating salt in his pantry." Gil shakes a cigarette into his mouth and lights it without missing a step. "Of course, Elmer sees things."

"I think something was on my bed last night," Martin says. "I found some fur there this morning."

Gil laughs, and then holds the smoldering cigarette in one hand as he coughs. "Teach you to leave your door open." He smiles, and his eyes, angry a moment ago, become brighter. Martin considers telling Gil about the strange sensations he got from smelling the sheets where the creatures had been—that he knew it was two bodies rather than one, how it set off his senses—but he doesn't want to explain why he was smelling the bed where something had slept.

The trees thin around them as they walk, and the two men emerge into a clearing. A round patch of dirt in a pool of tall, swaying grass is lit from above by the sun. It's the same spot he dreamt of when he fell asleep on his plans, or another similar spot, and without meaning to he says it looks familiar.

"You been here before?"

"Uh, I thought so, but . . . maybe not," he stutters, covering his tracks, unwilling to tell Gil about the dreams he's been having.

"Maybe you passed by here wandering around yesterday."

"Maybe," Martin agrees, but he's trying to remember exactly what happened here in his dream, and is trying equally hard to keep his face from revealing more than he wants to.

He might not be so reluctant if he knew the dreams Gil wakes from every night in a sweat, when he's able to sleep. Forty-some years since the war, since he slogged through all that mud and through jungles peeled clean by chemicals sprayed from above, and still the blood washes over his dreams and keeps him awake. It's gotten worse through the years until now he hardly bothers going to bed—the occasional cat-nap in his chair on the porch, or on his couch in front of the TV on winter nights, is the closest he comes to real sleep most of the time. As soon as he closes his eyes, his mind grows crowded with the shredded bodies and hollow voices of men whose faces and names he remembers as well as anything else in his life. The strange bushes and spiders and snakes, after years learning these woods and thinking he knew the world, only to find a whole green, wild world he knew nothing about. A world that knew nothing of him, not even enough to avoid groups of men and their guns.

The harder he tries to push all that out of his head, the more insistent the phantoms become until he gives up on sleep, gets out of bed, and pours himself a drink on the porch where he can keep an eye on the woods. It's worse since he retired—he hasn't had one good night's sleep since he stopped guiding hunters and stopped hunting himself, more or less—and the amount of whiskey it takes to come close makes the next day hardly worth waking up for. So he sits through the dark, night after night, listening to the forest around him, and somehow just sitting quiet for hours does almost as much for him as sleep used to do.

The lonely and homesick half-orphan, the old soldier haunted . . . they're types, they're familiar, as indistinct as I suppose you find one bear or fox from another. It's so easy to pay attention to the wrong parts of their lives and to get hung up on where a life comes from and not where it's going. Too easy to think the point of other lives lies in touching your own, in confirming how you know the world works, but why tell a story you already know?

We could go on about Gil's bloody dreams and the war he brought home, the map of some other place and its memories he laid over this land years ago, layered among all the maps and other memories spread out by one generation after another. But this story's not his. Gil's not the kind of dreamer I'm after. Martin is malleable, his desires as easily bounced off their target as a satellite dish knocked askew. His will is more easily replaced with my own, because so much of what makes him up is empty space. Gil's seen too much, he's too set in his ways and too sure of how little his life adds up to in the end, but Martin hasn't a clue what his own life is worth.

No more than he knows where this trail he's on leads.

As they cross the bare earth of the clearing, something green appears in the dirt. Gil crouches, balancing his rifle across one knee, and lifts a swatch of cloth from the ground. He runs the fingertips of one hand through the dirt. "Claw prints here, too. Looks to me our cat tore up some of Elmer's clothes in the house and dragged 'em outside." He crumples the cloth in his hand and shoves it into a pocket. He looks back in the direction of the house, now out of sight, and adds, "Must've hung onto this bit a while."

Martin almost points out how wholly Gil seems to have accepted the presence of an animal he denied a short time ago, but the satisfaction of saying so is outweighed by the shock of Gil's earlier reaction. So he stands speechless above his crouched neighbor, scanning the trees and the clearing, trying to reconstruct his dream. He remembers running through the woods, feeling like some kind of animal, and ending up in this place. He met something here, a man who didn't move like a man, and wasn't he wearing green clothes, or was he wearing nothing at all? Martin knows something ran into the trees on the other side of the dirt, and he pictures it sleek and leonine, but he would, now, wouldn't he? After the dream I seeded this with? With the mountain lion so much on his mind?

His dream—my dream—came to him only a few hours ago but has already faded, and the harder Martin pushes to remember the more distant it seems. Its signal has decayed over time, and he's so tired after his night without decent sleep, his body is so sore and battered, that it's hard to draw distinctions between what took place in his dreams and what really happened. It's hard for him know what's only fantasy spun and believed by his tired, fraying mind—his earlier, unlikely suggestion of a mountain lion dragging a man away into the woods.

Something moves in the trees, behind the curtain, and both men look up. "Did you hear . . . " Martin asks, but is shushed by Gil's upraised hand. A soundless shape slides through the brush, yellow and long, fading in and out of the dry grass and leaves.

Gil lowers one knee to the ground for support and raises the rifle butt to his shoulder. Martin takes an involuntary step backward, toward the path on which they arrived, away from Gil's gun and away from the shape in the shadows.

The mountain lion melts out of the scrub and into the clearing, head swinging back and forth on its shoulders with each liquid step. Its body is a vast stretch of ribs slung between thick, broad-pawed legs, and under the block of its head a triangle of tufted white fur slopes down its chest. The cat is only a few yards away, moving in slowly, and Martin is shocked by how casual its approach seems to be. Despite the weapon pointed right at it, the animal walks as if it's approaching a friend, like the gun is aimed somewhere else. It hasn't even bared teeth, but for all Martin knows about mountain lions, baring teeth isn't something they do. It's larger, but doesn't look any more threatening than the house cats that wander up to Martin's trailer from the town's houses and farms, waiting for milk from his cereal bowl.

There's a crack, then its echo, and a thin wisp of smoke twists away from the black tip of Gil's gun. At the sound of the shot, birds erupt into the air from the woods all around and for a second, before they disperse, the beat of their wings is a frantic heartbeat filling the world.

A red flower blooms on the white field of the animal's chest, and the cat crumples. Martin remembers a toy he had once, a tiny wooden man made of segmented parts held together by elastic string; when a button was pushed under his feet the elastic went loose and his body piled up on itself the way the cat's has.

Martin's stomach turns. His mouth falls open but he can't say a word. He's not sure why Gil had to shoot, and his mind replays what happened only a second ago, trying to find some threat of attack, some reason the cat should be killed. He holds his tongue and waits for Gil's explanation as his mouth fills with the acidic taste of the lump in his throat.

The cat, dying on the ground before them, has a look in its wet yellow eyes as if this was the last thing it ever expected. Maybe this is what Gil meant about animals forgetting their fear of mankind, their fear of getting shot. Maybe this cat has been reminded.

Gil doesn't offer the explanation Martin awaits. He's over the cat with a knife, jerking its head one way then the other, checking its pulse and its eyes, saying, "Give me a hand." Martin approaches, and the dead lion's fur ripples in a light wind through the trees. It's a false sign of life, though he half-expects the motion of the coat to slide into the legs, for the paws to stretch out and the tail to rise before the animal climbs to its feet. But the lion is very much dead.

"Hold him upright," Gil says, pushing the hind legs toward Martin, who grips them because he doesn't know what else to do. Then Gil's knife is in the cat's groin, dissembling it, the blade's motion as smooth as a zipper. Whether it's real or imagination or nausea, Martin feels the heat of the animal's exposed organs rising from the cut belly onto his face and it's all he can do not to vomit on the back of Gil's head and into the mountain lion's guts. He's holding the legs, but he's looking away.

"Quit jerking," snaps Gil, moving in quick, controlled, masterful motions, and already the lion is open; its hips would fall flat if Martin let go.

Martin looks away into the trees, he tries not to notice the anus and intestines Gil hurls to one side, he tries not to see as Gil unzips the rest of the cat and reaches up under the ribs to pull down the whole bundle of organs, as he stretches them away from the body. But he can't ignore it when the hunter commands, "Need you to make a cut, Marty. Right here."

So he kneels, lightheaded, overcome by the blood and the heat and sound of the shot that still echoes, at least in his head. Gil's holding the knife in a hand that is also holding the organs, so Martin must reach toward the kidneys, the stomach, the heart to take the knife from his neighbor. Even brushing them with the back of his fingers makes his own stomach lurch, but he manages, somehow, to receive the blade and to slice through a white membrane that tries as hard as it can to hold onto these organs, these parts of its body, along the inside of the stomach.

Then Gil says, "Underneath, Marty. Cut the gut sack free underneath." And Martin's arm—or an arm that is his but at a distance, another body he's watching, amazed and aghast—is in the cat's ribcage and slicing through sinews and arteries and connective tissues, then Gil has the whole bundle of organs and drops them to one side with a sickening wet plop.

What's left of the cat is a cavern—more empty, more missing, than Martin could ever imagine a warm body being. The carcass is pooled with blood, and Martin, this strange other Martin, helps Gil roll it over and pour that blood into the dirt.

Gil says, "Not bad, Marty. Not bad," and the firm pat on his shoulder brings Martin back to himself, worrying but not wanting to know how much blood and who knows what else of the lion Gil's touch left on his shirt. "Now let's get him on out of here." He looks around for a second, at what remains of the cat and at Martin, before saying, "We could drag him but I'd have to get back to the truck for a rope. Hell, we can haul him. Between the two of us."

Beside them, the abandoned organs are already bustling and buzzing with flies, no time wasted on mourning. Lives overlap, devouring each other, a river of time flowing through that one bloody moment.

Gil beckons for Martin to crouch, then lifts the hind-end of the corpse onto his shoulder so the legs hang down his back. Then Gil hoists the head and the chest so they rest on his own back and shoulders. When they stand, even the beast's gutted weight nearly brings Martin onto his knees—the body is so lean and looks so light, collapsed at the sides where they've hollowed it out, still it's all he can do to stay upright beneath it. He shifts the load to make it steady, and the heavy paws knuckle across his lower back. Then Gil starts down the trail, leaving the clearing in the same order they came, but now with the long, bloody weight of a dead mountain lion between them.

The taut body rubs Martin's cheek as he walks, and its short bristled fur scratches against his own stubble. The bowels and bladder clenched then relaxed when the bullet entered the heart, leaving a steaming, acrid pool in the clearing, and although the anus and bladder were cast aside with the rest of the innards, now the bouncing motion of walking dislodges the last clinging drops so they spill down Martin's back and onto the trail at his feet while the incision—if that clinical word isn't too much for the great, long cut down this cat—still bleeds into the air between his own body and Gil's, and drips onto the ground. The burning smell of the fluids and the heat of the body churn his stomach, and he fights to keep the bile down, all the way back to Elmer's farm.

It's nearly dark when they reach the crumbling house. The sheriff is gone and the broken door has been sealed with a board and some nails. There's a note tacked to the board and Gil walks up to read it with the mountain lion still on his shoulder. Martin stands below at the foot of the steps, and the steep angle of the cat's body increases its weight on his back, almost buckling him as he waits for Gil to descend. With its head on Gil's shoulder and hind legs hanging down Martin's back, the lion looks as if it is leaping into the air, pouncing toward something inside the house.

"Lindon figures this the way we do," Gil reports. "Elmer'll turn up in a couple of days, nothing to show but a headache."

Martin nods to acknowledge Gil's words, but keeps his mouth closed for fear of what might come out.

He's out of his depth in all this. Beyond all he's imagined. But he was the moment he came to the woods, and a few minutes later they're back in the truck, the big cat stretched behind them and bouncing in the bed with each bump of the road. Martin rolls his window all the way down and watches the forest scroll by. He opens his mouth wide and holds his head out so the wind washes away the bad taste.

Gil and the sheriff and other people in town seem so at ease with these strange events—people gone missing, and mountain lions; a hole in the ground full of bones. They're used to this place, and all of this seems strange to him, Martin assures himself, only because he isn't.

He's only half right. It is easier for the locals to accept strange events because they have someone to blame. They have me, and I have a name people around here can remember. As long as there's Scratch to attach these things to, and there has been forever, it's remarkable how much more willing they are to make sense of some things they probably shouldn't.

Gil and the sheriff and so many others are willing to believe this place is strange, that these woods are haunted—the way they would put it—by a restless spirit in the shape of a bear. More willing than they would be to consider the danger in this forest might be their own kind. It's a comfort, of sorts, to relax in the grip of something bigger and older and more powerful than themselves. They put up with this place so long as they aren't asked how it might involve them, how Elmer's disappearance or Martin's attack might be more than arbitrary. As long as it stays familiar—strange things may happen, but that's what they've come to expect—it's easier to endure what they've taken for granted as the ordinary fabric of local life.

Martin is more willing to notice that things aren't as simple as the locals want them to be. He notices, at least, that some things are strange. That's why he's useful to me. That's his appeal: he's more easily bent. But even he—right now, anyway—would have trouble believing the cat his neighbor killed and which he, Martin, hauled out of the woods on his own aching shoulder was, until a short time ago, Elmer Tully himself. This morning, Elmer found himself tangled in the sheets of his bed in an unfamiliar body with no idea he had ever been anything else but a cat, a cat trapped in the cage of a house from which he escaped. But when he saw Gil in the woods, some lingering dream in his animal mind marked the man as familiar, and he approached before animal instinct could override the attraction.

84

Unlikely, perhaps? Impossible? No more so than invisible stories that fly through the air.

Had he left behind those human attachments, Elmer Tully—or the cat he became—would have survived long enough to make his way into the woods. I had hopes he would, when I transformed him, even when I first coaxed the mountain lion into crossing his path a few days ago to set these events into motion. But there's only so much I can do. Sometimes a body is born to die.

9

WHEN MARTIN WAS TEN, HE AND HIS MOTHER WERE LIVing in an apartment that was actually theirs instead of space shared with a man. Across the street from their building was a park once inviting and green, but by the time Martin moved there the monkey bars had been bent down by restless teenagers grown up with nothing better to do than hang in the night. What little grass remained on the ground had been burnt by the sun and the sour fumes of traffic, or trampled by feet hurrying home through the dangerous dark.

Martin's mother was never home; she'd never been home, he was used to it, but now they had their own home and she was *still* never there. His ten-year-old head couldn't make sense of that: finally having her own place to be but not being there. So he decided to make his own home, somewhere else, by himself or with a family who let him run on their grass and sleep in their beds and take a long time to finish his dinner because he was so busy talking to everyone else at the table. He packed clean underwear and socks into his backpack, put on brand new jeans with bright orange stitching, and made as many peanut butter and jelly sandwiches as he could fit in his lunchbox while leaving room for a thermos of cranberry juice.

He locked the door to the apartment, picked his way down the crumbling, crooked stairs to the street, and looked both ways into traffic before crossing to the edge of the park. In the dead, dusty square Martin weighed all his options. There were six streets he could choose from, on all sides of the park, and he couldn't decide which way to go. He sat on the concrete support of what had been a bench, its wooden slats broken off to be burnt on one cold night or another, and he looked up and across the street at the apartment he'd left behind.

The sky was turning the blue-black of iron but there was still enough light to see into his room, to see it in shadow. On the shelf over what had been his bed for the past several months he saw model cars lined up in a row, and the baseball trophy he'd won in another town the summer before.

He saw the bottom corner of his World Series poster and the cap his mother's last boyfriend had given him the first time they met, still hanging on the post of the bed where he'd left it.

He wished he'd brought the hat. That boyfriend had promised to take Martin to his parents' farm for the summer but was gone before they ever went. Perhaps he should go back into the apartment to get it.

For a long time he sat on the bench, until he couldn't see through the window at all, until skeletal older boys emerged from their lairs to hang from the bent monkey bars with their knees scraping the ground. Martin ate two of his sandwiches and watched the aerials on top of buildings sway back and forth in a breeze so high he couldn't feel it down in the park.

He sat until he saw his mother weaving her way down the street on the arm of a man he didn't know. Then he ran back into their building, ahead of her so she wouldn't see, and he was doing his homework at their gray-flecked kitchen table when he heard her key in the lock and both her own laugh and a deeper one behind it outside the door.

It isn't as easy to run away from a life as Martin thought it would be. There are voices commanding us to remain in the places we come from, calling us back when we leave, even if we clamp our ears tight to the sides of our heads and pretend not to hear. Or do what it is each animal does when it doesn't want to listen, when it doesn't want to be called. None seem to work very well, though: the places and bodies we run from can't always follow, but their voices always echo across the distance we've stretched between them and us, growing louder and louder until they find our unwilling ears. It's hard to leave spaces empty; they want to be filled with something to take the place of what's gone. Something is always displaced, the coyote whose body you're wearing now or the mountain lion I replaced with Elmer Tully. If the life ousted in favor of something or someone else isn't given a new shape of its own, the wills of the new and the old battle for control of the body—the way yours is telling you to sleep and to howl and to run. You'll only need that body for a short time, so it shouldn't matter, but if you tried to keep it forever the conflicting desires would drive both you and that body mad.

It was no easier for Martin to leave an empty space in the life he had made with his mother; it was too hard to picture one of them without the other, at least until he became older. First when he went to college, then for the ladder he's climbed to reach his current life, and at last to his trailer out here in the woods where the ground is full of broken old bones and mountain lions look surprised when you shoot them. He moved miles and miles away from that ruined park in the city, but never filled that empty space with anything else, so it's no wonder he hasn't quite left it behind. It's no wonder the loudest voice in his life calls him to return to a place that doesn't and couldn't exist, that he's pushed by an unquestioned instinct to build it—or try to—the same as that bear he ran into is pushed toward hibernation each winter. Martin's not so different from any of us, suspended between where we come from and where we imagine we do, between a vague future and uncomfortable present and the safety of a past we can return to again and again because it never quite happened at all.

He'll build his houses based on some dream, some wild desire, as people have done here for centuries and as rabbits have burrowed, bears denned, and squirrels nested since long before that. But there's always a fox waiting outside your hole or a wind waiting to pull down your nest or another life to overwrite yours, to fill the space you've made for yourself.

MARTIN SITS ATOP THE TALL CHAIR IN FRONT OF HIS DRAFTing table and rolls it back and forth with his feet. He's eating a bowl of miso soup made from paste and drinking a bottle of water, thinking about the dead mountain lion he helped hang on a chain in Gil's barn, slouched like an old overcoat on a rack. He went home when Gil parted the first bright red meat from skin and bone, when the animal stopped looking so much like itself.

The cat's face comes back to him now, the white triangle of its chest clouding red in the seconds after Gil's shot. Its eyes swelling wide and its lower jaw slack. His mind floods with the choreography of the animal's death, the way its shoulders slumped forward and how the body pitched to one side. The lower jaw struck the ground hard enough for Martin to hear the rattle of teeth. A long, pink tongue hung out one side of the mouth, a sharp tooth driven up through it by the weight of the body's collapse. Dark blood spilled over the cat's lower lip and ran down its jowl in twin streams.

The cat goes on rising and falling in Martin's head, a short, silent film in a loop. He closes his eyes, pinches the bridge of his nose, and tries to drive the image away. He doesn't know when he began pinching the bridge of his nose, or how long he's relied on the gesture. It doesn't feel familiar, but perhaps he's been doing it all his life and has only noticed now.

As he slurps the last strains of soup from his mug, his tongue catches on the rough point of a tooth and he tastes the rusty flavor of his own blood. He's sure the jagged tip wasn't there yesterday, or even this morning, and he pictures the miniature landscape of his mouth, the tiny ridges and gorges on top of a molar, a microcosmic mirror of the hills around his new home. He had a cavity a couple years back that seemed able to swallow the tip of his tongue, but when the dentist held up the extracted wisdom tooth between two bloody fingers the hole was little more than a pinprick.

He runs a finger over the sharpened tooth, still slippery with soup. Though the mysterious dimensions inside his mouth make it hard to be sure, this canine feels higher than its complement in the opposite jaw. Perhaps it broke off without his being aware, leaving an isolated point like a tower and the illusion of increased height.

There's a show about dung beetles wrapping up on TV, and then one begins about birds—Arctic terns and their long, homeward treks, from pole to pole twice a year. The narrator calmly announces through the crackle of lousy reception how many birds die every season for the sake of getting back to where they began.

Martin spreads his map across the drafting table again, and works out where he and Gil went on their drive to Elmer's. The house isn't there, only a side road that looks on paper to end at no place, so he sketches it in complete with power lines and notations about the damage to the bedroom inside and backdoor. He guesses at the path they took through Elmer's yard, and adds hash marks to show the cornfield with a darkened swathe where he and Gil crossed it. The map shows the woods but not the clearing, so he draws in a rough circle and labels where the cat fell, where Gil fired his gun. He goes back to the cornfield to indicate where they found the first tuft of fur, then scans across the page to his own building site, and marks the clean white paper that stands in for brown, muddy ground to show where they dug up the bones.

With these new annotations and the others he's added, the clean sky of his map has grown clouded as pencil marks begin crowding the bolder black lines of printer's ink. The ink still dominates, Martin's plans still shine through, but the space is becoming a squeeze.

Evening has fallen quickly outside, sneaking up as it does in these last days of summer, and fireflies speckle the air. Martin steps to the trailer's collapsible stairs with a steaming mug of tea in his hand. The air is quiet and cool with the calm of a storm approaching; he hears thunder on the other side of the hills long before swathes of deep purple appear over their peaks. He sits on the top step and sips tea until the first raindrops fall, pinging the metal roof of his home and churning a tempest in his mug as the deluge picks up. The fireflies are gone now to wherever they go in the rain, and with the moon blanketed in thick, smoky clouds the only light is what slips through the blinds of his window and across the wet ground in thin strips.

He sits as the rain comes down harder, soaking his hair and tracing the lines of his face. Razor-blade lightning slices the sky, and Martin counts Mississippis before thunderclaps rattle the frame of his trailer and shake the stairs under his feet. He counts ten before the first boom, and he tries to remember if that means the storm is ten miles off or if each second counted represents half a mile and the storm is twice as close. He's still trying to decide when the next jag splits the dark, and thunder comes six seconds after.

He'd like to know why Mississippi: is it only the length of the word, or a chant learned from people missing that state? The prayers of stranded travelers reminding themselves between flash and boom what they had to live for and where they had to return, a prayer adopted by the rest of the country for reasons lost to history's swirl. Should we all find our own prayer for living, our own lightning counter, and what would his be if we did?

Each bolt bursts the trees into green silhouette, long enough for him to register the rippling of leaves, the shaking of branches and white towers of birch at the edge of the woods. He wonders where animals go when it storms, and pictures the bear huddled inside the fireplace as he was, ducked out of the rain. What does a bear make of thunder and lightning? Is it the end of the world every time a storm comes? Or does instinct assure them that this, too, will pass and they'll be back to routine by the morning?

Aino, the dog he spent that still week with, always ran to a particular closet at the first boom of thunder and curled in a deep corner until the whole storm had passed. She found a quiet spot to wait out the storm the way homeowners are advised to huddle in their cellars when a tornado comes.

Emptied of tea and set on the step beside him, his chipped enamel mug refills quickly with rain. He knows he could go into the trailer, stay dry, but the pounding on the roof is so much worse than wet taps on his face—the metallic echo inside is a headache waiting to happen—so he stays where he is on the steps. It only takes a few minutes for dark streams of water to streak across his building site and down the soft slope to the road. Raindrops bounce off the bulldozer's roof, a rush of eruptions on its yellow steel surface, and the teacup churns beside Martin.

He tries again to measure the distance between himself and the storm, opting for half-mile increments, but the thunder arrives before he gets to one, so close overhead it shakes the bones in his body. The echo bounces back and forth through the valley for several long seconds, so loud he imagines it might go on for years, that the town could get used to the permanent reverberation of a long-ago storm, even become a tourist destination for its strange, ceaseless sound the way some places offer spots in the road where cars seem to be rolling uphill. But soon the rumbling echo dies down, making room for the next thunderclap.

He hardly notices wet clothes plastered to him, his T-shirt transparent in places and his bare feet half-buried in mud at the foot of the stairs. He's lost track of time, of how long he's been sitting outside, and now the storm seems to be slowing. Rain tapers off until it leaves only a shower light enough for the burnt odor of ozone to rise through the air. Lightning flashes move into the distance on the other side of the trailer and far past the site, and the time between flash and bang increases with every set. The moon pokes its head out from under cloud blankets, a pale thumbnail over the hills, and fireflies emerge from their shelters to flit through the trees and gossip about the storm they've just seen. To speak in a language washed clean the way only thunder and lightning can do, the exhausted words taking on bright new life when faced with something so everyday, but so hard to explain all the same.

Now that the world is quiet again, Martin finds himself thinking of Alison, of his botched attempts to talk to her about something other than work. He wants to tell someone what happened with Gil, about Elmer's wrecked home and the dead mountain lion, and Alison is the first person who comes to mind. She's the only person he has had a real conversation with since he arrived, apart from his neighbor, and even those have been about the construction more often than anything else.

Buoyed by the reemergence of bugs and bats, and the many soft noises of nighttime, by the miniature spring that blossoms at the end of each summer storm, Martin forgets where he is and slips his phone from his pocket. There's a signal, for once, perhaps the air is electric after the storm and the whole world has become his antenna, so he scrolls to and dials

Alison's number. Three rings come and go and by the fourth ring he's back in junior high school with his friends, daring each other to call girls they know vaguely from class but with nothing to say if and when those girls answer—summoning the nerve to pick up the phone was the thing, to make the connection, reach out—the conversation merely incidental.

It's late. She might be asleep, or she might be reaching for the phone in the dark and pulling it to her head on a pillow. There's a faint chirp on the line that could be someone saying hello; Martin opens his mouth but his phone beeps three times to signal its lost connection, then falls silent as every call made from his trailer has done.

Embarrassed, he stands on the bottom step and stretches his back, and he feels—or thinks he feels—the whole of his foundationless home shift on the softened muddy ground with his weight. Then he climbs back inside and peels off wet clothes that have become claustrophobic and cloying now that the deluge has stopped, and he slings them over the side of the shower before sliding his sore body into its bed, where he falls asleep too quickly to feel himself drifting off.

11

H IS DREAM SELF IS BACK IN THE WOODS, BACK BEHIND GIL on the trail toward the clearing where they ran into the lion. He follows the hunter's broad back and orange cap ever deeper into the bush, ducking and weaving through branches and vines. He opens his mouth to say something, to ask some urgent question, but what comes isn't his voice: it's a soft growl, a rattle in the back of his throat, and rather than answer Gil turns with the gun held out before him, his eyes flicking over the trees.

Martin hasn't been seen. He's following at a distance, carving his own path through the scrub, parallel to the trail.

After swinging the rifle back and forth a few times, Gil adjusts his hat and keeps walking, and Martin draws even off to one side. He doesn't know why he's trailing the hunter but the urge is too strong to resist; his legs drive themselves, on footsteps softer and surer than if he was in control.

At last Gil enters the clearing and discovers the tattered green sleeve of the shirt as he did in waking life a few hours before. Martin moves in a circle around the old man, close to the edge of the trees but unseen, creeping sideways and close to the ground. His body feels dense, coiled, and another growl rolls unbidden up the back of his throat.

Gil starts at the sound, balancing himself on one knee with the rifle aimed at the trees, zeroing in on the source. The top button of his black-and-white checkered jacket is open, and Martin eyes the pale triangle of flesh between the collar of Gil's shirt and his red, ruddy chin—the stubble-specked stretch of his throat where it floats a few inches over the gun.

In the shadowed forest Gil's neck is a beacon, a lighthouse at sea, and the desire to pounce quivers in Martin's feet as he rocks forward and back on the ground. He crouches, legs tight, arms digging for traction in the packed earth. His body shuffles sideways, still coiled, until the gun is aimed where he was and not where he is and Gil's throat pools like milk against an emerald backdrop of leaves. Martin swings his full weight to his heels then hurls forward so it lifts him into the air. His familiar yet foreign body erupts into the clearing.

He and Gil move in slow motion—the short flight from the bushes into the light, the gun barrel swinging around. The world is frozen with him in mid-air, and Martin hears the scuttle of beetles under the brush and the rustle of bird feathers high overhead. His ears pick up twelve distinct tones in the wind, a complexity he's never noticed before, and he smells what Gil had for dinner, his soap, the cigarettes that cling to his fingers and the unopened package in his shirt pocket. The urine trail of a sick opossum passed through the clearing hours before.

He hangs in the air a long time, sorting the forest into finer and finer detail, his head buzzing with the conversations of bees and the worries of bats and the desperation of a young vole caught in the shadow of a circling hawk. And Gil crouches before him, rifle swung halfway around, his pulse resounding in Martin's newly-sensitive ears.

In his dreams I can make Martin more than he is. I can lead him to do more than he expects of himself. His body feels bigger, more powerful, and he's willing to use it in ways he wouldn't dream of in waking life. Where would he summon the strength to attack anyone the way he's dreamt of pouncing on Gil? If he could be that powerful in his own life, if he could drag that strength out into daylight instead of shaking it from his head when he wakes, he could take command of his world the way he wishes he would.

Not that opportunity is any guarantee of success. Look at how little Elmer Tully accomplished when I finally gave him the chance to escape he'd always longed for.

Martin isn't yet ready for what he's been offered. Even in a dream he fears his own strength, and wills himself awake before sinking his teeth into the old hunter's neck. His body runs with sweat and the sheets have been kicked to the floor. The trailer is dark in the minutes before dawn, until his eyes adjust to the world rippling around him. Nothing looks as solid as it did a few hours before. He's been jerked from sleep so abruptly his body feels unfamiliar—the way it felt in his dream. Heavier, somehow, the same shape with more mass.

95

He drags himself out of bed and into the shower. His chest and sides are still stained with bruises, but when he peels off the grayed bandages the cuts look almost inconsequential. They're five thin, parallel lines, capped by ridges of red and yellow scabs, and hardly seem the result of such a dangerous encounter. He expected more obvious damage from an animal's claws—infections and swelling and scars—but these are no worse to his eye than slices from a sheet of clean paper. If not for the more visible evidence of his dark bruises, and the pain in his ribs each time he stretches or twists, his body might hardly know it was attacked. He's glad now that Gil talked him out of finding a doctor, because the lasting injury hardly seems worth the awkward explanations he could have been asked to repeat to one professional after another. Like this town and its residents, the longer Martin is left to his own explanations, the longer he's cut off from any outside opinion, the easier it becomes to rely on a localized sense of how the world works.

That the cuts from the bear aren't any worse is surprising, but he's willing to believe it's a fluke; perhaps the bear deemed him unappetizing. He's more concerned with the dreams he's been having and how they're following him into waking life. It takes longer and longer each time he wakes to sort out what's happening here, happening now, from what went on while he slept. Sometimes, when he's not paying attention, it's easy to think of the bear that attacked him and the mountain lion Gil shot as vivid dream fragments rather than concrete events.

After a shower and fresh bandages, Martin examines his sharp tooth in the mirror. It doesn't look broken, so maybe the sharpness was there all along and only seems more pronounced now that he's noticed, or there could be a cut on his tongue making it more sensitive to the edge of the tooth.

With untied boots flapping their laces, he walks outside to his car. He needs to restock his groceries in town, and he needs to make a few calls, but he's going to start by having breakfast with the morning crowd at Claudia's, if only to hear the sound of other voices after so many hours spent by himself.

12

THE SUN ARCHES ORANGE OVER THE HILLS AS MARTIN DRIVES into town. The high grass between the road and woods glistens with last night's rain. He doesn't see another car for the first couple miles, until at last a truck slides by in the other direction as he rolls up to the grassy town square. Near the peaked bandstand where teenagers smoke and the occasional vagabond curls up for the night, twin iron cannons point to the east and the west, aimed up into the mountains. Outside Claudia's, two-toned pickups and sedans gnawed by rust—cars old enough to still be made of metal—crowd the small parking lot. Martin recognizes Alison's SUV and pulls in beside it.

There's a lull in conversation when he enters the restaurant, whether because of him or one of those passing silences that slide through a crowded place every so often. The world seems sharp this morning: every sound more distinct, every aroma more nuanced, and the busy dining room overwhelms him for the first seconds after he enters. The sudden quiet may have been his senses skipping a beat.

All of the stools along the counter are taken and there isn't a booth to be had, so he stands with his heel propping the door open, close to turning around and going home to find something else for his breakfast. There's a rhythm beneath the dining room chaos, the scrape of forks against plates and glass syrup carafes sliding back and forth on slick tables; the patter of heavy boots worn on feet made jittery by too much coffee too fast. The pop of a plastic jam packet seems louder than all the room's conversations, and Martin feels his dream senses still with him, hearing and smelling more than he can take in.

"Mr. Blaskett," Alison calls from a booth in the corner where she sits with a straw-haired boy who's all angles and bones. "We've got room for you." She seems to be smiling, but it's hard to be sure through the smoky haze of the diner.

He lingers at the door for a moment, eyes on a row of broad flannel backs hunched over plates at the counter, then weaves his way through the room. He steps aside to let Claudia rush past with a tray on her shoulder, eyeglasses on a chain around her neck and swinging to one side from the speed. Then Martin sits down across the table from Alison and the boy he assumes is her son.

"Morning," she says over a half-eaten pile of pancakes. "This is Jake, Jr. Say good morning to Mr. Blaskett."

The boy greets Martin without looking up from his bowl of green milk and a few remaining cereal shapes, stripped of their color and bloated beyond whatever forms they once had.

"Morning. Thanks for sharing your table." He greets the boy, says it's nice to meet him, but the shaggy blond head remains down as Jake, Jr. pushes cereal around in his bowl with a spoon. Martin pulls a laminated menu from its perch between a napkin dispenser and a bottle of ketchup. "And Alison, I mean it, call me Martin."

"Right. Sorry." She steers a forkful of pancake pieces through the last streaks of syrup on her plate then guides the glazed hunk to her mouth. Jake, Jr. swirls a finger in his milk and lumps of soggy cereal rafts ride the whirlpool.

Claudia comes to the table and pours Martin's coffee. When he orders she asks, "Eggs Benedict again? It can't be so good without the meat. Maybe you should try something else." In the end she talks him into an omelet.

"Went to Elmer Tully's yesterday," Alison says when Claudia has gone, and it takes Martin a moment to realize she's referring to him, not herself.

"Oh, yeah. I went along with Gil."

"What happened?"

"I don't know, really. Something knocked down the back door, and the house was a mess." Martin looks toward her son, to gauge his reaction, but he's absorbed in sailing his cereal shapes and doesn't seem to be listening. "No sign of Elmer, though."

"He'll turn up." Alison pours so much sugar into her coffee that it makes Martin's teeth hurt just watching. "He always does."

"We did, uh, run into a mountain lion. It may have been in his house."

"You saw a mountain lion?" the boy asks, interested now. "Where?"

His eyes are wide and the spoon freezes in his hand, still half-submerged in milk.

"In the woods," Martin tells him.

"Where did it go?"

Martin pauses, unsure how to explain that Gil shot the cat without upsetting the boy.

"Mr. Rose killed it, honey," Alison answers without looking up from her coffee, already aware of what happened somehow. "It was too close to the houses."

"Oh," Jake says, as casually as if he's been told that today is Tuesday, or some equally dull piece of news. He goes back to his bowl. A few seconds later he lifts his head and says, "I saw a fox. At the swing set. He was so cool, he wanted to play."

"Jake . . . "

"He did, Mom! He came right up and sniffed me." The boy turns to Martin and says with a conspiratorial tone, "I wanted to keep him, but Mom said no. She always says no."

"Okay, Jake. That's enough."

He turns back to his mother. "It's true! You won't let me have a dog, or a fox, or *anything*." He sits up tall in the booth, and crosses his arms over his chest. He turns his face to the window but one eye is still on his mother, on her reflection, and measuring her reaction. "It's not fair," Jake complains, but the passion of his performance has already faded.

Martin remembers begging his own mother to buy him a dog and her constant reply that they moved too often and it was too hard to find apartments where they could have pets.

Alison leans close to her son's ear and tells him to calm down. Then he pretends to be looking at something very important in the gray flecks of the tabletop. She turns to Martin and says, "Jake thinks a dog will take care of itself."

"No, *I'll* take care of it! I *like* animals. And they like me."

"We'll see," she tells the boy as Claudia delivers Martin's breakfast, sliding the plate onto the table beside him before he sees her coming.

"Anything else with that? Ketchup? A steak?"

"No, thanks," he answers, but she refills his coffee anyway, not counting that as anything else. The omelet is the thickest he's ever seen. He doesn't know how many eggs have gone into it and decides he's better off for it.

Alison lifts her mug for Claudia to refill it, and Martin sees the fine blonde hairs on her wrist and the muscles running under the rolled up sleeve of her shirt. As the waitress starts moving away he blurts out, "And an order of bacon." Claudia and Alison are almost as shocked as he is himself.

"Well, if you say so, hon." Claudia rushes off before he has time to change his mind.

"I thought you didn't eat meat," Alison says.

"You don't?" Jake asks. "Why not?"

"I don't," Martin tells them, scratching the back of his neck. "I just . . . all of a sudden I want bacon. I don't know why. I haven't had any in years."

"Don't you like it?"

"Not really."

"Everyone likes bacon!"

"Okay, now," his mother cuts in. "Stop playing with your cereal and finish it, honey."

Martin digs into his eggs, forking a too-big bite to his mouth with a long string of cheese still tying it to the plate. Jake picks up a blue crayon from the table and colors in a line drawing of the café on his placemat while his mother looks out the wide window toward the cannons on the town square and the forest and hills farther on.

Claudia arrives with the bacon, a tall pile of dark, fatty strips on a white plate, and now that it's come Martin can't imagine getting it into his stomach. Alison, her son, and Claudia all watch as he reaches for the first piece. Feeling obligated, he crushes it into his mouth. The bacon is both greasy and crunchy; one end is burnt and the other feels nearly raw, but he chews and swallows and pretends it is just what he wants.

"Now, that's not so bad, is it?" Claudia says. "I knew I'd get through to you if you ate here a few times." She laughs, and then heads toward the kitchen. Martin gestures to the high pile of bacon, urging Alison and Jake to help themselves. The boy grabs three strips in one hand, and eats them out of his fist.

"Jake," Alison scolds.

"It's okay, he can have it." Martin finishes his omelet, ignoring the bacon, listening to the topics of conversations around him—Elmer's disappearance, the week's prospects for rain, and an article about squirrels attacking picnickers in some city park. Someone tells a story about a lost tourist who swerved to avoid a skunk in the road and found his SUV with its nose in a ditch. "I hauled him out, sure," a voice says behind Martin, "but I made him pay me upfront. Suppose I owe the skunk a cut, if I can find him." Laughter wells up in the room. Already his stomach feels heavy and sour, his mouth crusted with the charred powder of the burnt bacon.

The skunk story reminds someone else of yesterday's news, of a farmer a couple towns over with a herd of buffalo—"Bison," another diner corrects—who claimed last week one of his head was killed by coyotes. "Investigators say he's full of shit," the storyteller announces. "Say he made it up for the insurance."

"They would say that, wouldn't they?" another voice asks. "It's better than getting the whole state in a coyote panic."

And someone else has another story, about a bear locking itself in a car, and there's one about new robot deer to catch hunters who shoot out of season, and there are wolves and snakeheads and a whole ark of animal stories one after the another, each more absurd than the last and no less true for it.

"Mom, are you done?" Jake asks, pushing his bowl of milk toward Martin's side of the table.

"Not yet."

"Can I go outside?"

"Don't go far. I'll be out soon."

The boy climbs over his mother and runs to the door. He looks both ways before crossing the street to the square—a city habit out of place in a town with no traffic—and sprinting toward the bandstand where some other boys his size already kneel on the ground in a ring.

Alison sighs behind her coffee cup. Martin watches the web of fine lines around each of her eyes, the way they compress and relax as she drinks.

"He's a nice kid."

Alison smiles. "He's a handful, but I'll keep him. You don't have any kids?"

"Uh, no, I . . . no. I've never been married."

"Neither have I." Martin looks for a way he might walk back that misstep, but she goes on before he finds it. "Jake's father was . . . he wasn't the marrying kind. Left before Jake was born."

Martin pushes yellow clouds of cooled egg around his plate, and eyes the last strip of bacon the boy didn't eat. "Does Jake still see him?"

"Not for years. Sees his grandparents, though. They're an old family, the Haspers. Lived in town since forever until they went south last winter." She turns to look out the window, toward her son as he swings from the eaves of the bandstand with his lanky friends. The boys work their way around the roof, legs swinging a couple of feet off the ground. "If his father has been back since leaving, no one told me." She shakes her head, and looks at Martin as if she hadn't known she was talking out loud. "Listen to me. Shit. You don't care about this."

"I don't mind. I had a . . . my father wasn't around, either."

Alison slurps the last of her coffee, then sighs. "You gonna stay here?"

"Oh . . . I'm almost done. Hang on."

"No, here. In town. I heard you were going to stay."

Martin looks away. Did Gil tell her? he wonders, Are there rumors around? He wraps both hands around his mug though it's long cold by now. "I think so. I like it. I might keep one of the houses we're building."

"It's not a bad place. Most folks're decent enough. Gets a bit . . . I don't know, far away at times. A long trip from anywhere else."

"Where would you go?"

"Hell, that's it, isn't it? I don't even know. Probably nowhere. It's nice to think I might, though. Sometimes. Move near the ocean. Someplace different. That's why I don't get him a dog, you know. I keep thinking we might want to move. Not that telling him so would go better than saying no to a dog."

"Can I ask you something?" He isn't sure what Alison expects to hear, but her face looks panicked, at least tense, before she takes control of it and nods. "What happened to Elmer . . . does that happen a lot?"

"Elmer missing? That happens all the time."

"But the mountain lion, and his house? Is that . . . I don't know, *normal?*"

Alison's eyes dart around the room before she gives an answer. "People tell stories. My dad did. I don't know what's normal, now, but things do happen. Elmer. You and that bear. No one's willing to say so, but yeah, there're strange things."

"Like Scratch."

Alison leans back, away from him. "Heard about that, huh?"

"Gil told me." He waits for her to say something else, but when it doesn't come he asks, "Do you believe it?"

She sighs, and scratches the side of her neck. "Is it that simple? I've always heard the stories. From my parents, my grandparents. Everyone."

"But do you believe it? Does Jake?"

"Well, it's fun for him, isn't it? A local monster. It doesn't mean anything. But the older I get . . . " Martin leans closer, attentive, awaiting the rest of her sentence. At last she says, "I'm not sure I want him to hear it any more. If it's good for him."

"Why?"

She's about to answer but a loud burst of laughter comes from the men at the counter and she looks away. She shuffles in her seat the way she might if a chill followed someone through the diner's door in another season. Then her son is at the end of their table on the other side of the window, palms pressed flat and blowing his cheeks wide on the glass.

"Cut it out," Alison scolds while tapping the window, but she's laughing, too. She checks her watch and says, "I'd better get him dropped off so I'm not late for work." She smiles, and adds, "Boss is a stickler."

"I'll be back to the site later on, Alison. I'm going to make a few calls and take care of some things. Keep digging and if anything comes up I won't be too long." He says all that, as if they need him on the site. As if she doesn't already know what to do whether or not he's there at all and his part of the work extends beyond signing his name and giving out checks now that the permits and plans are in place.

"Right. See you later, then."

"Bye."

Through the fog the boy left on the glass, Martin watches them climb into her car and roll off. Then he sits by himself in the corner with his back to the room. Conversations taper behind him and trucks pull away from the lot. On the other side of the square, he watches the bank manager swing the door open and prop it wide with a brick. The *Open* sign lights up in the market.

He can't help wondering what impression he made on Alison's son, and how he'll be remembered. As his mother's boss, a strange man in town, a vegetarian who gives away bacon? Or if he even registered in the boy's world at all. Perhaps he'll be no more distinct in a few days or weeks than the men Martin was introduced to by his own mother. She never called them by name after they'd gone, only "that last one," or "the one with the dog," or "your father." So that's what they've become for Martin all this time later—a job or a house or a car, some identifying detail that keeps one fragment of memory apart from the others.

If Jake, thirty years from now, is still in this town he might drive past those houses where the woods used to be and remember the man who built them. The man who paid his mother to build them, more like. Or they might be his mother's houses, to him.

The last drops of coffee are cold in his mug, and yellow streaks of egg have congealed on his plate by the time he stands and leaves a ten on the table next to a bill for six dollars and the lone strip of unwanted bacon. He stretches his back in the dining room's aisle; two vertebrae pop and his ribs flare. As he leaves the restaurant, the few remaining diners follow him with their eyes.

He leaves his car in the parking lot and walks across the grass to the market. Pushing his half-sized cart up and down half-sized aisles, he lifts the occasional box of dry cereal or cans of tuna fish shrink-wrapped in stacks of four. The store's stock is limited by its size but the vegetables are always fresh, most of it local, so the bulk of his shopping is green. His tofu and soup mix are specially ordered.

The market has only been open for a few minutes, and there are no other shoppers this early, only a teenaged cashier snapping his gum behind a car magazine and the middle-aged manager in her office. When Martin passes her open door between the chill of the dairy case and the lights of the bread aisle, she looks up from her desk with a wave and he waves back without knowing her name.

He buys a large plastic bag of lentils, as loose as water in his hands when he lifts them off the shelf. Then some toothpaste and dish soap before heading toward the cashier, who has already rung through a box of food labeled with Martin's name and kept on a shelf reserved for special requests.

When his shopping is finished the sun is barely into the sky and the grass of the square is still wet enough to soak through his shoes after a few steps. He's not in the mood to go back to his trailer quite yet, and he trusts Alison has things under control on the site. In the car he dials his voicemail, and when the robotic voice announces how many messages await his attention he sighs and almost hangs up without listening to any of them. But he does listen, and hears his partner urging Martin to call, to come down to the city—the financing has fallen through on some other project, one Martin hasn't been so involved with and, though it's unlike him, can't recall the salient details of. But his partner's urgency is clear enough. His concern. So Martin calls back, gets his voicemail and says he'll try again later, says they'll get things worked out, but he's relieved the conversation won't happen quite yet.

It's inevitable and has been for some time—the economy has crumbled, houses and offices and apartments are empty all over, so there's no reason they wouldn't be touched. No way their own projects would slip through unscathed. But these houses and this project are separate. Secure. He'll still need to sell them, they'll need to be filled, but the rest of the company—the rest of the world—could come and go and these houses of his would be safe.

There's nothing in his groceries that will suffer from staying out of the cold a little while longer, so he drives away from the square in the opposite direction from which he arrived. After bouncing over the train tracks on the outskirts of town, he turns uphill onto the deeply rutted dirt road that goes to the lake.

It's a long, bumpy climb through the woods. The wheels of his low sedan bounce in and out of the trenches left by the wheels of other cars and heavier trucks and he goes slowly. Struggling to hold the steering wheel straight against the will of the road makes his arms tired, at first, and then numb. Beads of sweat bloom on his neck and forehead by the time he reaches the water, and his armpits feel damp beneath his sweatshirt.

There's an almost-round patch of dirt at the edge of the lake, bordered by picnic tables and black iron grills set in cement. He sits on one of the tables nearest the water. Most of the lake's surface is still in shadow, overcast by high trees on the banks and by the peaks of the hills beyond them. Mist rises off the water and the green surface shakes in smooth, windblown wrinkles.

Tall pines encircle the lake, ramping upward into the hills on all sides, and Martin can almost see the path of the glacier's retreat that left all this behind. He thinks of the bodies that have been in this water, the footprints that have crossed the lake's shore—indigenes and trappers and fishermen; children and spiders and bears. Men like him, no more than a speck on a mote of the world. And for a second—one of those strange, blown-up seconds somehow infinite and fleeting at once—Martin knows what time is. He can feel it. He understands something he could never wrench into words, then the second is gone and the knowledge gone with it, so he's left with the residual nostalgia of *knowing* he knew, knowing something made sense, but once more unable to pin down quite what.

His stomach feels rotten, furious about the introduction of meat, and not just any meat but a few greasy bites of fatty bacon. It churns and grumbles its displeasure to be sure Martin knows.

He yawns, suddenly tired, and leans forward with his elbows propped on his knees. He's been sleeping more than usual lately, straight through the night instead of the insomniac hours he's used to, but however much sleep he gets he's still tired, still feels as if he could nap the whole day and only wake every few hours to eat. His dreams have been so active, so engrossing, they've left him worn out. He hasn't actually been sleepwalking, but it feels as if body, mind, and muscles alike have taken part in those dreams and emerged restless and frayed.

A loon swoops across the water and skips a few feet before diving. Martin waits for it to surface, counting seconds inside his head, and it's a full minute before he relocates the bird, now close to the shore where he sits, its black head bobbing over the water so the white stripe on its neck comes and goes. It wails, and the reedy call rises and falls then echoes back and forth on the lake. He isn't sure if the loon really stayed underwater that long or it took him a while to notice once it came up.

The bird hoots once more before its next dive, and he doesn't see it again after that.

It's cold near the water, in the shade, so he pulls up the hood of his sweatshirt and tucks his hands inside the front pocket. Leaning over his knees, he watches the mist, and a few minutes later he is asleep sitting up.

His sleep is anxious and he doesn't dream.

An hour or so later some teenagers grind up the track to the lake on their bikes, and the noise of their approach wakes him. They're as uncomfortable finding Martin there as he is to see them, and anonymous, half-comprehensible greetings are mumbled before he goes back to his car and rumbles away in the ruts of the road.

He drives around town after leaving the lake, past the elementary school with its windows wide open to flush out the stale air trapped all summer. There are stacks of desks and chairs on the grass in front of the school, and through the broad front door Martin sees a man buffing the floors, in preparation for the start of the term in a few days. He drives by barns with their roofs bowed as the sweep of a ship, and every other board in their sides pulled out or swung open, depending on the design. Long leaves hang from the rafters inside, whispering and rattling in wind that runs through the walls, and Martin hears their rustling chatter even inside his car.

He had a cactus, once, in a pot on his windowsill, but over time it turned brown and its skin shriveled. He asked gardeners he knew for advice, and they assured him it was doing fine, merely in a cold weather phase, but Martin remained unconvinced—he wasn't sure they knew any more about keeping a cactus alive then he did. When he could no longer deny the cactus was dead, that he had killed an unkillable plant, he wrapped it in heavy black plastic and threw it away. Beyond that one failed attempt, his experience of plants has been only in passing, whether through windows or on a walk; he has always been more concerned with the produce than with the plants themselves.

There are children everywhere after he passes the barns, hanging from trees in front yards and crowding the infield of a baseball diamond next to a church. They're squeezing the last hours out of their summer, up early and already at play. Maybe these children already know Elmer Tully is missing, or about the mountain lion Gil shot; perhaps they, like their parents, are so much a part of this place that these things can be taken for granted.

He can't stop thinking about how wide the cat's eyes were as it fell. He has played and replayed in his head the seconds of the shooting and still can't locate the menace Gil must have seen. He assumes it was there, though, because if he could sleep through a bear creeping up, why would he notice another threat coming? If Gil hadn't been there, he might have watched the lion until it attacked, until he was dead, still convinced the big cat meant no harm.

At some point while Martin is lost in his head, the town's meandering roads turn him around and he crosses back through the center. Two blond boys in matching red T-shirts—the uniform of a summer camp that ended last week—straddle the iron barrel of one of the cannons. They kick their heels in and out, cowboys spurring their steeds, and somehow their tan, skinny legs stand the heat of dark metal that must have been soaking up hot August sun all morning long.

When he pulls onto the strip of dry mud between the road and his trailer, several new foundations—the unpaved holes for them, at least—gape from the ground. Some of the crew turn at the sound of Martin's arrival, and one of them waves, then they all go back to their work. He scans the site for Alison, but she's invisible somewhere.

In the driver's seat he leans forward, arms crossed on top of the wheel, and he pictures the houses where they will rise: two flanking the entry to the development, on either side of where he sits now, with the new road he's mapped winding between. Their front porches will face the street at an angle, not quite parallel to Gil's house but near enough for the residents of those first homes to wave to the old man on his porch as they sit on theirs.

For months now—in the city all winter as he pored over plans, and during these weeks as he's watched trees fall and grades leveled—Martin has imagined the first house on the map as his own. Whether he decides to keep that one or chooses another, in his daydreams that first house has already been framed and wired and plumbed, painted and papered and tested with every possible arrangement of furniture he doesn't yet have. The house in his head is the closest he's come to possessing a home of his own, the most time he's ever spent laying one out and holding samples of color next to each other on unpainted walls, even if it has all been a daydream.

From the front seat of his car he walks his mind's eye through brand new rooms full of brand new things: carpets with the creases of packaging still pressed into their nap and silverware in a matched set, not a single piece scarred yet from getting stuck in a garbage disposal or caught in the pull of an opening drawer. He walks through the house without turning on lights, aware without thinking of which board will creak, when to step left around an end table and when he's reached the last stair in a flight. He reaches into an enormous refrigerator to pull out a beer without looking and pops its cap on an antique metal opener bolted onto the wall.

The opener, advertising an obscure Mexican beer he's never been able to find in a store, is the only part of his imaginary house that is already real. At the moment it's wrapped in newspaper and packed in a box, waiting for a wall where it can finally hang. He's been hauling it around unused for a long time, and more than any other tangible thing, mounting that bottle opener on his kitchen wall is what Martin looks forward to doing once these houses are built. Once his own is.

In his daydream, in the house he envisions, the back door slides open without a sound, firm but not tight in its frame, so well-crafted the door doesn't stick and doesn't need to be jiggled the way every sliding door in every house in the world does after the first use or two. He steps outside onto the porch and it's evening now in his head, the sun a red glow on the mountains and trees, and he sits in the kind of Adirondack chair he's always wanted, a chair with three identical mates arranged around it. He imagines himself in his chair as the last drops of daylight soak into dark hills and fireflies speckle the air, though the day beyond his windshield is bright and hot.

The road is quiet now in the real world, but in his daydream of evening it's busy with cars moving to and from houses he's made, coming home from jobs in the city with headlights shining. He pictures Gil across the street, drinking a beer of his own, in his own chair and on his own porch, the two of them moving almost in tandem. The red ember of Gil's cigarette bobs up and down in front of his face, and an electric-blue bug zapper crackles on a pole above Martin's yard.

The clatter of the excavator's shovel against the bed of the dump truck jerks Martin out of his daydream and back to the inside of his car, humid and hot now he's turned off the engine and the air conditioner with it. In daylight, back in the world as it is, he stares through the windshield at the hole in the ground where his house doesn't yet stand, his present and future at once under glass.

13

A T THE END OF THE DAY'S WORK, WHILE THE CREW FINISH their cigarettes and make plans to meet at one bar or another, Martin walks away up the slope of the site to inspect the empty spaces that will be his houses in time. The walls of each rectangular hole are laced with the same thin, gray roots he saw tangled with bones yesterday, and he thinks of blood vessels, of bodies, and the pink striations of muscle he saw beneath the mountain lion's skin as Gil peeled it away. Martin didn't watch much of the process, but it was enough to stick in his head.

From atop the hill that crowns the clearing he looks back toward his trailer and the crew preparing to leave. He sees Alison in conversation with the dump truck driver; her tall, lanky body beside his squat, rounded one resembles a large number ten. She waves her hand through the air, fingers pointed toward Martin or maybe the hole he's standing beside, and the driver nods his head at whatever she's saying. Those gestures, those flicks of her fingers, are a language he can't enter into, not from this distance, any more than he's been able over the years to translate the subtle gestures a crane operator is directed with from the ground. He runs these sites and these projects, on paper, but on the ground—in the hands of his crews—he doesn't speak the language of work. As the first few engines rattle to life and cars and trucks begin moving away, Martin walks down the slope toward the road.

"Alison," he calls while approaching her truck, though she doesn't seem in a hurry to leave. She smiles, and Martin waits until he's closer before saying anything else. "Things are coming along, then. Digging's going well. How's the crew working out?"

"They're fine. No problems."

He nods, frustrated with small talk when he really wants to tell Alison so much more, about his plans for making a home and about the dreams he's been having. He'd like someone else to know of these things, to make them more real, and hers is the most sympathetic ear he's found here. The one he most wants to listen.

"Should be done digging this week," she tells him.

With the workers departed, with the ground cleared, starlings descend onto the building site. Their speckled black bodies, dozens of them, crowd the churned ground in a battle for whatever seeds and scraps have been overturned and whatever crumbs may have been dropped by the crew.

"Martin," she says, "listen. This morning, when we were talking. You asked about the stories, about . . . you know, Scratch, and all that. Look. I don't know if I believe them or not. Maybe I do. Most people do. Or . . . well, people say they do and I guess the difference between believing something and saying you believe it isn't so much. Say it enough times and you'll believe whether you mean to or not, right? If you say you believe something long enough you're bound to act on it sooner or later."

He watches her eyes, glancing from side to side at the forest around them.

"They make me nervous. I didn't say that before. Sometimes I think about moving so I won't have to hear those stories again. So my son won't grow up listening to them. That sounds stupid, right? It's a nice town, and I like it here. Jake likes it here, it's his home. I guess anyplace'll have it's own stories and I'll get sick of hearing those, too."

Three of the largest starlings alight on the roof of Martin's trailer, all trying to claim the same few square inches instead of dispersing across the broad space.

"Anyway," she says, standing up straight and stepping back, out of the moment. "I just thought I'd mention that so, you know...so you knew about it. Guess I'll go now." Before Martin can say more than goodbye, she's in her truck and backing across the mud toward the pavement. He's still waving as the glint of her windshield slips around a bend in the road and vanishes behind some trees. He looks toward Gil's porch, but for once the old man isn't there—perhaps he's in the barn, or off in his yard, or maybe he actually does spend some time in his house—so Martin climbs the three steps to his trailer.

He turns toward his map, pencilling in his trip to the lake and some of the sights he saw on his drive around town that he hadn't spotted and annotated before.

Later, after a dinner of tuna forked right from the can, he stands outside his trailer to watch evening fall. A few birds sing their somnambulant songs in nearby trees and fireflies are just showing their faces when a hollered greeting from Gil breaks the quiet. At his neighbor's insistence, at his shouts from the edge where the road meets the site, Martin crosses to Gil's porch where a can of beer has already been opened for him.

"Lotta digging today," Gil says.

"It's coming along."

"Those houses'll be up before it turns cold. I'll get neighbors for Christmas." With bare fingers Gil turns three sausages on the blackened rack of his grill, and Martin doesn't ask if it is mountain lion. The same hand holds a cigarette, and fine flakes of gray ash settle onto the sausages and float in the hot updraft from the gas flame below.

"It won't be quite that soon."

"Be nice, though, kids around at Christmas. Get 'em over here singing me carols. Bringing me cookies. Awful nice."

"There's a long way to go before anybody moves in."

Gil plucks a sausage off of the heat. "Hungry?" Martin shakes his head no. "Suit yourself. Don't know what you're missing." The meat is gone in two rapid bites, and Gil washes it down with the better part of a beer. "Made these myself. Venison." Martin sighs in his head, sips his own drink, and listens to the sizzle and pop of sausage casings and the boiling juices inside them.

"Why no kids, Marty? Young guy like you." Martin is getting used to his neighbor's rapid shifts in conversation, and the strange turns they frequently take, but this one catches him off-guard and beer slips down the wrong pipe. He chokes, and Gil delivers a hard thump to his back.

When he's recovered, Martin says, "No reason, I guess, aside from the obvious. Maybe someday." He takes a drink. "What about you?"

"I used to shine my boots three times a day, even when it wore out the leather. We were gettin' shelled, or crawling in mud, or sitting around the base for weeks at a damn time and every chance I'd shine my boots. Pay attention to the little shit, Marty. Control what you can. Takes your mind off the rest."

Gil drains his can and tosses it over his shoulder into the dark, then opens another before going on.

"You have kids, it's like that. Keeps you busy. Spend all your time shining boots or paying bills, patching scraped knees, whatever you like. Y'know what you're doing. You have a place to be." He lights a fresh cigarette from the one that's burned down to his lips, and makes a sound that might be a cough or a self-conscious dismissal of what he's just said.

Martin watches as the skin of one burnt sausage splits in a smooth seam along its whole length, and clear, bubbling juices spill out of the fissure. Gil grabs it and it's gone before he seems to be chewing, perhaps faster than his mouth could know it should burn. In front of the porch and over the yard, bats screech and wheel as they pluck insects from the air and avoid each other by fragments of inches. And Martin still doesn't know if Gil has kids of his own.

Once, only once, he tried finding his father. He called the hospital where he was born, but they told him if the birth certificate had a blank space there was nothing they could do to fill it in after the fact. He called his mother's sister, an aunt he has never met, on the west coast where she moved long before he was born.

"No," she told him, "I never knew. We were out of touch long before that."

They talked about his mother, about her last days and the funeral her sister couldn't attend—it was so far, so expensive, they hadn't spoken for so many years—and about Martin's business of building homes. When the conversation dried up between them, their awkward fumbling of hasty excuses overran one another and Martin hung up the phone before he began asking questions he didn't want answers to. Why his mother was thrown from the family, and why he'd never met any of them. Whether or not he looked like anyone else in their bloodline or if he'd gotten to be all he is from his father.

For a few months he wondered at each masculine face in the street that looked older than his, each man in a boiler suit or a tuxedo, driving a luxury car or wheeling a shopping cart full of cans on the side of the road. He wondered if he'd come from there, or from there, or from there.

Only once did he let himself think he'd come close, in a Chinese restaurant down the street from his office. He watched a man with white hair stretched thin as cirrus clouds speaking softly into a cell phone at a table for one, and there was something familiar in how his voice hesitated, the way he paused before every sentence. He sounded the way Martin sounds in his own head—as if he is only speaking because something needs to be said, not because he knows what it is.

The voice made him set down his spoon and sit over his soup until it grew cold, listening. The man, his maybe-father, had a round belly as if something was hiding under his shirt and his legs spread wide at the sides of his chair because they couldn't quite come together in front. The thick fingers of one hand marched back and forth on the glass tabletop, and those holding the phone to his ear marched the same way on its black plastic shell.

Martin knew he was watching himself. Not that this man, older and fatter and with far less hair, reminded him of what he saw in the mirror—it was something much more than that. The man in the Chinese restaurant moved when Martin knew he would move, looked from one side of the room to the other above his open mouth before speaking into the phone the way he expected him to. He understood what the fat man was doing, what he was *going* to do, as if he'd been watching the movements of this swollen body for all his life.

Martin nearly stood up from his chair when the man ended his conversation and set down the phone. He nearly crossed the width of two tables between them and approached the body hunched over a fan of papers covering the Chinese zodiac placemat beneath. When the man sighed Martin recognized the intonations—a subordinate not taking care of a project, or a contact giving him a hard time; something not getting done the way it needs to be done and the realization you'll have to step up and take care of it yourself, assume the awkward position of being the hard guy. He heard the man's sigh as a wish to have no one above or below him, no one else to rely on or relying on you.

It was the sigh that kept him from standing. It was the sigh that would not let him speak. He knew, in that soft rush of breath and the brief droop of the eyes that came with it, that this man had no need for a son whether he'd ever had one or not. No need for another life laying claim to his own, another voice to make him nervous about using his own. He understood the stranger so well that he knew the disruption his question would cause. He knew that the slight, absurd chance this man could be his father, the slim possibility that a random diner in a Chinese restaurant could somehow be related to him, wasn't enough to destroy the man's careful routines and the delicate scaffolding he had no doubt constructed around all sides of his life.

Who was he to overwrite this anonymous man's lifelong story?

Martin's maybe-father set his phone down on top of the papers, hoisted the last bites of lunch to his lips with careful chopsticks, and dropped a single large bill at the side of his plate. He packed his papers into a briefcase and checked his watch, dabbed his mouth with a napkin then folded it on top of the table. He squinted as he walked outside into the sun and turned left. Martin watched him cross three full-length windows between the restaurant's door and the edge of the building, a tall, bulging body half-hidden by Chinese characters painted backwards on glass.

Then the man melted into the city, into the millions of men who might be Martin's father, any number of whom might have wondered what became of that woman they slept with once or perhaps a few times, the willowy blonde with the S-shaped scar on the ridge of one eye. They may have wondered where the scar came from, or recalled an explanation she'd given—a game of tag and a branch that hung low, not looking where she was going—or she might not have crossed their minds ever again.

He doubted it had ever occurred to his father, or to any of them, that she might have a son and they might, too. That their child, now grown, sat over cold soup in an emptied-out restaurant, lingering late at his lunch, wondering what they wondered about, all those men he didn't know. All those men who are his father.

He gave up the search for good after slurping down that bowl of cold soup, after watching a man he didn't know talk on the phone and walk away. The disruption to both of their lives, had his father been found, seemed too great to surmount, too much to reconcile, and somehow a betrayal of his mother's wishes.

If she'd wanted him to know, she would have told him.

She would have filled in his whole birth certificate, or listed a name on his Emergency Contact cards when he was in school. Instead she left those spaces and so many others blank all his life, and those blank spaces left room for him to build the life he has made. Because that's the nature of spaces—they need to be filled. If a niche is created something learns how it's best occupied. There were larger bears once, in these woods—grizzlies alongside the smaller black bears like the one Martin met—and he's lucky for that. But the smaller bears devoured the forest more easily, fed more widely and quickly and efficiently until their larger cousins moved on. And now those black bears, like so many others who live in these woods, have found the niches and cracks in the town—the dumpster always overflowing with food, the gardens so easily raided. The dead air of conversation waiting to be rent by a bark or a howl, and the lives so easily entered and bent.

Gil's third sausage is still on the grill, crusted with char, and when one round end finally bursts it sprays hot juice onto Martin's arm. "Shit!" he cries out, leaping up and waving his arm, then he collects himself and fishes a can of beer from the pool of melted ice in the cooler between his chair and Gil's as if that's all he'd stood for in the first place. He holds the cold can against his burnt arm, and when he looks over to see why his neighbor hasn't said anything in response to all that, he discovers the old man is asleep. Gil's head has drooped forward, his eyes are closed, and the tiny orange nub of a cigarette pokes from between his chapped lips. He's snoring, but only softly, more softly than Martin would have imagined.

He reaches toward Gil's face and tries to pull away the cigarette. But the ember is too short to get a grip on without burning his fingers or pinching Gil's lip, and when he tries the old man's mouth opens with a loud snort and the ember falls to the porch. Martin grinds it into the boards with the toe of his shoe, and then opens the beer that's been cooling his arm and drinks most of it in one go.

A few minutes later, after extinguishing the gas flames of the grill and leaving Gil asleep on the porch, he crosses the street and soon falls asleep in his own bed, with the window at the back of the trailer open between him and us. His dream self feels our hot breath slipping in through the screen from our panting snouts and dry tongues. His dream self knows where we are, what we are, but doesn't tell his bound, slumbering body as he wanders into the woods once again.

14

I T TAKES A FEW STEPS TO GET USED TO THE WAY HIS OWN body moves. He bumps against trees with his shoulders and trips on oversized feet before deciding to move on all fours. The motion is instantly natural. Peepers sing his way through the forest, fireflies light a path, and he knows without knowing what everything is and where everyone's going and what they will do when they arrive. All the creatures and plants of the forest are doing what they know to do, and this strange Martin is moving among them.

When he pushes at the ground there's a thunder he's never known, a power that swells to his shoulders and shivers his hips. He feels that he could, if he wanted to, punch his hands into the ground and fell every tree in the forest with the rumbling vibration of that impact. He lets his body gain speed as it rolls through the woods. The surer he becomes of these unknown legs the faster he lets them run, the longer the strides they may take. Smaller shadows and shapes scuttle out of his way. Squirrels dash up trees, birds hide their heads under wings, even crickets fall quiet as he passes.

As quiet as they become, stone still as they hold, he knows where each one of them is. He smells every junco and chipmunk and fox, every lichen and fern and touch-me-not bursting up through dead leaves on his trail. His nose knows the difference between a skunk cabbage half-furled and one a single day past its prime, between a stump claimed by a wolf and one marked by a mere family dog.

His breathing gets heavy and hot and he hangs his mouth open so his tongue rolls out to swing in the air as he runs. A breeze rills the ridge of his back, and seized by an urge he can't explain or control he drops to one side in a patch of soft brush, rolls onto his shoulders and writhes so the ends of his body sway over green velvet leaves and overnight dew soaks into his skin.

Then he's up again and he's rumbling, plowing into saplings because he knows that he can, that they'll give but not break as they bend to his will and his weight.

It's miles and hours of running until the trees thin, until he stands on a ledge where the moon hangs mere feet from his face. He sits on his haunches and roars, but his is an inexperienced, unconfident roar that is more of a moan. And though they are not wont to do so, not without the influence of the strange, daylight dreams that I've woken them from, Martin's call—the wild sound of this version of him—is answered by other animals on other ledges, atop other hills in this forest.

Buoyed by these answers he wasn't expecting, by these nocturnal harmonies to his low tone, he fills his lungs to near-bursting and lets the roar swirl up his throat once again, his song spiraling into the air so much surer this time, so much louder, a voice that knows what it's saying and knows it is being heard.

Then his body is off down the ridge, running again toward the lights of back porches and the high fences of yards. Toward spotlights shining up from the grass of the square, casting their beams at the black iron cannons and the vacant flagpole that rises between them, its empty line clanging and echoing across the dark town. Toward the neon flickering *Closed* in the window of Claudia's Café where a few hours from now the town will ingest its eggs and digest its morning news.

And they will have news to digest.

He slides past white picket fences and stone walls without mortar, past night-blooming flowers that fill his nose with their scent and beehives abuzz with soft sleeping songs that hum from the trees where they hang.

This body, this Martin, climbs over a fence—only posts, only rails, no barrier to a body like his—and into a yard, a long rectangle rolling away from a house where all windows are dark. A child-sized bicycle lies on its side beneath the back porch. A blue vinyl swimming pool mourns summer already, collapsed and deflated in a patch of dead grass with a visible tear. Beneath a striped crossbar a single swing sways with its chains creaking, and the rest of the world holds its breath. There's no reason the swing should be moving, no wind in the air and the weight of no body upon it, no reason for such a cinematic cliché except that this is Martin's dream and sometimes clichés are how he sees the world.

He lies down in the grass now, tired. His chest heaves and his tongue stretches to its limit out the side of his mouth, a dowsing rod searching for water. He lies in the dark with mosquitoes and flies colonizing his back, with dew soaking his legs, until a fine orange thread is pulled through the sky where night is so loosely sewn to the ground. The seam starts to fray, the backdrop shows through, and a round edge of sun appears over the hills to the east.

A light comes on in the house, a window is suddenly flooded, and a shadow hardly shows as it crosses the low edge of the sill. Then bare, padding feet—too quiet for Martin's usual hearing but thunder in tonight's ears—make their creeping way down the stairs and through the kitchen where bed-sweaty skin squeaks on linoleum in need of wax. The glass door slides open a few steps above on the porch, sheer white curtains are pushed to one side, and the shape of a man—only smaller—stands in silhouette between the house and the yard, between asleep and a dream or the town and the woods or whatever you would like these two poles to be. This yard is the border between them.

A Martin of sorts, an out-of-sorts body, crouches close to the grass where moisture melts into air. He lingers on the ground near the swing that sways empty and waits for the body in the house to come closer. Its scent has already reached him, and the rising heat of its furless shape already coils up his nose, stirring a new kind of hunger from deep within.

15

H E WAKES SLOWLY THIS MORNING, AND IN HIS HALF-SLEEP
feels the tickle of warmth like a fly so he swats at the sun on his
face. The smack brings him into the world and the first thing he
knows is how sore he is, then how clammy and sticky with sweat.
A sheet tangles his ankles and it takes his fingers to free them.

The small window above his bed is cranked open, and a spider has laced
a fresh web across the gap of the frame and its extended glass. A brown
bead of a body huddles at the web's center, eight long legs tucked under
itself like some innocent flotsam caught on the wind. She'll wait all day for
something else to get stuck, then her legs will unfurl and she'll cross the
strands of her web as if they are air. All she needs is something edible to
spring the trap.

Martin knows something has happened since he went to sleep. He's
awoken aware the world is different somehow, that it isn't good, and he
lingers in bed for as long as he can to avoid finding out where this feeling
of dread has come from. But quickly the sardine can of his trailer is too hot
to bear, the air-conditioning off so he could sleep in a breeze that came
with the night. So he switches off the alarm before it has sounded and he
takes a shower, gets dressed, and brings a bowl of cereal to the front steps
on bare feet.

The hills look the same as the previous morning. The mud hasn't
changed, and the building site hasn't grown its trees back or filled in
the holes to be homes. Gil's house is still on the other side of the road,
across pavement cratered with potholes still unpatched so long past the
spring thaw.

Gil waves from his porch, still sitting where he fell asleep. Martin
crosses the street with his bowl of breakfast in hand. The old man rocks in
his chair, wearing the same grease-stained pants and heavy brown boots,
the same thin white T-shirt over coppery arms. His lap holds a paper plate
piled with sausage and eggs, and the grill is fired up again with the metal

sheet sizzling upon it. Martin can't tell if Gil has moved from the chair at all since last night, or only reached out as far as the food and the fire he keeps close at hand.

They sit on the porch eating breakfast, and watch the occasional car. "Got that cat into the deep freeze," Gil says. "Never tried mountain lion before. Pretty good, though."

Martin nods over his bowl with a mouth full of cereal and milk. He slurps and Gil snaps into his sausage. A skinny gray squirrel skitters head-first down a porch column flaked with paint. Its tail curls and waves while it searches for food and assesses the threat of these men.

"Git," Gil grunts through his breakfast, and the squirrel turns mid-climb to vanish over the eave and back onto the roof. Martin follows the footsteps by ear as it rushes up the slope of the porch then jumps to the low-hanging branch of an oak. An acorn shakes loose, thumps onto the shingles and rolls over the gutter down into the overgrown yard.

"Oughta mow that," Gil says, the same way he did two days ago, and two days before that. Martin's never had a yard he was responsible for mowing himself, but he thinks Gil's grass can go a bit longer before it looks too bad.

He still feels uneasy, convinced something is wrong, but the longer he sits over his cereal talking to Gil, the more that ill feeling fades. Until a few minutes later when the howl of a siren comes over the trees between the house and the road into town, quickly followed by the sheriff's car pulling up. The siren winds down but the blue lights keep flashing.

"Gil," the sheriff pants, out of breath over his gut as if he's been running instead of driving a car. The other words are swallowed by his gasps but the point of the message is clear and Gil is already standing.

He scoops a flannel shirt from the floor by his chair and pulls it onto his arms. "What happened, Lindon?"

The sheriff's breath is coming back to him now as Martin and Gil walk down the steps to the yard. "A kid's gone missing in town." He pauses, closes his eyes and his chest swells with a deep breath. "Followed some fucking animal."

"Who?" Martin asks, but his question is lost as Gil asks what kind of animal it was.

123

"Don't know. It's Jake Hasper's son, right out of his own goddamn yard." The name doesn't mean much to Martin at first. Jake, Jr. must have his father's surname instead of Alison's, at least to the sheriff, and a lump swells in his throat. He pictures Alison's son alone in the woods, that skinny body from breakfast mauled by a bear or something else, and he hopes the boy is just wandering scared. It seems a benevolent wish for a child to simply be lost in the woods, under these circumstances, after all Martin has seen in recent days.

Gil's bent down in the grass tying his shoe but he stops and looks up. "You don't know what the animal was?"

"No, but whatever it was, he followed it." Martin almost asks how they know, but holds his tongue, remembering every other exchange—or lack thereof—he's had with the sheriff. "We're gettin' a search party up on the square. Want a ride?"

"I'll come in my truck. Gun's in it already."

Martin crosses the street to get his boots from the trailer, then comes back to climb into the cab beside Gil without being asked. Without being told. His boots and socks are still in his hands as the old truck grinds to life and careens out of the yard to the road, the three-tiered gun rack rattling against the window behind his head. He hopes that this search will be more successful than the last one, and won't require guns—he hopes the boy will be found without incident, and without blood.

Gil's shirt is open and flapping, the flannel so faded it looks inside out. "Son of a bitch," he mumbles while holding a pack of cigarettes up to his mouth, letting the truck and the road shake one loose at the top. It's all either of them says while they ride.

Martin is more surprised to *not* be surprised by news of the boy's disappearance than he is by the news itself. It's almost *déjà vu* but more real, more certain, as if he already knew this had happened. He can't remember the dream he woke from clearly enough to know how close it was to waking life, but the confirmation of his earlier, ambiguous dread and the strange, violent events of recent days are enough to make him afraid for the boy, and for his mother, too. Without the attack by a bear and without Elmer gone missing—and without his strange dreams—Jake wandering off would be scary, but with all that's been going on it could be much worse.

Gil takes both hands off the wheel for a second. One holds the cellophaned packet of cigarettes and the other stabs at the broken plastic knob of the lighter until it sinks into the dashboard. It's not long enough for anything to go wrong, but in the time while no one is driving Martin thinks he can feel the truck slipping toward the edge of the road. The lighter pops out of the dashboard and Gil reaches for it without looking. The orange glow reflects on his face, and when the hot metal coils connect with his cigarette, the cab fills with the scent of it burning. Smoke swirls up Martin's nose, and he feels a sneeze coming, but stifles it for a reason he can't explain as Gil stares ahead at the road.

Martin leans down to pull on his socks and boots. He props one foot at a time on the plastic woodgrain of the dashboard while tying the braided brown laces, and he's pulling the second knot tight as they roar into town, into the jumble of cars and rusty trucks crowding the street on all four sides of the square.

Their concern is impressive, even to me, but Alison is growing too close to Martin. There's too much potential between them, too much chance she might change his story and undo all I've done. That's why her son had to be taken—it's not punishment, just pragmatism. A necessary step if I'm going to get Martin where he needs to go. Where I need him to be. And the boy was so easily led, far more than his mother would be. As easily as Martin was, because they both want so badly to trust in the world around them, to believe it is open to them and they are a part of this place. The boy wanted a pet, a companion, and I gave him one in my way. His lonely desire left him open.

I've had young of my own—not in this body, but others—so I'm not wholly callous to Alison's pain. There have been times I kept the same shape for so long that it began to feel like my own. I grew older. I gained and lost weight and hurt myself in ways that left lingering pain and changed how that body moved. I've laid eggs and sired fawns and have walked through the night with my every sense tuned toward protecting a passel of hairless, blind opossum joeys clutching my back. I know what it is to be part of something, and then alone, because in the end my young always died, and were gone—even if they lived a full life—while I used up one more shape and went back to drifting through these woods disembodied.

But this isn't Alison's story, and it isn't her son's, so I couldn't leave them in the way. I couldn't let them make Martin whole, which I'm sure you could see was where things were headed. They've stumbled into the story, but to no greater extent than the millions of bees killed by phone calls crowding the air, by selfish signals laden with meaningless gossip and chatter yet able to push whole colonies off course to die, are part of those conversations. Sometimes that's the price of a story worth telling: other lives, other colonies, torn at the seams.

Saying so wouldn't surprise these men wielding rifles and crowding the cannons on the grass of the square, hollering to be heard above one another and shaking their guns overhead. The scene is absurd but no less dark for it, and it puts Martin in mind of old movies and their torchlit mobs armed with pitchforks pursuing some creature or another across empty fields, less concerned about finding the right monster than willing to settle for any villain at all so as long as there's something to chase. Looking around at all the guns and angry faces, he isn't sure the weapons are meant to shoot anything or a convenient way to fill idle hands with iron-clad courage. His own hands feel conspicuously empty and useless, so he shoves them deep into his pockets. He recognizes several members of his construction crew among the crowd, some with rifles and some without.

Alison sits in the long shadow of one black cannon barrel, dry-eyed but dazed, surrounded by Claudia and a number of women he doesn't know. She looks up for a second in the direction of his gaze, and he forces a smile that he hopes will look caring, not cheery, but she looks down again without any change in her expression. He isn't sure she's noticed he's there, or if he should expect her to under the circumstances.

Sheriff Lindon stands at the center of things, raising his palms to the crowd as he urges, "Calm down, everybody, calm the hell down. We've got to get organized here."

Martin tries to convince himself all this tension is premature, that the boy is simply lost in some part of the woods he's been walking through and playing in all his life. That he followed a neighborhood dog, a familiar playmate, and will be back before long or will be found a few feet into the forest, safe and sound with some funny story. The worst of it will be missing his breakfast, maybe teasing about getting lost in his own woods. Martin wants to believe that, but he can't—not because Elmer is already missing, or because of the bear that attacked him and the dread feeling he woke with this morning, but because he knows in his bones and his soul something really is wrong. It's unscientific, an unfounded hunch; he couldn't take it to the sheriff or to Gil to be offered as proof any more than he could his strange dreams, still he knows the way he knew by scent those two bodies—our bodies—had been in his bed.

"Terrible," says a stooped, white-haired woman on Martin's left. "Just awful." She's in what he takes for a robe, sky-blue fabric printed with puckered, darker-blue flowers, and fuzzy, heelless slippers to match. Either she rushed out before getting dressed, or she dresses this way.

"Do you know how it happened?" Martin asks as the growing crowd surges behind him, pushing a knee or a hip into his back and throwing his body off-balance.

The old woman looks into his face with clouded, watery eyes. She's hunched so far over her neck is almost parallel to the ground, her back a high hump, so her head twists rather than rises to meet his eyes. "He was playing on his swing set. Very early."

Martin remembers the swing in his dream, how his dream self crouched in the grass and was ready to spring. He feels sick but wills his stomach down.

"What is wrong with boys?" The old woman sniffs, congested or on the verge of tears. "Why don't you know better?" Her voice drops lower the longer she speaks, until he can make out only the occasional word of her mutter, something to do with staying inside.

Dozens of voices rise and fall in murmuring swells that are almost a rhythm, and Sheriff Lindon stands before the crowd with his hands in the air, offering what are meant to be calming words.

"We need to shoot the son of a bitch," someone hollers. Martin can't locate the speaker.

"Who?" someone else asks.

"No one's shooting anything," Lindon yells. "There's nothing to shoot so shut up and listen, now. All you."

The old woman at Martin's side says in little more than a whisper, "It's always happened this way."

"What has?" Martin asks.

"Folks gone into the woods. Same way when I was a girl. We'd got the tractor, then, and could work more acres than we did with mules. So Pop and the other men expanded their farms, cut back the trees, and we could grow enough extra corn for me to have a new dress for school in the fall. He sold all that extra timber and Ma got a pearl necklace—real pearls!—that first Christmas, and I think Pop beamed bigger than her."

She keeps talking, but as far as Martin can tell it isn't about the disappearance of Alison's son anymore, or about anything else he can follow. He wants to prod her back onto the track of whatever point she was making, but a loud engine roars and car doors slam, cutting the old woman off. Martin picks Gil out near the front of the crowd, arms crossed on his chest and his shirt buttoned now. Lindon stands high on the wheel of one cannon with Alison below him on the ground, and Gil looms beside her with his mouth closed and his eyes on the assembly. The sheriff urges everyone to calm down as he tries to organize groups for a search, but the angry voices grow louder.

At last, Gil climbs onto the other wheel of the cannon, across the barrel from Lindon, and holds up a hand. The voices settle, a little, with the novelty of a new speaker, and Gil talks to them. He doesn't seem to be raising his voice but his words boom over the square.

"Now then," he says, as if he's beginning any old conversation.

Martin watches the rifles and the hands holding them up pause in the air, and all those eyes turn toward his neighbor. He asks himself, for the first time, what it is about Gil—he isn't the sheriff, he isn't in charge, but people defer to him. He's done it himself ever since he arrived. He saw it in town meeting and he's seeing it now, the way whatever Gil says, whatever direction he gives, supersedes every other as if there is no other way things might go.

"Good boy, Gil Rose," says the old woman. "The old families know how things are."

Martin asks what she means, but gets no answer. He isn't sure she's heard but he doesn't ask again.

Gil has the crowd quieted now, and they wait while he jabs a cigarette into his mouth. He lights it then slides both hands into his pockets, and the crowd stays calm through it all, waiting for him to speak.

"What we'll do," he says, "is split up. Boy's gone missing near his house, so we'll start there. Fred and all you head west from the yard. Leslie and you all from the sawmill go east. Lindon's boys are checking the houses nearby. I'm going north toward the ridge."

The crowd pulls apart into clusters of men and guns moving toward cars and trucks around the edge of the square.

"Hold on, now," Gil says. "I hear he was following something." He looks down toward Alison who gives a slight nod. Gil reaches down a hand and helps her onto her feet, and asks her to tell everyone what she saw. Her voice is steadier than he anticipates; she looks worried, terrified, and of course she would be, but she sounds in control. She sounds strong.

"I didn't see much, so I don't know how much I can help. Just Jake in the yard, looking at this fox we've been seeing lately." Martin's nausea comes back in force at that revelation, as she goes on. "It came up to him and before I could get out there to chase it off he'd gone along behind it. I got into the woods quick, but . . . I don't know . . . they were faster, somehow." She's engaged in a visible battle to keep from breaking up now, struggling in front of all these people who expect her to come apart and probably feel she has the right to. That she should. "I guess I don't know what else to tell you. Thank you all for . . . for . . . "

Gil lowers her back to sitting with an arm on her shoulders. "Alright, you heard her," he says. "Boy's in the woods. I'm betting he hasn't gone far. I don't want to waste any more time here, but don't you all get worked up and start blasting away out there. Woods're gonna be full of folks. Be smart, now."

There are sounds of assent as he steps down from the cannon and the sheriff goes back to talking. Lindon explains the state police are in touch, and are sending a team. The women in the crowd move toward Alison, surround her with comforting hands, and Martin wishes he could be near her, too, but the men are going in other directions. The division of labor strikes him as almost a kind of resignation, as if the town's women know their time is better spent comforting the mother, the one they can help, rather than searching for the boy who is lost. He lingers at the back of the group around Gil until other men begin moving off and he can step closer. Lindon spreads a map over the curve of one cannon and Gil trace routes through the woods with his fingers. Martin leans in to see what they're seeing.

"Figure we'll find him around here," Gil says as he swipes a bent knuckle across a line of low hills behind the neighborhood where Alison lives. "Probably taking a nap."

"You don't think he'll be hurt?" Martin asks, over their shoulders, and the other men turn, only now seeing he's there.

"Why would he be hurt?" asks the sheriff.

"He . . . well, if something took him . . . "

"What do you mean 'took him'?" the sheriff growls. "You heard her, the boy's followed a goddamn fox." He looks away, but mutters, "Took him, for fuck's sake."

Gil says, "Not everyone bumps into a bear when they take a walk." Martin feels his face flush and looks down. Lindon laughs, and so do the other men, a darker laugh than he's heard from these same men talking over the counter in Claudia's.

Martin doesn't say anything else as the map is discussed and, in time, folded up. The last men hurry to their vehicles, rev the engines and roll away from the square. Women shuffle in groups toward their own cars and follow the men down the road with Alison somewhere among them. Martin trails Gil to his truck and climbs into the passenger side where a primer-gray door stands out like a storm cloud against the forest-green cab. He rides silently, wanting to press the issue of first Elmer missing, now Alison's son. He wants to tell Gil about the dreams he's been having and about the fox he saw on the edge of the woods, but he doesn't know where to start—there isn't any one part of his story that would make more sense than the rest, so he doesn't know how he could tell it without sounding crazy right from the first word.

A long line of vehicles snakes through town, heading east toward the turnoff for Alison's road, and there are already dozens of people parked and piling out of their cars, tightening laces and pulling on caps, lifting their rifles from rear windshield racks and backseats.

There's an energy welling up in this town, and in these woods. It's the charge of aimless fury and helpless rage. Rifles are growing heavier in those calloused hands the longer they wait without something to shoot. Someone to blame for their loss, someone who isn't part of their world, caught crossing borders along which they're unwelcome.

They're flailing against their own loss of control, against the world slipping out of their grip, and we can't fault them for that. Everything fights when it's cornered, from beetles to bears. So we'll need to follow them carefully, keep our distance from all those guns, because getting shot isn't part of my plans and those men and their guns have grown ravenous. They've found an outlet the way their dogs do every night, sneaking away from backyards for the forest, returning raptured and bloody by breakfast, no questions asked because no one wants to know where they've been.

16

THE SHERIFF WAITS BESIDE HIS CRUISER AT THE SIDE OF the road, and Gil pulls in behind him to park. A split-rail fence runs between the pavement and a yard Martin recognizes, swing set and all. Faced with the actual site, his hazy dream becomes clearer and his stomach more ill. He looks up from the yard at the house it belongs to, Alison's house. The porch is where he knows it will be and five steps lead up to it the way he remembers. Above them is the window he watched a small shadow walk past.

Gil swings himself over the fence in one fluid motion. Sheriff Lindon walks around and lets himself in through a gate but Martin lifts one leg over the top rail, and then balances himself with both hands on the head of a post as he hoists the other foot into Alison's yard.

Gil kneels by the swing set, running his fingers through grass thin enough for dirt to show through at the foot of an orange- and yellow-striped pole. "See here," he says, and both Martin and Lindon lean down as if he's talking to them. They nearly bump heads, and Lindon squints out at Martin from under the shadow of his dark blue baseball cap. Martin stands and takes a step back as the sheriff bends over the ground where Gil's pointing.

"Here's your fox prints," Gil says and the sheriff makes a noise that might be agreement. Gil slides the palm of one hand back and forth in the grass, slowly and close to the ground. "Little one, too."

Martin steps closer to look at the prints, but the sheriff stands and holds the crossbar of the swing set with one hand, blocking Martin's approach with his back. "Follow those tracks, we'll find the boy," Lindon says.

"I figure." Gil stands up from the ground, brushing dirt and grass from the knees of his pants. "Let's get along, then."

He and the sheriff walk toward the fence, and Martin crouches to find the footprints for himself. He sweeps the grass the way he watched Gil do it, but doesn't see anything resembling a paw in the dark soil around the stripes of the pole. The grass has been recently mown, because there are short, broken blades all over the ground, and the agitation of his sweeping hands stirs up the smell. Whatever the other men saw on this ground remains hidden from him.

"Coming, Marty?" Gil calls from the other side of the fence, and they move toward the road where other searchers stand in groups, waiting to enter the woods.

They pace their way through the trees, spread in a line with a few yards from one person to another so they can always see the next searcher. Gil beats the bushes to Martin's right and there's an unfamiliar young woman on his left, pushing branches and thorny switches aside with a ski pole as she walks, a thick braid of brown hair swinging behind her.

Every face is firmly set, even Gil's, as if they're expecting the worst, however casually Gil and the sheriff dismissed his concerns, and how calmly they spoke of the fox prints leading them to the boy. As if they know more than they're telling, something he's felt more and more from his neighbor. But, he admits to himself, I know more than I'm telling, too.

He thinks of Alison, pictures her out in these woods, one of the dozens of voices he hears calling, "Jake," and, "Hello," and, "Come on out, son." Or she might be inside somewhere, waiting, too terrified even to look. If he had managed to run away for real when he was a child, if he had remained sitting on that bench in a broken-down park or wandered off even farther, would his mother have knocked aside trash barrels and light posts to find him, plowed her way through the neighborhood calling his name? Or would she have waited while the sirens and shouting grew louder and darkness fell, figuring he'd come back in time to pack for their next move?

His mind is far away, his eyes set on the past instead of the forest around him, until he trips on a loose stone and comes down hard on his face. Pushing himself up with both hands on the wet, spongy ground, he hears the woman searching beside him ask if he's alright, then Gil says, "Careful, Marty, look where you're going," from the other direction. There's blood trickling from his nose and he feels his lip swelling into a bruise to match those on his chest. He gets to his feet, keeps walking with a handkerchief pressed to his face, and the bleeding stops before long.

The line of bodies weaves through the woods. There isn't much conversation, but the calls of the search drift between trees on the wind. It's hot beneath the canopy, humid where the ground they move over is wet and sometimes swampy. Streaks of sunlight slip down from above as thin branches crackle with a sound nearly the same as all those feet crunching over dead leaves and downed sticks, or paper balled in a fist.

Whistles blow but don't mean anything, just a scrap of the wrong T-shirt discovered or an old sneaker. They're always remnants of some earlier passage, perhaps other children lost on other days, taken by other animals or by their own kind or clothes gladly shed when they were out at play, and none of them point toward the disappearance at hand. Each time a whistle is blown the curtain of searchers stops short, closes in on itself around whomever the sound has come from, and breath is held until someone determines how long the object turned up has been in the woods. Usually it's a long time, and Martin wonders if whoever lost this sneaker, this shirt, is grown now, moved on, or if their family is still looking somewhere for a body that fits into these clothes that should have been outgrown and forgotten years back.

During that long week he spent alone with Aino, he tried to teach the dog how hide-and-seek works but the overeager canine couldn't catch on. She always followed him to hide instead of waiting to search, or lay grinning behind his legs when Martin finished counting and opened his eyes. He gave up on hide-and-seek, so instead they just walked. A deep, muddy ditch marked the boundary of his host's property, but he slid down one sloppy, wet side and scrambled up the other with the help of a low-hanging branch. Aino barked once or twice as if stuck in the bottom, then switchbacked her way up the slope to where Martin waited on top.

On the other side of the ditch, farther into that landscape than he'd walked before, he found a sneaker in the shade of a tree. It was a blue canvas high-top the same as his own, the same red star and white background printed on the inside ankle, but his own star was bright, still shiny, while this one was rubbed almost away. From the toe to the laces the lost shoe had been torn or chewed on by something, and a creeping green vine had grown through a hole in the toe and woven itself into the eyelets and laces, tying the whole shoe to the ground. He stooped to inspect it, not touching, while Aino squatted to mark the territory on which it was found. He held his foot over the sneaker, comparing its size to his own, and the shoe on the ground was an inch or two longer, meant for a foot bigger than his.

For years he has wondered not how the shoe came to be lost in the woods—that's easy enough to imagine—but how it came to be by itself. It makes sense to lose shoes in a pair: you go swimming and don't put them back on. Or they're tied to the frame of your backpack while hiking, waiting to be worn in camp; the knot slips, they fall off, and it's miles until you notice they're gone. But a single shoe suggests something else, something darker or dangerous. It suggests something has happened to prevent the shoe being worn.

The searchers walk through what remains of the morning, into a section of forest where tree cover is thin. When Martin crossed the cold asphalt to sit on Gil's porch, the sun had barely risen over the trees. Now it burns straight overhead, following the back of each person's neck as if on a pole attached to their shoulders. He's left the bowl from his breakfast sitting beside Gil's rocking chair and it's still half-full of milk. At least, it was until some squirrel or raccoon surely gulped down the rest. He imagines the squirrels from Gil's yard trying to drag his bowl up their tree, and smiles despite his serious mission.

Mixed in with the footsteps and calls of Jake's name are the occasional squawks of walkie-talkies, one search party checking in with another to ask if they've had any success. Every quarter-hour or so Martin listens to Gil tell Lindon or one of his men no, we haven't found a sign of the boy, we're away from the neighborhood and deep in the woods.

In the early afternoon they come to a road that runs parallel to the foot of the hills. On the shoulder are a couple of vans and folding tables stacked with sandwiches and hot coffee and bottles of water bound together in sixes. Searchers in twos and in threes and sometimes alone sit by the side of the road, dangling bare feet down the slope they've come up while sweaty boots and socks dry beside them. Very few people are speaking, only the women giving out sandwiches and listing what kinds of meat and condiments they contain, and the sheriff and his deputies mutter over a map with a few other men, drawing out the afternoon's proposed routes in red pen.

Martin looks around the group for Alison but can't find her. She would be involved in the search; his earlier doubt seems absurd. She's not a person who could sit quietly, he tells himself, letting others look for her lost son. She'll be doing whatever she can.

He tells himself he's done the right thing by withholding his dreams and the story of his own walk in the woods, that the appearance of two foxes on the edge of the forest at two different times doesn't mean anything more than the presence of two birds in the sky. He assures himself speaking up would only cause more confusion rather than help anyone find the boy, and would only make him look crazy or stupid or worse.

He sits on the bumper of the town's one ambulance, and sunlit chrome warms the backs of his legs through his pants. He wishes he was wearing shorts, that he'd taken the time to find some before setting out in the cool morning, but then looks at the legs of some people who did, scratched by brambles and streaked with dry blood, and decides he'd rather be hot.

Of all the sandwiches stacked on aluminum trays and provided for the search party, the nearest Martin can come to a vegetarian option is a layer of turkey thinner than all those around it—perhaps it was the last sandwich made, when ingredients were running out. He peels apart two slices of spongy white bread painted yellow with mustard and pinches off the poultry between finger and thumb. An eager brown Labrador sees what he's doing and waddles over, then sits so its tail slides back and forth on the ground as it wags. Martin tosses the turkey in an arc toward the dog's nose, where it disappears with a gulp and the slapping of gums and nothing the least bit like chewing. Sated, the dog turns tail on his spent benefactor and moves away to where other people are eating.

From his perch on the bumper Martin listens to the crowd, following several conversations at once. They're all about the boy's disappearance, of course, and the search party's lack of success. The old woman he stood beside on the square—no longer in her dressing gown—stoops behind a card table and takes charge of a dented silver percolator. She's speaking to a much younger woman who pulls cling film from plates of brownies and Rice Krispie squares.

"Just because no one's saying it doesn't mean we don't know," the old woman says, voice as wrinkled and loose as the skin on her throat.

"Oh, Ma, come on. Don't start about that again." The daughter rolls her eyes and gazes over her mother's head as she speaks. "That won't help anything."

"Can't *be* helped. That's the point. Scratch takes him and he's not coming back. That's how he does."

The daughter flaps a hand in the air, urging her mother's voice down, and looks around at the crowd as she does. Then she hisses in what seems to be meant as a whisper, "Ma! Shut up! Don't talk that way. She could hear you!" Martin looks for Alison, but again doesn't spot her in the crowd.

The old woman huffs, and her shaking hands bang the percolator back and forth on the table as she tries to secure the lid. "*Some*one's got to face facts. We all know what's going on."

"For the last time, Ma, enough. I'm not a kid anymore. You can stop making up stories. These woods are enough on their own. And I hope you don't go on this way in front of the kids when they spend the night. They don't need bad dreams."

The mother snorts, and mutters something Martin can't hear.

A few minutes later, when he throws his paper plate into a gray plastic barrel lashed to the same silver food truck that's been coming his work site each morning, mother and daughter stand together pouring coffee and offering dessert, the argument over and gone. But Martin, moving through the assembly of faces sometimes familiar but almost all without names, picks up whispers of "Scratch," as if his passing draws the word out.

They invoke my name so easily but in such soft tones, unwilling to acknowledge what they're all thinking. They want to give a name to the cruelty I've caused, because that's easier than accepting the arbitrary loss of a child or an unintended disaster. As long as there's me to believe in, to blame, atrocities are marginally more gentle to bear.

And it is cruel to secret a child away, I admit, but no more so than the rifles and poisons and traps that cost so many other creatures their young. None of it's random. None of it's chance. There's always the intention of killing, whether you target a specific body or are willing to settle for whichever becomes your victim. You don't set a trap or spin a web without knowing what the outcome will be. A trap and a web and a rifle all count on one thing. My reasons aren't any worse than the greedy desire for a wolf's head on a wall, or the skin of a bear on a floor.

And besides all of that, the boy isn't dead and won't be anytime soon. Not by my intention, at least—I didn't plan for Elmer's death, either. So let's put that to one side of the story, and keep up with what the townsfolk are doing.

After lunch the searchers keep searching, but their lines are less rigid, their fanning-out folding in. Martin walks closer to Gil, close enough for them to talk as they move through the trees. Gil pushes branches and brambles aside with the barrel and butt of his gun while Martin fends them off with his hands as much as he can.

"Do you think we're going to find him?" he asks.

"He'll turn up. Probably found some shelter. Waiting for us. If he's a smart kid . . . "

"I think he is."

"If he's smart, he'll sit still. Won't walk around. More you move when folks're trying to find you, the longer it's going to take. Gotta stay in one place. Keep calm and wait for who's coming to come."

"But if something was leading him . . . if he was following something, couldn't he go a lot farther?"

It's a hot day, and Gil's cheeks are flushed. His eyes squint as he looks ahead, deeper into the forest. "Don't get carried away, Marty," he says, his voice raspy and tired. "He's not gonna follow once he knows he's lost. Besides, a fox wouldn't let him follow that long. No animal would."

"What if the fox . . . well, wanted to be followed?"

Gil turns his face toward Martin but keeps walking forward. His eyes are pinched and cold. "The hell are you talking about?"

"Nothing." Martin hangs his head while he speaks, avoiding Gil's eyes as long as they remain fixed on his face. "It's just . . . a lot of strange things have been happening, haven't they? The bear that attacked me, Elmer missing, now Jake?"

"How do you know what's strange?" Gil's voice is flat but gruff, as if he's daring Martin to say something.

"I don't, I guess, but . . . "

"But what?" Gil lets a spent cigarette drop from his mouth to the trail and grinds it into the mud. It's still smoking when he pops another one into his mouth.

Martin takes a gulp, and asks, "What if it's Scratch?"

Gil doesn't answer as he knocks a branch aside and moves forward. But after a moment he says without looking at Martin, "Keep your eyes on the woods instead of making things up, now, huh?"

Martin kicks at the ground, his blushing face lowered. He tries to remember his dream, to replay it in his head, but the ending won't come. He sees himself lurking in the backyard, by the swing set, watching the dark windows upstairs. Then the boy pads down to the kitchen, drinks some orange juice from the carton, and comes out through the sliding glass door to the porch. Did the boy in his dream see a man crouched in the grass, and if so, did he recognize him?

Martin tells himself it was only a dream, that any real boy in any real place would scream at a naked man in his yard. Of course he would. That if any of what he saw in his head had been real, if it had any connection beyond coincidence to what's happening now, he would have known to tell his story. There would be some clearer sign than the coincidence of foxes and a few unusual dreams.

The image of his body crouched in the grass doesn't feel right to Martin—in the dream he didn't feel like himself, he didn't feel human at all. And suddenly he can feel the heaviness of his dream body and the thundering run of its legs. The long, echoing note he sang from the top of a cliff and all the answering voices.

All these details returning make him feel better. When he recalled only the bones of the dream, that he watched the boy enter the yard, it felt so close to the truth Martin worried he might be somehow to blame, even if he couldn't remember doing anything to the boy. Now that he recalls himself not being human and the other impossible details of the dream, the part of his mind afraid he'd done something, afraid he was somehow involved in all this, is assuaged and the coincidence of his vision feels further away from real life. It doesn't make enough sense anymore to be believed.

But he still can't reclaim the end of his dream. Did the boy come down off the porch and sit on the swing? Did he go back inside? Martin thinks he awoke before the moment reached its conclusion but isn't sure.

They walk without speaking for hours, only calling out the boy's name and gathering around infrequently blown whistles. In time the search party approaches a bluff, a high, flat rock face they won't be able to climb without ropes and that Jake couldn't have scaled by himself. As they step into its long afternoon shadow, Gil's radio crackles.

"What?" he hollers into it, then listens. "Dawes Bluff. No, we're just getting here."

All Martin can make out of the other speaker is static, squawks rising and falling in pitch. Gil talks a few seconds longer then turns the radio off and speaks so the straggling searchers all hear. The party gathers around him. A map is spread out on the ground and held at the corners with stones. Martin takes in the faces of the search party, sweaty and streaked, stained with dark sap and speckled with scraps of leaf, all of them tired and heavy with worry.

"Talked to Lindon," Gil tells the group. "They aren't doing any better than we are. It'll take us 'til dark to get outta the woods, so we're gonna head west here. Come out to Pine Street and someone'll pick us up there, get you all back to your cars."

A murmur rolls through the crowd, the sighs of bodies allowed to relax despite their worried minds, and the popping of shoulders burdened with worry and failure.

"What about the boy?" someone asks. "He'll be all alone."

"We aren't gonna find him in the dark," Gil insists. "Don't have the gear for it. I'm not big on leaving him either, but we can't find what we can't see. Staties'll be looking tonight. We'll head out again at first light if we have to. Let's hope we don't. But we'll all need rest to keep at it. Get tired and we'll get lost ourselves."

The voices aren't happy, they don't like his answer, but the bodies know Gil is right and start moving west along the granite face of the bluff. They walk in a clump now, their straight line abandoned. Occasional pleas to the lost boy still ring through the trees until after a few miles even that calling has stopped, and the empty space left by their voices is filled by the chatter of birds and the rattle of leaves and the soft squish of heavy boots on moist ground.

The sky is purple when they emerge from the woods to a row of waiting cars. Their headlights are on, washed over trees still lit by the last trace of sun, and the effect is a double shadow on everything, a world with its edges in motion. The cars aren't rescue vehicles, but mini-vans and hatchbacks and an avocado green station wagon with wood-veneer panels held on by duct tape. The drivers are townspeople who weren't out combing the woods and volunteered to pick up those who were.

Gil tells Martin he'll meet him down at the truck, that he's going to wait for the sheriff so they can look over the map, and that he should get another ride down the mountain.

Martin watches the face of a woman Alison pointed out once in Claudia's as the town's fourth grade teacher. She waits by the open door of her cranberry van. The thick lenses of her glasses exaggerate the moist eyes behind them so her face shimmers with twin liquid pools. Her mouth is set in a quivering line.

There's more coffee, in tall silver urns with brown pumping tops that stand on the hood of one car, and though they're sweaty and hot each person leaving the woods fills a foam cup and drinks it black. They stand on the road's shoulder for a few minutes, or lean against the sides of idling cars, waiting for the group to assemble. Then everyone piles into one car or another without speaking. No one pays any attention to who they ride with, or where they are going; away from the woods is enough. They duck through whichever door's closest and roll down the mountain toward town, to cars and trucks of their own still parked on Alison's street and toward the beds where they won't fall asleep easily no matter how tired they are.

Martin gets into the green station wagon and his clammy T-shirt adheres to the vinyl seatback. He can't find a seatbelt to buckle so gives up looking and clutches a handle at the top of the door as they rattle along, bouncing up and down over a wheel with dead shocks. He cracks his elbow against the armrest three times, and twice jostles the woman beside him, but her eyes are closed and she doesn't look up. Her body is there in the car but her mind is elsewhere, still out in the woods second-guessing how hard she searched, afraid she could have done more. And also afraid there was nothing she could do that would matter.

17

AT THE BASE OF THE MOUNTAIN WHERE SEARCHING BEGAN, at the edge of a dark neighborhood, Martin waits by Gil's truck. He watches other cars pull away, their taillights shrinking into the dark, and it isn't long before he's alone. There are still a few cars standing by empty, so he assumes another group of searchers is on its way down the mountain and his neighbor will be among them.

On the other side of the fence around Alison's yard, the swing hangs from its frame, a dead pendulum in a clock no one wound. In the dark, the orange and yellow stripes of the swing set blur into a uniform shade of dull grey.

Martin climbs into the bed of the truck to wait. He's noticed before the tailgate is always lowered, and now he discovers the hinges are rusted and stuck in place; it's been a long time since the gate could swing shut. He stretches his body across the ridged steel of the bed with his head at the open end, raised slightly by the tailgate's low angle. He yawns and looks up to find the stars as clear as he's ever seen them, emerging in ones and twos as the evening grows darker. Right now, after sunset but before night really falls, before the moon gets higher, there's no other light source to wash the stars out and the blurred streak of the Milky Way and a pink dot he suspects is a planet are vivid far off.

He knows how to find the main constellations, Orion and the twins and both dippers, and he knows there's a bear around the larger one though he can't quite pin down its shape. His guesses at the North Star are often right. But his stargazing is all stories and shapes, not a navigational tool. He couldn't follow their map unless the sky realigned in a long blinking arrow with his name sparkling bright in the center. It's something he's always wanted to learn—not where the stars are, but where they tell him to go—and stretched in the bed of Gil's truck he promises himself once again that he will.

He picks out a single red star and knows from a staticky mention by a

TV weatherman the night before it's Antares. As August trails into September, he said, the star becomes bright and hangs at the scorpion's heart, but Martin can't find the shape of the body or even its claws.

After walking all day, his legs cramped up as soon as his body fell still, first in the car and now in the back of the truck. He bends one knee at a time to his chest, trying to limber them up, and his joints and vertebrae crackle and pop their complaints. He unlaces his boots and pulls them off, letting them drop with a clang at his side, then rolls two sweaty socks down past his toes. Steam rises from his feet and their skin prickles as it dries in the cool evening air. His ankles are webbed with pink creases where his socks bunched up in his boots, and he rubs them smooth with both hands.

An airplane passes high overhead, visible as a row of blinking red lights and the shadowy line of a wing. All those people up and out of the world, some on their way and some going home. Planes overhead still make him feel the way he did as a boy waiting for his mother in the long hours of night—apprehensive but eager, excited for the arrival but holding his breath until it actually happens, in case something goes wrong in the final seconds of the approach.

His vision is hemmed in by the walls of the bed, and he stares into the sky while sinking toward sleep. Suddenly, there are noises near the truck—the swishing of footsteps through grass, the rattle of fence rails when the weight of a body leans on them. He holds his breath, his first instinct to hide, then wills himself upright to find out what he hears but still can't convince his body to move. There's a long exhalation followed by a sad sniffle, and the fearful moment is broken—the sounds are distinctly human, and distinctly distressed.

He rises into a sitting position, startling Alison where she leans on the fence. She gasps a loud, "Oh," and takes a step backward into her yard. "Martin," she sighs, coming forward again. "I didn't see you."

"Sorry. I didn't mean to scare you." He stands and stretches in the back of the truck, and for a moment he towers over the road and the yard and over Alison, too, leaning her arms on the fence, wrapped in a brown afghan despite the day's warmth lingering beneath the cool breeze. Then Martin steps from the broken tailgate to the ground and is no taller than the rest of the world. His bare feet and cramped legs protest their sudden call into action, his knees quiver, so he reaches for the head of a fence post to balance himself.

Nearer now, he sees the shine of her tears and the dark shadows under her eyes. He hazards a weak smile but it isn't returned, and she pulls the blanket tighter around her shoulders. Across the backyard, in Alison's house, Martin sees some of the women from town washing dishes and drinking tea. The whisper of their conversation and the clatter of plates come to him through open windows.

He stands in front of Alison but on the other side of the fence. "Are you okay?" he asks, because he needs to say something and it's all he can find. "I mean . . . as much as . . . "

"God," Alison says without looking up, and it's more a plea than an answer. "I don't know. I don't know if I'm tired or hungry or angry or . . . one minute I can't believe all of this is happening. The next, I want to go back out there and keep looking. He's alone, and hungry. Cold. What do I do? I should be out there right now, I should . . . "

Martin struggles for an answer to offer but finds none to give.

"I'm tired of people in my house. I'm tired of . . . help." Her face looks worn out, her body a scarecrow that only keeps standing because it is held up by the fence. She seems shorter than she did the day before, seems to take up less space in the world. All of a sudden she looks right into Martin's face with her hands crossed on her chest and holding together the ends of the blanket.

"Where is he?" she asks. "Where did he go?"

"I don't know." The words feel useless as stones in his mouth. He heard her description of what happened this morning, but asks again in case he can glean more details, discover something about the strange junction of his dream and events. Something that somehow escaped the notice of Gil and the sheriff and all the other men who know this world, these woods, so much better.

Alison closes her eyes. From inside the house, through the window, comes a loud rattling of plates. "It was so early," she says. "He never gets up before me. I heard him in the hallway and thought he was going to the bathroom. I didn't think anything of it." She wipes her eye with a corner of the blanket, and then pulls it tighter around her body. "I didn't even hear him go downstairs before the backdoor slid open. So I went to the window."

She pauses, overtaken by crying, and Martin's arm jerks toward her but settles instead on the rough wood of a rail.

"He was in the yard, on the swing, and I started to open the window to call down to him. There was a fox. I mean, I think there was, but the whole thing felt like I was dreaming, like it wasn't real except . . ." Her words trail off into sobs, and she covers her face with the blanket.

Martin's legs still ache from standing up, and he flexes the muscles in his sore thighs. When he releases the tension the shakes are gone for a few seconds.

"The fucking thing was just *sitting* there, by the swing set, and Jake was talking to it. I ran downstairs, to the back door and out on the porch so I could chase it off, but when I got there . . . when I got outside I watched him follow it into the woods." She reaches out from under the afghan and points toward the dark edge of the woods. "Right there, into that hole."

Martin looks, but the shadows all look the same to him and he can't pick out the entrance she's pointing at.

"I ran after them, into the woods, and I was shouting, but . . . I didn't see them at all. Nothing. Where did he go? How did he just . . . *vanish*? How does that happen?"

"Does he know the woods? I mean, does he know his way around, what to do, that sort of thing?"

Alison sniffs, and pushes on each of her closed eyelids with the tips of her thumb and forefinger. "I don't know. Yes, I guess, he's been to camp, and Cub Scouts, but . . . I don't know."

She wraps her hands around the top rail of the fence and shakes it. "I should have put up a stockade fence, something solid," she says in almost a snarl. "Instead of this goddamn thing." She rattles the rail in its sockets, and the posts at either end of that section sway back and forth. The fence seems to be new, relatively, though already weathered, and at first Martin thinks he should stop her before she knocks it down. But it might be what she needs to do. "What good is a fence that can't stop animals from coming in? Isn't that why we have the damn things?"

He lays his own hands back on the rail as Alison shakes it and the wood scrapes against his palms. Her mouth curls and quivers as tears slide from her eyes not in individual drops but in small, steady streams; she's been holding them in and now they're all coming at once. Finally the length of wood in her hands pulls out of one post and clatters against the lower rail as it falls. The other end stays in its socket, and the beam lies at an angle between them, sloping up from the ground.

"Fuck," Alison says, and kicks the downed rail with a heavy brown boot so its high end comes loose, too, and the whole beam tumbles into the grass.

They stand on opposite sides of the collapsed fence without speaking. Without the top rail running between them, there's nowhere for Martin to lay his hands and they hover useless before him. He wants to hold her, to offer some comfort, but he looks through the window at the kitchen full of women and hesitates. What comfort could she need from him with all of these people already providing whatever they can? People she's known all her life, not an outsider with whom she has only an unrealized vision of houses in common.

But she steps forward against what remains of the fence, then leans across it against him. She's nearly as tall as he is, so he rises onto the balls of his feet until her wet eyes reach his shoulder. Her tears spill onto his neck, dampening the collar of his T-shirt, and he wraps his arms around her with the blanket between their bodies. He lays his hands lightly upon her, not pressing, not holding, just there.

"I'm sorry," she says, and he feels the movement of her lips on his skin as she speaks, a tingle straight down his spine.

"No," he says, "it's okay. Don't be sorry." She says more, but he can't hear the words, only feel them. It's been a long time since he has held or been held by a woman, since his last girlfriend got tired of waiting for him to move in or propose or break up or *something* and finally gave up on waiting. He doesn't know what to do with his hands, especially with the angle of contact between their bodies made awkward by the bottom rail of the fence against their legs.

They stand holding each other in the dark, Alison's arms crossed over her chest and clutching the blanket against herself, and Martin's hands high on her back. Lightning bugs flicker around them and peepers sing to the fiddling of crickets. Conversation goes on in the kitchen but the clatter of dishwashing has stopped and the voices sound far away now. Overhead, bats circle the peak of a pine tree, darting in and out of the crown. Their squeaking chatter is no more or less clear than the words from inside.

"Here you are," a loud voice says behind Martin. He drops his hands from Alison's back and steps back from the fence as she moves away in the other direction. Turning, he finds Gil on the road, across the hood of the truck. "Been waiting long?"

"Not really." His face feels hot and he looks at his bare feet on the gravel shoulder between pavement and grass.

"How y'holdin' up, hon?"

Alison pulls the afghan tighter before she answers. "Okay. Thanks."

"He's alright. Probably made himself a lean-to somewhere, having a campout."

"Guess I'll go in now. G'night, Gil. Thanks." She looks at Martin, and he's sure her eyes are asking him something. He looks for some excuse to stay with her, to send Gil home alone, until she says, "Thanks, Martin," and turns.

He watches as she climbs the steps to her porch and enters through the sliding glass door, then the women inside converge on her and she disappears from his view. A few seconds later the curtains are drawn in the house.

Gil smokes and leans on the truck. Martin yawns. He has no idea what time it is now but he hasn't eaten since the mustard sandwich he shared with a dog. His stomach growls and cramps on cue, as if it's been waiting for him to notice.

"Well," Gil says quietly, "let's get on home. Another long day tomorrow. Longer maybe."

"Why longer?"

"We'll have to walk rougher terrain. Look farther out. If the boy wasn't close to home, he could be anywhere." Gil finishes his cigarette and flicks the stump into the road. "Longer it takes, more chance something happened."

"I thought you said . . . "

"Well, what am I gonna tell her? Not much hope we'll find your son, good night? Don't think about it now, Marty—save it until we're looking or you'll keep yourself awake. Get it in your head. You don't want that. Believe me."

They lift themselves into the truck, and Martin peeks through the window at the back of the cab to make sure his boots and socks are still there. They pull away from Alison's house without speaking, but a minute or two later Gil fills Martin in on the day's fruitless search and what other groups walking other parts of the forest reported.

As they pass Elmer's driveway, Martin leans his head through the window into the breeze but can't see the house set way back on the hill. A mailbox stands next to the road, a rectangular tube of corrugated tin sheet Elmer must have made for himself. Newspapers and bills and catalogues selling things nobody needs hang out both ends. If the mail doesn't get picked up soon, there won't be room for any more, but it won't make any difference to Elmer.

"Do people go missing around here a lot?" Martin asks.

Gil turns his head a couple of degrees so the smoldering nub of his cigarette points across the bench seat at Martin. "No more than anyplace." Then he seems to understand what he's really being asked, and adds, "It's a coincidence, Marty. Don't make anything of it."

The cigarette has no filter, and Gil has let it burn down so far it's almost an internal glow sneaking out of his mouth, an ember inside his body. How he can smoke them so close to the end without burning himself is beyond Martin. His own throat is scratchy from shouting all day and breathing the particles and pollens that swirl through the woods, and he strains his neck muscles to clear it with a wet, rattling growl.

"Couldn't it be something else? More than coincidental?" he asks, shocked by his own unintended directness and the implied challenge in the tone of his voice.

Gil turns away from their conversation and spits the end of his cigarette out the window into the night. In the side mirror Martin watches it collide with the ground. It explodes in the road behind them, a tiny display of orange fireworks as they roll on.

"What? What do you think's going on? 'Cause it's nothing. Elmer's a drunk, Marty. He gets lost all the time. It's nothing."

Martin watches a string of gray lumps get larger ahead of the truck. A raccoon edges along the side of the road and four smaller versions follow behind, struggling to maintain a straight line as they sniff each weedy white flower and discarded cigarette butt planted in the soil of the soft shoulder. They remind Martin of pictures he's seen of war refugees leaving their homes, endless trails of peasants in shabby brown and gray clothes following one another to the next town, and when they're inevitably driven from that one, too, on to the town after that. The mother raccoon stops every few steps to check on her young, keep them moving, get them wherever they're going before the bright light of morning gives them away.

"What about Jake?"

Gil sighs, a slow-motion cough. "I don't know what to tell you. You seem hell-bent on seeing something that's not there. Kids get lost in the woods. They're kids, they wander. Weren't you ever a boy? Didn't you play in the woods? And yeah, sometimes they run away. " He pats around on the truck's deep, dark dashboard until he finds a half-empty package of cigarettes. He shakes one loose and stabs at the lighter.

"But he was following a fox . . . "

"Hell, Marty, we've been through this. A fox won't let himself be followed. It's nothing."

"What if it wasn't a normal fox? What if . . . "

"What you asking me? What do you want me to say, damn it?"

Martin pulls at a patch of peeling green vinyl where it hangs from the dashboard, exposing yellow foam underneath. "I followed a fox, too. Sort of. That's how I got lost the other day."

Gil laughs, and his laughter gets harder and louder until he starts coughing and pounds his chest a few times with a fist. The lighter pops out of the dashboard and he draws it to his mouth, the blazing coils of wire reflected on the skin of Gil's face. "Hell, you may *think* you followed a fox, but I'll bet you the fox didn't think so."

"But you said yourself the animals have been acting strange. What if they want to be followed? What if it was trying to lead me somewhere? And Jake, too?"

"Oh, for Christ's sake, fine. Maybe you saw a fox. Maybe you followed it a little. But I don't think it picked up a ten-year-old boy and carried him off. Yeah, I said animals were coming up closer to houses. Not that foxes're kidnapping folks. Shit. They're rifling garbage cans, Marty. Scaring cats and old ladies. Damn it."

"People were talking about Scratch when we were searching. Saying . . . saying that this is what he does, taking people away from their homes."

Gil sighs and stares straight ahead at the road. "Look, Marty, it's late. I know you're worn out because you're talking nonsense. Things you don't understand and they've got you worked up. So we'll get home, get some shuteye. Find the boy in the morning and he'll tell us what all happened. No sense jawing about it when we're both tired."

"But do you think there's something going on? Whether it's this Scratch or . . . something else? You're the one who told me about him, and everybody else seems to believe it."

"Damn it, I said let it go. I told you a *story*. I didn't think you were fool enough to believe it. I was trying to take your attention off what I was doing to those cuts on your chest. It was a fucking distraction. That's all. Now drop it. I'm tired. So are you."

Martin is sure that Gil's avoiding something, pretending to know less than he does. But his neighbor's anger is piqued enough he doesn't push, and lets the rest of the ride go by without speaking. He thinks of the conversation he overheard in the woods, the daughter's insistence that Scratch isn't real and the mother equally sure that he is. Martin has never been prone to believing in things he can't see but this town and its forest are testing his lack of faith—there's too much he can't explain, even Gil's angry reluctance to ask what could be going on.

I could tell Martin what he's found, if he knew to ask. People here believe something's out in the woods, they believe that something is me, but no one wants to admit they believe it. Same as Martin, their sense of how the world works, their faith in what they think they know, has been tested by what happens here so many times they've gotten used to it all whether they meant to or not. But that doesn't make it any easier for them to explain, to each other or to an outsider. For so long they've grown up with the stories, one generation after another hearing the same half-humorous threats from tired parents to children refusing to sleep, they can't *not* believe anymore. The stories are so much a part of this place it makes no difference, to them, whether or not I'm actually here. It's like Gil told Martin—I'm a convenient distraction.

And he doesn't know how right he is, or how often he's the same thing for me.

Martin is jostled from his thoughts when the truck bumps over the rocky lip of the road at the edge of Gil's yard. Before the headlights cut out with the engine, he sees the white curve of his cereal bowl perched on the porch, a tin camping spoon projecting over its rim.

"You riding with me in the morning?" Gil asks, and Martin nods as he swings the door open and steps out of the truck. "Be out here about five. Get in the woods for first light."

"I hope the police find him before that," Martin says. "I hope they already have."

"Well, I hope so, too. But those boys aren't from here. They don't know our woods."

Martin isn't sure why this matters, and almost mentions that a town full of people who *do* know these woods couldn't find the boy so far, either, but he holds his tongue. Then Gil says good night and climbs out of the truck. They separate and head to their homes, or the closest things they have to them. Martin watches from his front steps as a light comes on and goes out on the first floor of Gil's house, then another flares behind the curtains upstairs. He lets himself into the trailer, home to the same pile of socks he left on the carpet this morning, the same glass of water standing alone on the counter. He peels off his shirt, damp and ripe, and steps out of his pants in the door to the bathroom. His boots, he remembers, are still in the truck, but he can get them when they leave in the morning. It's only a few hours away.

He stands in the shower without moving, leaning against the wall of blue- and green-speckled plastic. He lets the water slide down his back, a brown eddy whirling around his feet over the holes of the drain. The bruises on his chest and sides have lightened in shade from the eggplant of a few days ago. The pain around his ribs is less, too, but they're still sore enough to feel each drop of water as it lands on his skin. He imagines Alison's son somewhere in the woods, huddled in the shade of a tree, knees to his chest and arms wrapped around them, crying himself to sleep or, long cried out, rocking back and forth in primordial comfort.

The steam makes him tired, and his eyelids hang half-closed in a blink that has stalled. He collapses onto the tangle of bedclothes without drying off, without getting dressed, and a cool breeze through the slats of the window runs icy fingers up and down his wet body.

He isn't quite sleeping but it's the most restful state he has reached in days and in nights. He lies with his eyes open wide and his body melting beneath him, spilling into the mattress. He's more relaxed than he's been for so long. He's awake but feels deep in a dream, his muscles fully replenished. He stares at the ceiling, the textured plastic panels and bolted seams over his bed, but sees something else altogether.

He sees the forest, the woods he walked out of a short time ago, and the long shadows of trees drawn out by moonlight. He's in the forest and in his bed at the same time, but somehow he's knows that it isn't a dream and it isn't a memory, either. His eyes zip between trees, dodge around boulders and through bramble twists, and he knows that he's seeing things as they are right this moment. He forgets that his body exists, that he's sore and tired and lying in bed, as he slides through the woods with the fluid grace of thin air.

And he knows where the boy is now, too. He can see the thick oak with exposed roots on its downhill side, forming a shelter into which Jake has huddled. He's in pajama pants exactly as Alison described them, printed with a parade of lassoing cowboys marching up and down each of his legs. Both of his arms are pulled in through the short sleeves of his shirt and they cross his chest under the fabric, bulging over his ribs. He's murmuring something, telling himself a joke or a story or song, distracting himself, but his eyes are shut tight and his feet are muddy and bare and every muscle is clenched in his body.

Even without his ears and their body, this projection of Martin can hear the boy's stomach growl.

He knows where this tree is and he knows how to get there and the knowledge feels so natural he doesn't ask where it comes from. It's as basic as telling apart red and green, or knowing a hand from a foot, and it seems foolish now that he ever thought two trees looked the same, that they were all more or less identical.

Immediately he's out of the bed, pulling on the clothes he's just taken off, and is out the door on the way to his car. Then he turns and goes back to the trailer, pulls three plastic bottles of water from their shrink-wrapped cardboard case because the boy is bound to be thirsty. He shoves a handful of energy bars into his pocket and pulls the blanket from his bed before leaving the trailer again and making sure that the door is closed fast behind him.

He drops the blanket, food, and water into the passenger seat of his car then goes for his boots. The night is especially dark and he moves slowly, afraid that Gil will be on his porch, maybe even awake. He creeps onto the pavement strip of the street, eyes peeled, and though the moon is covered by clouds, and there aren't any lights on in the house or hanging over the road, he can still see. Not daylight, but enough to know the porch is vacant for once, enough to pick his way through the grass without tripping on any rocks or low stumps. The chorus of crickets and peepers goes quiet in waves as he passes and starts up again once he's gone by.

As he approaches the bed of the truck, he hears the whir of a fan in Gil's window and the faint groan of snores filtered through the hum of the blades. He considers waking his neighbor, asking him to join this second search, but he imagines what he'll be told—to go back to bed, get some sleep. And how could he convince Gil to help without claiming to have had a vision of where the boy is? Who would believe him?

Martin decides, in the end, it's easier to go by himself and explain how he found the boy later when he has proof he was right, or to keep all of this quiet if he turns out to be chasing geese. He sits on the lowered gate of the truck and pulls on his socks and his boots, already moistened by dew and night mist. Then he rolls onto the road with his headlights out, and leaves them that way until he's far enough from Gil's house they won't shine through the dark windows.

18

THE DREAMS ARE BECOMING AS REAL AS HIS WAKING HOURS, the woods as familiar as the streets and houses and paperwork jungles Martin has navigated for years. It doesn't feel new to him so much as it is waking up, a rediscovery of something or someone he already knows but hasn't seen for some time. Like an adult climbing onto a bike for the first time since learning to drive, or a father slipping on an old baseball glove familiar as skin before he plays catch with his son.

He drives through the dark until he reaches the shores of the lake once again. His strange hours of waking and sleeping have knocked his sense of time out of balance, and he can't determine with any certainty whether it was one day ago, or two, or even three since he last sat here. He parks his car beside the picnic table and looks across the onyx sheet of the water. The moon is so low, so close to the surface, that its yellow trail of light has the look of a ladder he could climb all the way to the source.

He tightens the laces of his boots then rummages in the trunk of his car until he finds a faded red backpack. He stuffs in the blanket, the water, and the energy bars. As he walks away from the car it chimes twice to tell him it's locked itself, and as strange as the sound was earlier, on the site, it's stranger still here—the artificial voice of a bird in a place where real birds are asleep overhead. Strange enough for those real birds to go on sleeping, none of them waking to answer the car's robot call.

A moment later Martin plunges into the forest where it thickens at the edge of the lake. He's farther from Alison's neighborhood than the search party roamed during the day, beyond the cliff where they stopped and a few miles deeper into the woods. No one imagined the boy could have wandered this far, up sheer faces and down steeper slopes, mile after mile, hours of walking. Those who were expected to know, Gil among them, assumed he would stop when the going got rough, would try to turn back or sit down where he was and stay put, but now Martin knows better. He remembers how far he wandered on his own trek, driven by the desire in his legs long after the fox that sparked his motion had fled. Jake could be anywhere, however far it might seem, and if his own experience is any indication the boy has no idea which direction he came from or how to retrace his steps. No more idea than Martin has at this moment that he is being led once again, and will be as easily lost as he was the first time.

His feet soon burn with blisters from a long day spent walking, and the straps of his pack cut into his shoulders right through his thin fleece pullover. He would prefer to be wearing his weatherproof jacket, but it lies in the building site's dumpster, shredded by claws and caked with blood, not much good for keeping rain out.

He trundles through the woods, energized despite his earlier exertion: his lungs seem bigger, strides longer, and he plows through low-hanging branches and the gripping tendrils of briars without stopping, only ducking his head sometimes to protect his eyes. Martin is coming to know his way through these woods, to know what to watch out for and what to ignore, to know what the real dangers are and, relatively, how few exist. Mosquitoes are so much more common than bears, and there are ten million gnats in the world for every lion or wolf.

The moon can't break through the tree canopy, but his eyes have adjusted and the trail seems as clear as if it were day. It's not a wide path, one made by deer instead of by humans, but it meets his needs at the moment and in the back of his mind where the vision still hangs, he sees the whole lay of the trail to where the boy waits. He sees the thick tree trunk and wedge of mud walled in by roots where Jake curls in a ball, and he tightens the straps of his pack without stopping, stretches his stride now that he's limber, and sings a low song to himself in the back of his throat.

As he walks he thinks about Alison, waiting at home for word of her son, as exhausted as he is from searching all day plus the extra exertion of worry, of woe, of believing all this is her fault even if she understands that it isn't. The strain of being the lost child's parent. He tries to imagine himself in those shoes—of having a son, of having him lost—and for the first time in his life he feels close to getting it right. That he almost knows, as much as he can, how Alison feels. That he can empathize with her loss, and the need to have her son found.

He wants to worry that much, to be so concerned about someone else it hurts. He returns to the house in his head as he walks, the one he daydreams about, and rearranges the furniture for the ten-thousandth time, clears out his office upstairs to make it a room for a child, moves his desk and his papers to the small den on the first floor instead. He moves all his clothes to one side of the walk-in closet he has imagined, and leaves the other side free for someone else. He takes down half the wall hangings to make space for another aesthetic, a taste that isn't his own, and he buys four extra place settings to stack in the kitchen cabinets.

Then he walks through the house, through his daydream here in the dark, and three times he trips: over a chair he wouldn't have chosen, and toy trucks parked on the stairs. Over a cat that shrieks and dashes under the couch when he steps on its tail, and it's this that is most unexpected because Martin is a dog person. He isn't allergic to cats, he doesn't mind them so much, but he wouldn't bring one into the house if left to himself.

Is that what it is, he wonders, to share a home? Tripping over things you didn't know you owned, and compromising on pets you don't want? Being surprised in your own space? Tracing and retracing his steps from kitchen to porch, from attic to basement to den, he finds that the furniture in his head won't stay still. The house he has imagined so fully, the space he has mapped to such fine detail, is changing with each step he takes and has gone beyond his control and he doesn't mind.

He smiles as he walks through the dark forest, pulling the backpack straps away from his chest to let fresh air swirl beneath, to dry his clothes where sweat has already soaked them, again. What has been missing from his visions of home, from his floor plans in their minute measurements, is some other will to share his house with, other bodies and minds to keep him on his toes. To move chairs where he might trip over them and leave toys where he might break his neck, and to keep him from paying all his attention to his own life. He understands now what Gil meant about shining shoes. As many times as he's imagined sharing his house with other people, they've never before appeared in his dreams—they were always in some other room that he couldn't find, leaving no sense of their lives in the objects filling the home.

He thinks of the families who will buy his houses, all of the people who will be his neighbors and their individual lives tangled together the way noises swirl in this forest. All coming and going each with their own intentions as the deer and coyotes and caterpillars do in the woods, and he can hardly wait for construction to finish, for those parents and children and pets to arrive so he can tie his own life together with theirs and the life of the town that sleeps on the edge of the woods.

Lost in his thoughts, Martin trips over something in the path with a clang. He swings face-first toward the ground but breaks the fall with his palms so he's suspended over the trail on all fours, hands and feet flat and head tilted up on his neck as he looks ahead. He rights himself, and looks down to see a thick, rusty chain stretched across his trail. It's been there long enough for vines to wind through it, tying it to the ground, and it snakes from the scrub on one side to the scrub on the other.

He keeps walking, thinking again of Alison's son, who the boy longs for, alone in the dark—his mother who's waiting, or the father who isn't around? Who does the boy imagine reaching him first, making the rescue? Whose arms does he rush into again and again while he waits to be found?

The forest is full of bright eyes: sparkling spots between the shadows of trees, dashes of yellow in all that black and dark green. The ground on either side of the trail is thick with crickets, trilling up and the down the rasped ridges of their legs in conversation with one another.

"I'm a cricket, I'm here."

"I'm a cricket, too, and I'm here."

Martin walks through the dark, watched by the eyes of the woods. Sleeping birds whistle and chirp overhead, the round balls of their tufted bodies perched on branches with their heads tucked under their wings. Bats swoop and circle over the ceiling of leaves, picking mosquitoes out of the air. Louder sounds echo from farther off, the howls of coyotes and the singing of wolves that always comes from some other direction, those packs of low, sleek gray bodies left to their own part of the forest while the rest of us stay off their path, out of their teeth and away from their claws.

They aren't as succinct as the crickets, those wolves, but they don't waste words or time, either. They'd as soon kill me as hear the end of this story, and even though I would lose this body without losing myself, it's an experience I'd rather avoid. So I stay out of their way when I'm wearing a shape that is no match for theirs.

Martin was amazed, in his dream, when I allowed him to overhear the forest's full dialogue, but it's not always worth knowing what's being said around you. Crickets aren't much to understand unless you're a cricket yourself; you're better off letting them fade into background, letting what passes—for them—as conversation lapse into generic night sound.

Sometimes I still listen in; sometimes I take the shape of a cricket and join their orchestra in all its fiddling, but never for long, a few days or weeks, until I tire of the same notes again and again. I think Martin would know what I mean, if I told him. I think he'd find being a cricket as mundane as I do. There are better animals he could become. More interesting voices to understand, voices with something to say.

Simplicity doesn't make the cricket any less vital than the largest of bears or the deepest of fish. It doesn't make them dumb bugs. Crickets have perfected their language; they can tell all the story they need to tell with a few notes, a few strokes of a leg, nothing wasted. Everything one cricket needs to know of another—have you found food, do you want to mate—can be carried in those quick tones.

Maybe the rest of us are, over time, learning to tell our stories with the efficiency of a cricket, learning how to not mince our words or our growls and to harness the spasmodic motions of bodies that so often leave room for doubt and confusion and violence. I could have told you this tale as a cricket, but I suspect you would have been less keen to listen.

Or I might have worn the long shape of a wolf, but your kind are still as afraid of the wolf as most others are. Even when other animals lose their ability to plant fear in your hearts, when the howl of coyotes or the rumbling of bears makes your heart flutter with the nostalgia of ignorance, and you feel yourself drawn back to nature—as if you have ever been able to leave—the call-and-response of a pack in the hills sends you scampering back to your cars, onto the roads, out of the mountains toward home where you lock double-paned windows and pull down heavy shades and turn up the lights as bright as you can. Is there anything else left in the forest as frightening as wolves?

There's me, I suppose. There's still me.

Martin arrives on a ridge overlooking a valley, and knows the boy is below. The moon is straight above now, trapping his shadow beneath his own feet. A long way off in the forest he sees the flicker and flash of lights in the trees, too big to be insects and too bright to be eyes. They move like headlights on a road full of curves but there are no roads down there. It must be the state police, still out searching, swinging their flashlights through the forest and talking on radios he's too far off to hear.

He hoists his pack higher, cinches it with a jerk on each strap, and descends with his feet turned out. Something darts into the scrub as he nears the foot of the hill, long and orange and maybe a fox, getting out of the way of his coming.

The woods in the valley are thicker than on the ridge above, and damp with dew. Martin rests for a moment at the foot of the slope, taking deep breaths and stretching his back. He stands still long enough for the crickets he quieted with his arrival to start telling their stories again, re-tuning their legs and picking up where they left off.

He knows, without worrying how, that he's nearing the tree, and the boy who leans into its bark for some kind of comfort. From his vision in bed he recognizes the rock that he's passing and a spot where the drooped branch of an ash arches over the trail. Buoyed, he hastens his step and hurries toward the boy's rescue.

Then the tree is in sight, a tall oak with its first branches high from the ground, one of the oldest trees in this forest. Old enough for generation after generation of seedlings to have burst through the thin glaze of topsoil and grown their first inches only to smother and starve without light in the looming shade of their source. The ground at the base of the trunk has been given over to bushes and brambles and other plants that make due with a thin trickle of sunlight and suck leftover moisture from damp mud too shallow for thirstier roots.

Martin sees the trunk now, but the base is still obscured by the scrub. He breaks into a run, his pack swinging and dragging the damp fabric of his shirt back and forth against his shoulder blades. "Jake," he calls as he approaches, then he calls out again. He bursts through the brush between the trail and the tree, the thin sails of root visible now, buttresses between the trunk and the ground, and the notch where Alison's son should be huddled.

Was huddled.

And where he was there is only a pair of small sneakers. Around them is only the scuttled, scarred soil where the boy sat for so long, the marks of his shoes so smeared in the mud that no individual footprints can be picked out, only the swirling tread pattern stamped all over itself.

"Where . . . ?" Martin asks the bustling woods, or the tree, or the abandoned sneakers before him. He collapses to the ground in the crook of the roots, and mud soaks the knees of his pants. He was so certain the boy would be here, in the spot he occupied in the vision, that supposing otherwise never once crossed his mind. And now that it has, it's brought in so much more doubt along with it.

"Jake?" he asks the dark and again he gets no reply.

Martin pulls the shoes into his lap, scuttles backward against the bark of the tree so the hard walls of root squeeze at his sides, tilts his head to the trunk and closes his eyes. He draws long, chest-swelling breaths with his mouth open wide, and listens to the night birds who chat overhead as if gossiping about his failure.

Something skittles and skitters on the other side of the tree and he sends his legs the command to leap up but his body ignores him, or tries to obey but it can't, relaxed in the wedge of the roots and tired again now that he's still.

A porcupine shuffles into his field of vision, circling the trunk of the oak. A bright red T-shirt clings to the animal's body, collar around its spiny abdomen, dragging across the ground behind it. The porcupine is struggling to free itself from the shirt, rolling and clawing and grunting. It can only move forward, through the collar, because earlier attempts to back out of the shirt have snarled the fabric in bristling quills. The animal waddles closer, so intent on its efforts that it seems oblivious to Martin's presence. Its stubby tail bobs up and down and its quills roll. As it approaches his feet, Martin reaches with jittery fingers and grips the tail of the shirt. He extends his arm as far as he can and leans his face away, because he's never been told a porcupine cannot, in fact, launch its quills. At last the animal heaves through the shirt, the force of its effort causing it to tumble when the grip of the collar is released. It stands as if dazed before Martin.

The logo printed in white on the fabric is the one kids in town have been wearing for weeks, the marker of the summer camp they all went to, Jake, Jr. included.

"How did you get . . . " Martin begins, but stops because he's addressing a porcupine, which only wiggles a pink triangle nose and stares with its navy bean eyes. Then he notices a smaller scrap of fabric stuck on a hind claw, and as he reaches toward it he's almost sure that the porcupine swivels, lifts its hind end and lets him pull the remnant away. Holding the cloth in front of his face, Martin makes out small cotton cowboys on small cotton horses, and a lariat cut off at the edge of the scrap.

"How did you get that?" he asks, and the porcupine turns toward him but doesn't respond. Then the strangest idea slides into Martin's head, the kind of idea he would have rejected a few days before but now, with all he's seen in these woods, makes as much sense as anything else.

"Jake?" he asks, leaning forward, but if he expects a reaction it doesn't come as the porcupine scratches its neck with gray claws. Then he feels stupid for asking, for indulging the notion at all. Boys who become porcupines, animals wearing cowboy pajamas—he shakes his head and laughs at himself, willing to believe but only so far.

Martin hunches against the rough bark at his back, knees pulled close to his chest and skin cooling fast as the sweat he worked up on his hike dries away. The porcupine stands between mud-covered boots, looking up with its head cocked to one side the way Martin has only seen a dog do in the past. Then it yawns, eyes squeezed tight, and a long strand of pink tongue rolls around its mouth. It turns, quills heaving at its sides as hips roll underneath, then shuffles into the brush. A few crackles and the rustling of leaves from the scrub, then it's gone.

He draws his phone from its pouch on his pack, just in case, and for once it has a strong signal—deep in the woods, under these trees, its indicator is as full, even fuller, than it has been since he came to these woods. Who to call? He has his partner far off and all his suppliers, strangers he speaks to in numbers and checks. He has the number for the town clerk in an office still closed for several more hours, and he could try 911 but isn't sure that service exists in such a small town. There's Alison, right at the top of the list in his phone, but what could he say? I almost found your son but I failed, I was no help to you and now I need you to help me? The person he'd like to call, the person who would know what to do, he has no number for. He hasn't needed it, with Gil's house right across the street from his trailer, almost always in sight and within a shout's reach.

He remembers, then, that police departments are always or often the same, an area code and exchange then 1212, and he doesn't know if that's the case but it's worth a try. What area code, though, and what exchange? His own phone is ungrounded, tied by its numbers to the store where he bought it but not where he lives. There's a code for this place but he doesn't know it, so he copies the first digits of the number for town hall and hopes that will work.

But when he finally dials, his phone, so deep in a signal it hums and gets hot in his hand, can't connect. He tries, and he tries, dialing and dialing and dialing again, there's only that hum. A hum that isn't the signal he's after but a signal that's older and stronger and overwrites whatever weak stream might still make its way to his phone. All this forest's stories, its voices and rattles and roars, cracking and splashing and croaks, memories and dreams . . . all that converged on this tree, this great mast in the depth of the woods where they're oldest. Think of it as an antenna, if it helps, but not one that was raised in an afternoon by a gang of men with a crane; this spot is where signals converge because it's been here the longest. Because it has listened the most.

His phone is receiving a signal, but not one he knows how to hear. He doesn't know yet how to listen. If he was willing to believe a boy could give way to a porcupine, or a man to a mountain lion, he might be more at ease. If he could take seriously things it's so much easier for him—and for you, too, I expect—to dismiss. Or he might be more afraid. It's hard to say, sometimes, how any mind will react to discovering more things are possible in the world than it knew. He would certainly know his search is over—he set out to find the lost boy and the boy has been found, though not in quite the same state. Martin is free to turn around now, walk back to the lake and his car and drive to his trailer for some well-earned sleep. But he doesn't know all of that. He thinks the boy is still missing, that these scraps of cloth are his best clues, and he should keep on with his search of the woods. That he needs to move deeper into the forest, farther away from any place he knows, if he's going to find out what happened to Alison's son.

19

MARTIN SITS WITH THE PAIR OF SMALL SHOES IN HIS LAP, and runs his fingers over the laces as if reading Braille. He drinks a bottle of water before hoisting himself to his feet. Exhausted after two long walks in the woods without sleep, standing up is enough to send the blood rushing away from his head so he steadies himself with a hand on the trunk. He eats one of the energy bars, stuffing the foil wrapper deep into the pack where it won't blow away, then leaves his shelter between the high roots of this tree.

There are toadstools, or mushrooms—he can't tell the difference—growing in the deep chasms formed by those roots. Moss reaches from one side of each root up and over the other, woven with vines, and fine white flowers with feathering petals peek out of the shade. This ring of earth is a landscape all its own, grown up with the tree as its heart and its mind, deciding in its own passive way which stories linger and which are erased. For decades this giant has shaded out some lives to make space for others, a whole drama scripted by time in which the actors appear to stand still.

But Martin doesn't see any of that as he looks away from this tree and into another, where several feet overhead a maple spile extends from a trunk, rusted and forgotten and raised out of reach by the passage of time.

The birds are waking above him, and their chatter grows lively. The first orange streaks pick their way through the treetops, splashing bleach spots of light on the dark ground. Then a thick shaft of sunlight pierces the canopy and dozens of starlings and grackles and finches and wrens begin shrieking and squawking and carrying on as if they've picked up where they left off last night, as if sleep was a lull in a long conversation. Martin hurries away, out from under the noise, as a headache takes shape in the back of his skull, aroused by the din of the birds and his exhaustion and the frustration of knowing where the boy was but arriving to find him gone.

He circles the edge of the clearing made by the tree's shade, searching for a break in the scrub that might be a trail. If the boy isn't here, Martin reasons, and if his shoes and his clothes have been left behind, then he must not have left by his own power.

There's a spot in the brush where stalks are bent back and leaves are pressed into the mud as if something heavy passed over. It doesn't look wide enough or damaged enough to have been a person, or even a large animal, and he has no way of knowing if it's a fresh trail or days old or older than that. But it is the only lead he's discovered, so with Jake's shoes dangling from a carabiner clipped to his pack, and the red T-shirt and scrap of pajamas in hand, he follows whatever it was that forged this trail. Before long he gets hot, and ties his fleece top to the pack, too.

The sun is up and Martin is sweating, jittery and strung out the way he gets without sleep. When he's been awake this long the semi-conscious rattle at the back of his head comes to the fore and the muttered ramblings his brain cycles through all the time without telling him become as loud and insistent as the birds in the trees. He can hardly think straight for all the snippets of songs and repeated words and jumbled images crowding his mind.

After the obvious gap near the tree there isn't much of a trail. He spots the occasional broken twig or bent sapling, or a branch that perhaps caught on something to pull it in the awkward direction it's facing. Martin takes these as clues, as signs of some passage. The sweaty fabric of his shirt bunches up, sticks to his chest, and when the folds work their way under the straps he feels the heat of blisters beginning to rise.

His feet are sore, too, cramped in his boots for all of the previous day and most of the night. The ground here is fairly soft, and mostly free of sharp stones and sticks, and though it may be a result of his tired state and muddled thinking, Martin decides to walk barefoot until his feet have cooled off and his socks have dried out.

He lashes his boots to the pack next to the much smaller sneakers, and weaves the wet socks through their laces. His naked feet notice each tiny pebble and the edge of each leaf, every shift from dry ground to wet, and the shock of moving from the sauna of shoes to the cool breeze of bare skin prickles him with gooseflesh. He's more careful about placing each step, and it's a while before he stops feeling squeamish about wet, black mud, but soon he's moving along as fast as before and the new realm of sensations entering his body has woken him up. He's amazed at the comfort of walking this way—his feet feel expanded to their full size, though they never knew they'd been compressed.

A mile or two away from the tree, heading into the sun, the trail trickles away without a trace. There are bald spots on trees with fur pinched in the bark where deer have left each other rubbings, and the shredding and gouging of bears, but they aren't signs Martin knows how to read. He finds moss on a trunk and remembers that—supposedly—it always points north, but even if that's a truth it's a useless one at the moment because he's following a boy, not a compass. He kneels in the mud, head sideways and parallel to the ground. He's looking for footprints and he finds them, dozens of impressions in all directions, hooves and claws and his own naked feet. He picks out the swing of a snake and can tell right away a raccoon went by with a bad leg—it must be his tired mind playing tricks, calling up knowledge he imagines he has, or unconscious trivia about tracking he picked up from TV or a poster of animal prints on some classroom wall years ago. He even sees the steps of a pair of coyotes creeping under the scrub to a secluded spot.

But none of those prints point toward Jake, and now he isn't even sure how to get back to the tree or retrace his steps to the lake and his car, so he presses on into the brush, hoping another sign will appear to keep him on track.

He's annoyed with himself for getting lost again, and this time he has no excuse: he thought he could find the boy, that he could be a hero and win the town's praise and Alison would be grateful. But he doesn't have Gil's tracking skills, he doesn't have a history in the woods—not a good one, at least—so what the hell he was thinking to wander alone off into the forest in the dark dead of the night?

The search party will end up searching for him, once they know he's missing—he didn't appear to meet Gil this morning, but his boots are gone as is his car so it won't appear anything's wrong until someone visits the lake, and even that might not raise an alarm. He imagines Gil waiting by the side of the road, then pounding on the door of the trailer before driving away on his own to rejoin the search, grumbling about selfish, irresponsible city people. Or, perhaps, relieved Martin is gone with all of his naive questions. In retrospect, he wishes he'd woken Gil before leaving in pursuit of his vision, come up with some way of convincing the hunter to come along without trying to explain why he was going, but Martin can't think of any way he might have claimed to know where the boy was without sounding guilty or crazy or both. He can't imagine why Gil would have come along rather than tell him to go get some sleep, and wake up making sense in the morning.

He walks on with bare feet, his breathing heavy and stomach growling, and the forest gets louder around him as the birds and the squirrels and the black lines of marching ants all emerge to begin their own days.

The forest in morning wants to be watched, all singing and squirming and cacophony. It's a performance. Birds spread their wings for a stretch and a song as downy rabbits emerge from hollow trunks to sniff the air with pink noses, begging for someone to coo. The forest in morning is a child showing off.

In the dark or the near-dark of evening, there's no one to be impressed, no sentimental sense of rebirth or of everything made new again. It's not new, it's old, as old as the forest itself: every evening for millions of years the woods have awoken, owls and opossums emerged from their lairs, and the nighttime world set to its business. Morning wants you to look, it demands your attention, but evening doesn't care if you're there. Morning only offers a story because it knows someone's listening. Evening talks to itself.

But Martin plods blind through this performance as overzealous birdsongs give him a headache and he passes unfurling ferns, oblivious to their reemergence. He has more on his mind than flora and fauna. He stumbles along, feet too tired for working together and each going its own direction, his drive to move forward battling the weight of his pack. The smells of the forest are coming awake, the hot, sticky rot rising off the ground and the aromas of so many night-sleeping flowers piled up all at once they've become a mud of perfumes. He keeps his body going with a second energy bar but it does nothing to fill his stomach, gnawing at itself and releasing an occasional growl.

Sky-blue berries cling to the underside of a branch and he almost plucks a few off, nearly drops them into his mouth, but his mind talks his hand out of it: he's hungry, he's dazed, but he isn't that desperate yet. Or that stupid—he doesn't know food from poison out here, and he's still conscious enough to recall that.

There's no hint of a path, no suggestion of the route Jake or whatever is leading him traveled, not even a guarantee what Martin thought was a trail ever was: as far as he knows, there was a missed turn or an unnoticed sign miles ago and now each step leads him farther away from the boy. He can't even go back the way he's come, because he isn't sure where that is. His feet, still bare, feel tender but more awake than the rest of his body.

The scrub grows thicker and the morning more humid as low leaves trap rising heat. He enters a shadowy copse, a stand of tight trees with no spaces for sunlight to wriggle through. It's so dark his eyes need to adjust but he walks on without giving them time.

His nostrils fill with the sharp tang of wet fur and an animal body. He moves cautiously, trying to remain alert in the shadowy copse, afraid of what could be moving beside or behind or even above him. Then he trips over something, comes down hard but never reaches the ground. The impact buries his face in a thick blanket of fur, wrapping him in the smells of rancid meat and old clothes. Martin rears back. He rolls onto his knees with his palms splayed over the lukewarm lump he has fallen on top of, and when his eyes become used to the almost-dark he can tell, he can see, that the mound of fur and fat before him is the body of a dead bear. Its fur is dark brown, almost black, with streaks that catch light like molasses.

The animal faces away from him, and he has landed on its upturned side. The forelimb he can see, the one not pinned under the body, drapes over the head, claws dangling beside a round ear and almost scraping the ground. The bear's legs scissor across the ground.

He pulls his hands away, skittering backward, and lands on his haunches in the mud. His body tells him to run, to get up and drop the pack and rush away down the trail—what there is of one—but his mind reassures him the bear's body is dead.

It must be fairly fresh, because where his fingers find flesh under the fur it's still warm as rising bread dough and almost as soft. And it doesn't smell yet, at least not of death. It's the same smell as before, the same as the last bear, the smell of hot meat and wet dog.

He can't resist trying to roll the bear over, to look at it more closely, but the bulk is too much to move on his own. So he leans forward, pressing his stomach and legs to the corpse, balancing with his hands deep in the fur as he cranes his body over the mound of dead bear to look at the front where already beetles and flies and worms have arrived, where microbes and time are at work, breaking down the bear's stories into so many small tales of their own.

One ear is chewed up, the fleshy rim mangled, and its long snout hangs open so the tongue drags in mud. The brown-orange eye facing up toward him is fogged like breathed-upon glass, and he's half-tempted to wipe it with the tip of his finger.

He leans farther, trying to see the whole face, then loses his balance when his head gets too low, when his reach pulls his feet away from the ground and his body tilts over the fulcrum of the bear's side. He tumbles onto the ground in a curl against the corpse, his face touching the bear's cold leather nose, his warm breath spiraling into its airless mouth, and Martin is paralyzed with the bear's dead, cloudy eyes locked on his own.

Stunned, he lies on the ground, staring into the calm face of the creature before him. In time he feels something sticky and wet on his hands and his chest and looks down to finds them glistening red, smeared with cool, thickened blood. He stands, and wipes his fingers on the scraps of cloth he took from the porcupine, staining his palms and the remnants of Jake's pajamas the same crimson that clouds the front of his shirt. Grunting in frustration he pours water from the last bottle over his arms and rubs them hard against each other, but the blood has already set. He only manages to spread it around; he only makes himself look like he's been trying to wash blood from his hands.

He looks down at the bear and sees a dark, oily stripe running the length of its side, a ribbon of blood under the fur. Martin shoves the stained fabric shreds into his pocket, and tries in vain to clean his hands on the back of his pants.

It was a fall onto a jagged stump that did the bear in, and a dream about walking in a particular spot. It wasn't anything to do with this bear, not personally, but I needed a bear-shaped hole in the world and this bear had to do.

The smell of the bear has grown sharper, filling the air under these trees, and with a grimace Martin smells it also coming from him. The bear's death is all over his body, his skin draped in its scent.

Suddenly he wants to keep moving, to get away from this place, and he pulls the pack high on his shoulders and continues in the direction he had been headed before the bear blocked his path. Flies crowd his hands and his chest while he walks, alighting on spots of blood as they dry. At first Martin swishes the insects away as he walks, but in time he gets used to that, too, and stops noticing the feathery fan of their feet. As blood congeals on his chest it pastes the fabric of his shirt to the skin underneath. His cuts don't hurt very much anymore, but the sweat running into them under their bandages still itches and stings.

He hurries away from the bear's body, out of the shadowy copse and into the pale, dappled light filtering down from above. Before long he hears voices, not the insomniac chatter in the back of his mind but actual voices, drifting to him through the trees. Buoyed, he moves toward them, pushing branches and brambles aside, taking long strides and heavy steps. The stabbing pebbles and twigs beneath his bare feet keep him awake. He's out of breath, wheezing in rasps that growl up from his lungs, but he keeps moving. Soon the sounds come into focus, the voices speak actual words, and he spies flashes of safety orange through the browns and greens of the forest.

He bursts through a thicket and stops, facing a line of men holding rifles and the sheriff with a black radio in his hand. The search party gapes, a squared off firing squad with Martin before them.

"Where the hell have you been?" Lindon barks. One of his deputies whispers something to the bald, bearded man beside him and both of them frown, shaking their heads.

"I got lost," Martin says. He feels as unprotected in his bare feet and sore body as he would appearing naked before all these strangers.

One side of the sheriff's face tightens as he asks, "When? Gil said he couldn't find you this morning." Lindon scans Martin's body, looking over his blood-stained shirt and muddy jeans, the dirty, uncovered feet and two pairs of shoes—one big and one small—dangling from the sides of his pack. The T-shirt and scraps of red-clouded cowboy-print fabric poking over the top of his pocket.

"What's that in your pocket, son?" the sheriff asks. He leans toward Martin from the waist, feet planted firmly below his round gut.

Martin reaches down to tuck the scraps of clothing in deeper, away out of sight, but checks himself. "I found it," he says. "I think it was Jake's."

The search party shuffles, a wave moving through them in the form of stamping feet and shifting weight, rifles changing hands and baseball cap bills adjusted. The deputy rolls a long-ashed cigarette from one corner of his mouth to the other and aims dark, beady eyes at Martin.

The birds have stopped singing and the woods have been hushed, but it's only due to a large group of men being there rather than a response to the tension of this human moment. The birds don't care what these intruders are talking about, they only want them to leave.

"Gorman," the sheriff snarls over his shoulder without taking an eye off of Martin. "Call in and confirm that description. Find out what the Hasper boy was wearing."

The deputy pulls a radio from a clip on his belt and tells it something, then waits while it squawks in response. "Cowboy pajamas and a red T-shirt, sheriff," he repeats.

"That's what I thought." Lindon lowers a hand to his belt. "Lemme see those." He steps toward Martin, reaching with one hand, and the mob surges forward behind him as if they're tied to his legs.

Martin slides the ruined clothes from his pocket, imagines them a magic show scarf stretching on for miles while everyone waits for the end to emerge. But they pull free right away, and he drops them into the sheriff's waiting palm, bronzed with tree-sap.

The sheriff holds them up to the light. "Where'd you find these, now?"

Martin tells Lindon about the tree but not the vision, that he found a porcupine tangled up in the clothes, about the body of the dead bear and falling in its blood at the side of the trail. He tells the whole story of his night in the woods and the morning so far, and as he recounts all that's happened he struggles to have it make sense. He can see in the face of the sheriff and his posse that the harder he tries to explain, the more skeptical they all become. The more he tries to shape his account into something coherent, the more ridiculous it sounds even to him.

"All that's well and good," Lindon says, eyeing the bear's blood on Martin's chest, "but what the fuck were you doing out here? Middle of the night. By yourself."

"I . . . I couldn't sleep, and, ah . . . thought I'd keep looking."

"In the dark?"

"I don't know, it didn't seem to be such a bad idea until I got lost." The search party erupts out of its silence, and the pitying laughter of men fills the forest before a sideways look from the sheriff brings back the quiet.

"How'd you'd get here?"

"I drove. Not here, I mean, my car's at the lake."

The sheriff's eyes widen, and he turns to his deputy. Martin watches the faintest of nods back and forth between the two men. "Long way from the lake, Mr . . . "

"Blaskett. Martin Blaskett."

"Right, right. Martin Blaskett. The builder." Behind him, the men are in motion, splitting into two streams and moving around Lindon's flanks as if they're merely a group of friends walking, out for a stroll, as if all of them decided to set into motion at the same moment out of pure chance. Martin takes an unintended step backward in the direction from which he arrived.

"Whoa," the sheriff says, "don't get jumpy. We're just talking here."

It's a bad police drama, the kind of ridiculous story that pours through open windows at night: the sheriff's assurances and the false calm in the forest, the smiling men surrounding him and waiting to pounce. Martin feels as if he's been scripted and needs to turn and run from these men, get back into the brush as fast as he can so the sheriff and the others can chase him down. That it's his role. He pictures himself on the run through the woods, stopping to pick off one man at a time, a shadowy beast. Already his muscles are itching for flight and pursuit, his body surging with an energy he shouldn't have after the past two days of exertion and a long, sleepless night on his feet.

He feels the way he has in his dreams, bigger and stronger than when he's awake, so close now to sleep that his mind might be playing tricks. The sheriff moves closer and Martin's arms tense and his fingers curl in on themselves as if they are claws. His body urges his mind to set it in motion, to take to the trees, but he stays where he is. As convincing as his body can be, his mind is so tired it would rather let Martin rest here in danger than keep him running on fumes. He stops after that one backward step and the hands poised to strike relax at his sides.

The sheriff comes closer with one hand held up in front of his body as if to offer himself protection. His other hand rests on the radio clipped to his belt, a cowboy walking into a showdown. "We're just talking," he says again as he moves toward Martin.

"About what?"

"What you saw, what you found . . . nobody's suggesting anything." The sheriff's voice is meant to be reassuring, but Martin isn't convinced: he knows what the men before him are thinking, knows he should have left the clothes where he found them and buried his own after he leaned into the blood of the bear. Better to be discovered a naked man in the woods, to be branded a freak, than to emerge from the forest looking like a kidnapper or something worse.

"Let's be calm here," says Lindon and he lays a hand on Martin's arm. His voice is soothing, professional. It isn't the sheriff's normal voice, it isn't how he talks to his friends. It's a tone he puts on to talk criminals down, to talk jumpers off buildings, or it would be if there were any buildings high enough to jump off in town.

Then the men crowd around, and the sheriff's hand on his arm is a vice, and the other one clamps his opposite wrist. Martin is twisted and turned on his feet, his arms bent behind him and strained at the shoulders. He groans, and one of the men he doesn't know barks at him to shut up. He's handcuffed, pushed to his knees in the mud and one of the men steps on his pale, naked toes with the heavy sole of a boot. Martin feels something break, hears that same something crack, and grimaces without making a sound.

"Take it easy, boys," Lindon tells the impromptu posse. "I meant what I said about talking."

The men mill around, muttering to one another and smoking. Their pinched, angry eyes are all cast on Martin who looks up at them from the ground. He hears "killer" and "pervert" and worse, can see rifles itch at the hands that hold them. A voice behind him tells someone else, "Told you there weren't no fuckin' Scratch. Motherfucker's the only monster out here."

Without looking up from the leaves on the ground Martin says, "I told you, I didn't see Jake. I just found his clothes."

"And that's what we're going to talk about," the sheriff says. "Where?"

"At the foot of a tree."

The men snort and laugh. "That isn't much help, son."

"No, I mean a really big tree, the biggest I've seen. There aren't any others around it."

"Back that way?" The sheriff waves an arm toward the woods in the direction from which Martin came.

"Right. A few miles."

"You're gonna have to lead us back there, Mr. Blaskett."

"I can't . . . I got lost, I don't know how to get back."

"You're going to try." The sheriff stands up, speaking into his radio, but he steps away with his back toward Martin and his words are muffled then mute. Martin glances sideways at the men glaring down. His legs and back ache from kneeling, from walking and being so tired. He's still wearing his pack, and the weight pulls on his shoulders, urging him to collapse.

He wants to sleep, wants to fall on his side and curl up on the ground and when he wakes all these men will be gone, he'll be in his trailer stretched out on his bed and Gil will be knocking to wake him so they can return to the search for Alison's son with the rest of the people from town.

The sheriff steps close to Martin, the radio still in his hand. "So you got lost," he says, as if there had been no pause in the interrogation.

"Yes. I don't know how to get back to the tree."

"But you're parked at the lake? You started out there, and went into the woods?"

"Right."

Lindon repeats all this to his radio, instructs someone to check on the car. Then he tells the deputy and a man in a blue flannel shirt cut off at the sleeves to take Martin back to the station, put him in a cell until he, the sheriff, can arrive. "And leave him alone," he warns them. "I mean it."

The deputy and the now-deputized stranger grumble assent, then lift Martin's slumped body between them, pulling on one shoulder each so as he rises his arms pull hard in their sockets. He grunts, and the man on his left laughs. He has a blue eagle tattooed on his bicep, clutching arrows dripping with blood, but the tattoo is old and the arrowheads may simply be blurry.

Martin is dragged between the two men with his hands chained behind him, on the far side of his pack so his arms are overextended. First they cramp, then go numb, and after a few minutes in that position he only feels his hands at all as an itchy tingle. He is convinced these men are going to kill him, that they will haul him back to the station and beat him to death or maybe not even wait until they arrive—they may stop at the side of the trail and hurl him off a cliff, or batter his head with a rock. Or torture him until he gives up the confession they want to hear, whether or not it is the real story.

As he stumbles along between them, his chest tightens the same way that it did while he waited alone in the dark of the burned-out foundation, the way it did when he was a boy afraid of the world beyond his black window. He watches the woods for a chance to escape, some muddy patch he could use to knock his guards off-balance and run, some slope he could shoulder them down. A stage for the kind of grand gesture he's seen on TV. But nothing presents itself, no chances emerge, and he's dragged all the way to the road, bent into the back of a cruiser, and carted to town sitting sideways because his pack pushes him away from the seat.

He expects a lynch mob to be burning him in effigy on the town square with pitchforks and torches waving over their heads. He expects Alison to be standing in front of the crowd, her face streaked with tears and eyes black with rage, waiting for any opening to kill him herself. He expects a vat of hot tar and a pile of feathers, or a gallows hastily erected on the town green. But there is none of that when he arrives, no angry crowd and no straw man on fire—nothing to indicate the town knows he exists. The green is empty except for its cannons, the bandstand hollow and still. There aren't even any cars parked outside Claudia's because everyone is in the woods, or if not in the woods yet on their way there after getting this news from the sheriff.

Deputy Gorman parks in front of the station, and pulls Martin from the back seat by tugging the chain between his wrists. His shoulders lift in their sockets and burn. The other man pushes him from behind, shoving the backpack until the prisoner is inside the building where at last they unbuckle the straps to avoid removing the cuffs.

He is fingerprinted and searched and shoved so hard into a cell he falls on the floor, cracking his jaw on the steel frame of a cot as he drops. Gorman slams the door closed and the other man snarls, "Now shut the fuck up in there, sicko." They're the first words either man has spoken to Martin since leaving the woods, held until each of them was safe on his respective side of the bars.

Martin is deep in the world of men now, locked in a cell without windows so he can't see the sky or the ground. He doesn't know which direction it is to the sun or how long he's been sprawled on the floor. Every organ and inch of his body aches, each muscle is burning and cramped so he couldn't stand up if he wanted to. Which he doesn't, right now, because his empty, starved stomach has been gnawing itself into pulp and if he moves he will surely vomit.

He imagines himself to be somewhere else, wandering the woods of his mind and feeling the wind instead of staring at the gray walls of his cell. Instead of reading the desperate graffiti of other confined men and women, so panicked for voices apart from their own they invented them on the walls of the jail, scratched out their stories with fingernails. And this cell is only a stopover, the kind of place you get stuck for a short time before getting stuck somewhere else for a far longer time.

Martin may claw the walls later; he may scratch his own story into the concrete if and when he opens his eyes. But for now he is sinking into the floor, into his mind, and despite himself and his terror he is actually falling asleep. He's so tired he can't resist and why should he try: dreams are the only place he can escape to, the only place he can be his real self for a while.

And that self, that dream Martin, is outside the cell and outside the building, standing on the town square. He eyes the brick walls of the police station on the other side of the road, a large box with a small box inside it, a small box with his waking self buried inside. Then the Martin who is free turns away.

This Martin is the one who had a vision last night, the one who rolls through the woods, a force too strong to be stopped. Something as primal and wild as a bear, a Martin who doesn't worry whether or not he belongs, because he belongs wherever he goes. This is the Martin we have been waiting for.

20

THE MASS OF HIS BODY HAS CHANGED, ITS CENTER OF GRAVity shifted, and it takes a few steps to adjust—his belly pulls toward the ground until he learns to push himself forward rather than up, to walk on all four of his limbs. Martin walks in wet grass and sniffs out last night's events as he crosses the square: the knotted scent trails of three dogs at play, and the comings and goings of raccoons and cats in the small hours of morning. The drunk man who couldn't get home before relieving himself on the wheel of one cannon, leaving a sloppy stream of his scent. Faint nocturnal footsteps still dent the lawn, but bent blades are springing back into shape as the sun comes over the hills and dries them of dew.

The town is too quiet, too still, as if all the people are gone: no one notices this new Martin crossing the street in an animal stance, a naked man crouching low as he lumbers past the front door of the bank, by the dumpster behind the market and along the library's front walk. No one shouts or screams as he slips unseen into trees beside the elementary school, or follows his new body on its way out of town, into the forest and hills, where it pauses to lap streams of water and pluck berries from branches with nearly prehensile lips.

Then at once the forest around him is gone, a curtain pulled on his dream.

"Up, Blaskett, wake up!" the sheriff is yelling while banging his nightstick across the bars of the cell. "I'm talking to you!"

Martin rolls into a sitting position before his sore legs can complain, and he blinks against the fluorescent light overhead.

"We're going to talk," the sheriff says, no longer in his talking-down voice. It's no-nonsense now. "You're going to tell me where the boy is."

"But I don't know," Martin answers without lifting himself or his eyes from the floor.

"You might after we've talked." Lindon unlocks the door to the cell and swings it wide with a rusty squeak from the hinges. He sits on the edge of the bed with his feet spread wide on the floor and one heavy black boot on either side of Martin's body. "Now. Tell me again what you were doing out in the woods."

"I couldn't sleep," Martin stutters, "so I thought I'd keep looking."

"Why there?"

"I don't know, it . . . " He trails off as he considers telling the sheriff about his vision, about how he knew where the boy would be—or had been, as it turned out. Then he decides against sharing the source of his knowledge and says, "I know Jake likes the lake so I thought he might go there."

"His mother didn't say anything about that. Him liking the lake."

"He said at breakfast, he said . . . " but Martin can't remember what the boy said, if he said anything, and he feels the meat of his lie coming off of its bones.

"Said what?" Lindon asks, lighting a thin brown cigar from a match. Smoke fills Martin's nostrils, sticky and earthy and warm. He sits without giving an answer, staring at the sheriff's shiny black boots. Either he's put on a fresh pair since coming back to the station or else they were cleaned after leaving the woods.

"Said what?" the sheriff repeats, louder now, angry, as he shakes out the match only inches away from his prisoner's face.

"Nothing. He didn't say anything." Martin's stomach sinks into his legs then keeps going all the way to the floor. He closes his eyes, willing himself back to the dreams that, although troubling, have become more of a comfort than this waking world. In one breath of the sheriff's cigar smoke he abandons his hopes of getting out of all this, resigning himself to prison, or worse.

Lindon leans forward from the side of the bed. His cigar weaves through the air and leaves ribbons of smoke where it travels.

"Listen son. Here's the deal. You tell me whatever you know. *Everything* you know. You're in deep shit, I won't lie to you, but you tell me where the boy is and we might work something out." He makes his request with no intonation, his voice as flat as the fluorescent light that falls into the cell. "If you know where he is you should tell me."

Martin hangs his head and stares at the painted gray concrete of the floor, speckled and scuffed by the boots of other jailed men and women, other lives locked in this cage for a day or a night or a week, people who sat until they sobered up and went home or were hauled somewhere else, bigger jails, smaller cells, and some of them probably still behind bars. Some must have gone free after a few hours in here, but others perhaps should have and didn't.

"Let me ask you something, Blaskett. Don't bullshit me. Did you see anything . . . *strange* last night in the woods?"

Martin looks through smoke at the sheriff's pocked face. The lawman's eyes are intent, open wide and awaiting an answer. He can't tell if the sheriff is actually asking what he seems to be. Lindon seems to expect the sort of strange story Martin has been so reluctant to tell him, the kind of story that involves having visions.

"Strange how?"

"Something, ah . . . " the sheriff scratches the shadow of beard on his chin, and looks around at the walls. "Anybody out there, in the woods? You know, anything . . . animals or something. Anything that didn't make sense. Sometimes stuff happens out there. I hear things."

"Scratch?"

The sheriff stands at the sound of the name as if he's received an electric shock. "Now don't . . . I . . . we don't need to get so specific." His voice becomes angry, thickens to a phlegmatic snarl. "Just tell me did you see anything."

Martin almost mentions the monster that chased him and crushed Gil with a log, or admits seeing himself as a creature stalking Gil and Jake, Jr. both. Even that he was led to the tree and the clothes by a vision. Lindon seems to be asking for this kind of strange explanation, he seems to expect it, but Martin isn't sure if the sheriff can be trusted. The invitation could be a trap.

"No," he answers at last. "I didn't see anything."

Lindon sighs and turns away from his prisoner, still on the floor. "Okay then." He exits the cell without looking at Martin, fiddling with his cigar as he leaves, but the back of his neck and the rims of his ears are flushed red. He slams the door hard before walking away, leaving the echo of iron.

Martin rolls backward to stretch himself across the cool concrete floor. He closes his eyes, tries to make sense of whether or not the sheriff really believes Scratch is out there, if he believes in the stories Gil has refuted so sternly. But after he thinks about it a bit, he decides that Lindon couldn't believe in the stories. If he did, if he really believed a monster had taken Jake, Jr., then he would have already let Martin go. Unless there's a reason for keeping a prisoner he knows to be innocent.

Outside the cell, down the hall in a part of the station Martin can't see, he hears an argument between several male voices. One insists they should get back to the woods, make the suspect lead the search for the boy. Lead them to where he found the clothes. Another says they've found his car, they're retracing his steps, the state police know where to look now and they'll find the boy for sure. Says it's better to wait here, out of the woods, instead of giving Martin a chance to escape. Instead of spending another day in the wild.

Then a more familiar voice enters the conversation, booming over the others to tell them, "You all know he didn't do shit. Let the man go, for Christ's sake."

Martin sits up, shocked by how relieved he is at Gil's arrival, how his stomach pulls away from the floor at the sound of someone he knows and to hear that someone speaking in his defense.

"Now, Gil," says the sheriff, "let's not jump to conclusions. He was in the woods, and he had the boy's clothes."

"Well," Gil says but doesn't go on, and the whole station falls quiet, from the front door to Martin's cell, everyone waiting for him to finish the thought. Gil must already know how they found him, about the explanation the police don't believe—the tree and the bear, and stumbling onto the clothes. He hopes Gil suspects something else, but doubts it's anything close to the truth.

"I'm telling you, Gil," Lindon says, "it doesn't look good."

A moment ago the sheriff seemed eager for an otherworldly explanation for all of this. Now he seems just as eager to pin it on Martin, and to convince Gil of his guilt, too. He imagines Gil rubbing the back of his neck as he thinks, sliding a cigarette into his mouth. And he's right, because he hears the scratch of a match before the smells of sulfur and smoke drift into his cell. His senses seem keener than normal, but it may be the hallucinatory effect of going so long without any real food or sleep.

"Lindon, do you think he did it?" Gil asks.

There's a pause, an audible shuffling of feet, and Martin leans close to the bars, as close to the conversation as he can get. There's a balloon being blown up in his throat, and if there wasn't he might yell, shout his own innocence down the corridor of the station.

"No," the sheriff says at last, and other voices mutter and mumble. "Shut up," Lindon barks, then answers a question Martin can't hear. "It's a hunch. I don't know. How much do you know about this guy, Gil? Do we even know why he's really here, if he's been in trouble before? Hell, it's not like he's building those houses himself."

"No," Gil replies and the balloon in Martin's throat bursts. He leans his forehead into the space between two of the bars, a cold metal rod at each of his temples, and lays a palm on the back of his neck.

"But I don't want things getting out of control," Gil says. "We all need to keep calm here and figure out what really happened to that boy. We don't need this kind of trouble on top of all that." Martin doesn't know what trouble could be worse than what's already happened—for himself, but also for Alison and her son.

"Damn it, Lindon. He told you there was a bear. That he got its blood on him, right?"

"Yeah?"

"Well, there was a damn bear. Few miles down trail from his car. That city boy left tracks as wide as the bear's. I followed him all the way from the lake, first to a big oak where he sat around, then to where he met you. And there was a dead bear, bloody. I think our boy tried rolling it over. For some goddamn reason."

Other voices speak, but they're too low or too far away for Martin to follow. Gil says, "Wasn't any blood on the trail until I got to the bear. Then he dripped it the rest of the way. Don't know what the hell he was doing, but that blood didn't come from the boy."

"So where is he?" asks Lindon.

"I don't know, but we need to keep looking. Must've been where the clothes were, so we oughta get Marty back out there to help."

"I don't want him out there," Lindon insists. "If he did it, he isn't going to tell us. If he didn't, folks won't care and someone's liable to take a shot at him. I don't need a search party turning into a lynch mob. Besides, he said he was lost. You already found the place easier than he could."

There's a pause, and Martin holds back his next breath. The bars at his temples feel tighter and squeeze the sides of his head.

"We'll leave him here. In the cell. At least we'll know where he is." There are murmurs of agreement, and Gil's reluctant assent, before the voices move away and a door clangs shut. A chair scrapes on the floor as someone sits down. A newspaper shakes open.

Martin leans away from the bars, and then scuttles across the floor on his hands and the backs of his legs. He rests his shoulders against the edge of the bed and closes his eyes over the dull ache behind them. His breathing is raspy and strained, overtired, and the stench of himself is as strong as it's ever been, meaty and sharp, almost acrid—his own stale sweat, but also the smell of the bear and its blood and the forest. Every inch of his body is dirty and sore, even the muscles he calls on to close his eyes.

His broken toe throbs, but the rest of his digits and limbs hurt almost as much. His jaw aches, and even his tongue is scraped and sore. The bandages wrapping his chest are dirty and damp, and the cuts are so close to healed he can't need them any longer, but Martin doesn't want to remove them because his ribs ache so badly he'd rather not touch them at all. His whole body is out of sorts, sluggish, his head filled with the unintelligible voices of his exhaustion and hunger. The porcupine and the bear and the vision last night all seem so far away, as if they happened to somebody else, somebody other than Martin.

In his mind he returns to a familiar story, himself in his house with his tables and chairs. But half of the bedrooms are empty, the closets all bare. The spaces he'd imagined Alison and Jake, Jr. filling around him have been cleaned out. His mind seems unwilling to imagine a future for them together, or the boy having a future at all, or that Alison will even speak to him again after this. He tries to rebuild the house bit by bit, to walk through the rooms and put it in order, but each time he sees himself turning the knob and swinging open the door the walls fade away and he's left adrift on the muddy sea of the site.

Somewhere in the police station, down the hall, a phone rings three times then stops. It sounds like his phone, but the ring tone isn't uncommon so he can't be sure.

His stomach growls, rumbling and low, and he tries to quell his hunger by picturing the bloodiest, rawest slabs of meat he can imagine, something that will turn his stomach away, put him off food for a while, but he's so starved the idea of a dripping cheeseburger, a barely-seared steak that still practically moos, actually makes his mouth water.

He lies back and dreams of meat, so exhausted that raw, carnal urges override his normal desires.

In the box of his cell he thinks about leaving, and envisions grand schemes for escape, because he hasn't been locked up very long. That's the thing about boxes: once you've been in one long enough you can't picture being outside, you can't imagine what's beyond the walls of your cage, and will go out of your way to stay in a trap so familiar it seems to be safe.

He stretches his arms up over his head and pops his back twice. He spreads his mouth wide in a roar of a yawn, smacks his lips, blinks his eyes, and then frowns as the reality of the situation weighs on his mind. The hours pass as indistinctly as the gray concrete of the cell's walls, and he has no way of knowing what time it is except the fluorescent tube in the ceiling hasn't yet been turned off for the night, assuming it will be.

Sometimes tired voices drift down the hall, and he hears the occasional squeak of the station's front door, someone coming or going. He stands at the front of the cell with his fingers wrapped around cold, rusty bars, and cranes his neck in hopes he can see down the hall. But the angle of the walls is too sharp, and all he can see is more of the same shade of gray.

There's a conversation in the front room, but he can't make out what the voices are saying. Before long, heavy footsteps approach. It's Gil, rubbing his eyes as he walks, orange cap hanging askew to one side.

"Did they find anything, Gil?" Martin asks, and the older man frowns at his eager voice.

"Marty. Listen. I'm going to get you out of here. Folks aren't too happy about it."

Everything Martin's been waiting to tell someone comes bubbling out all at once. "I didn't do anything," he pleads. " I just . . . I found the clothes, but . . . " the porcupine shuffles into his mind, but he ignores it. "That's all, I found the clothes by the big tree, but Jake wasn't there. Really, I . . . "

Gil sighs. "I believe, you, Marty," in a tone that is less than convincing. "I think Lindon does, too. That's not the point. He'll let you go, but you might be safer staying in there." Martin slumps against the bars. Gil may believe he did not take Alison's son, but has doubts about something else, and Martin feels that doubt, that disappointment, deep in his belly.

"I can't stay here. I want to go home."

"We can do that. Hang on a few minutes. Let me tell the sheriff." He shuffles away from the cell, his body more bent than Martin has noticed before, feet moving more slowly across the worn cement floor and turning the corner at the end of the hallway. For the first time he looks like the old man he is. Martin strains his ears to listen from the front of the cell, but the conversation isn't drifting his way. Whatever is said stays between Gil and the sheriff.

Soon Gil comes back to the cell with the sheriff beside him. Lindon unlocks the door without a word, and swings it wide to let Martin out. The three of them walk down the hall to the front room where desks cluster on either side of a narrow aisle and a woman with wiry gray hair and thick glasses waits for a phone to ring.

Martin braces for an angry mob in the street, torches and pitchforks and demands for his hanging or burning or both. He steels himself to the knowledge that Alison will be right outside, at the foot of the stairs from the station down to the sidewalk, and she'll give him a look that says more than any words she might choose. A look to confirm that his daydream of a house with room for more than one person, of a person who might want to fill up that space along with him, is foolish and stupid and a waste of his time, that her son is missing and he is the reason and his dream is not going to happen.

Gil's told him the town is upset. Word spread quickly he was to blame and the correction has been slower to travel. People want someone to have stolen the child—they want a reason why Jake is missing and they want that reason to walk on two feet, in shoes, and to wear pants it puts on one evil leg at a time.

Gil opens the station door and late sunlight flares through the hole. Martin squints, his eyes unused to the sun, and looks away at the tile floor of the lobby. Then he walks into the late afternoon with his eyes still averted, braced for the impact of the first stone.

But no one is there. No mob in the street, no impromptu gallows thrown up on the square between the bandstand and the cannons. The supermarket manager who waved from her office is crossing the street toward the station and though she looks up she doesn't greet Martin this time. A mousy brown dog cocks its leg on a mailbox and casts an eye toward the two men without breaking its stream. The dog shakes its head and walks away.

It's worse this way, Martin thinks, to be so worthless and low no one even shows up to make sure I know it. To not even be worth the trouble of hating.

"Truck's around the corner," Gil says, letting the police station door swing closed on its own.

21

THE RIDE HOME IS QUIET. IT WOULD BE SILENT IF NOT FOR bumps in the road and children shouting and the kind of dogs that will bark at a truck rolling past as soon as they'd howl at a skunk or at their own tail or shadow, more concerned with the attack than the target.

But today Martin makes everything personal, each dog that bares its teeth at his passing and each stone that kicks up from the road and pings off the truck; all of it is directed at him. This town, these streets and these houses and dogs, are all telling him to move on, pull up stakes, track the rest of the construction of his houses by phone—if he'll even be allowed to complete their construction—and get out of here as soon as he can. He'll find a new foreman, someone from out of town, because he assumes Alison will be unwilling to work for him now, that an absolution from Gil or the sheriff won't carry much weight with the missing boy's mother. He'll follow his development's progress from an office far away in the city he's come from or some other he doesn't yet know. He'd prefer not to go back to the city, he'd prefer to stay here, but doesn't see much of a choice. He could find another place as nice as this one, perhaps, but there's no reason things would go better for him there if he did.

He doesn't feel welcome here now. He no longer feels as if this place wants him, but he's more wrong about that than he has been about anything else—this place wants him to be here more than he can imagine. Or, more precisely, I do. I know where Martin will fit in exactly, a space he was born to occupy. And now that he's given up on his domestic desires, on his daydreams about Alison and her son and a house they might share, he is untied from the world of humans around him and as available to me as he will ever be.

I'm not punishing him for anything. I'm not doing all this to be cruel. On the contrary, I'm helping Martin become what he wants—what he *needs*—to become. I'm offering him a place to belong to, which is the one thing he's wanted for so very long.

And if there's something in it for me, too, then so be it—I never claimed to be altruistic. Would you expect me to be willing to sacrifice Alison's child, to turn her son into a porcupine and leave him to wander the woods, and not have my own stake in this story? I'll get what I want when Martin gets what he needs—we're bound together, he and I are, whether he knows it or not.

He was given back his phone when he left the station, along with his backpack and boots, and now tries to check his messages more to avoid speaking to Gil than because he cares what they have to say or is confident he'll be able to hear them at all. His partner has called again, and again after that; he sounds panicked, he pleads for Martin to call him, to come back to the city, their problems have only increased and projects are in jeopardy. There's little left and they'll need to act fast to salvage whatever they can. But the details are vague, rendered less real by the static and inconsistent connection, or it seems that way to Martin because it all feels so far, far away. So abstract and intangible after these recent hours of sore muscles and blood.

This isn't my doing, this other collapse, these bigger turns in the world. It isn't part of my story and I didn't expect it to be part of Martin's, but I won't pass it up, either. Everything is always in motion, everything turns, and if you wait long enough—and time is what I have the most of—it turns your way as often as not. Each severed tie leaves fewer strands in his web, until there's only one path he can take. And that's the one I've put him on.

When Gil's truck rattles to a stop at the edge of the site, Martin sees that the muddy ground is pale and cracked. Fine lines fissure the surface in all directions the way he imagines a desert might look, but his trailer is right where he left it, the bulldozer and dump truck still where they were parked such a long time ago and not so long at all, either. Nothing has moved except him. There's no sign of any work having occurred in his absence while his employees were out combing the woods with every-one else.

He looks at the lot nearest the road where his imagined house stood, in its way, a short time ago, over a hole full of ground up animal bones. He digs into his mind but can't make a single wall rise from that dead patch of ground. The view from the back porch and all the furniture he'd selected and the wide oak floors it stood on have become an expanse of cracked mud, as pale and unproductive as his own bare skin.

At last he asks about Alison's son, if the search has been successful, and Gil tells him the state police and most of the town are still looking, but after this long it doesn't look good.

"Gil," Martin says, with a lump in his throat, "I need to tell you about something."

Gil's mouth tightens and his eyes go dark. "What did you do?"

"Nothing. Nothing, but . . . " Martin takes a deep breath. "I've been having these dreams."

Gil's body relaxes. "You want to tell me about *dreams*? Christ, Marty, you scared me. For a second I thought I was wrong about you. I thought you'd hurt the kid."

"I've been having strange dreams, about the woods. About being an animal. And I had a dream about Jake, kind of, after we came back from searching. That's why I went out to find him. I thought I knew where he was."

"Hell, you went off in the woods in the middle of the night because of a dream? Thought you had more sense than that."

"I know, but I also had a dream before Jake was gone. About him going missing. I think I had something to do with it."

Gil exhales a sticky cloud of cigarette smoke, and it darkens the windshield in front of Martin. The spaces of the site in front of the truck vanish behind the stain.

"They're dreams, Marty. Nothing to do with what happened. I have dreams all the time, doesn't make me a real astronaut. I dream I got blown up in the war, but I didn't. I dream my house is on fire and my legs get chewed off and, shit, seventy-four bikini models show up at my door on my birthday. None of that's worth a goddamn. You didn't do a thing to that boy by your dreaming."

"But I think there's more to it. I think . . . "

"I were you, I'd stay close to home. Folks aren't too thrilled at you being released. And don't go talking about these dreams of yours, neither.

Let things be. Don't get stupid. Don't try to make it all better because you won't."

Martin opens his mouth to say something, to insist again on his own innocence, but he can't come up with the words.

"You know I don't buy it, but still. Safer for you that way." He lifts Martin's confiscated backpack from the floor of the truck and holds it out at arm's length.

Martin takes the bag and holds it away from his body. He climbs down from the seat and slams the door against its tight hinges, then the truck rattles forward a few feet before turning into Gil's yard. Martin turns and walks up the gentle slope of the site and it feels steep to his sore, tired legs. He hears the thunk of a truck door behind him as he climbs the collapsible steps to his home. Then he seals himself into the hot, cramped space of his trailer.

Everything is the way he left it—the boxes of water bottles stacked by the door and the wheeled stool rolled away from the desk. The map still spread across his work table and weighed at the corners with a can full of pencils, a gray tape dispenser, and two round stones that almost match.

Before he's done anything else, he is driven to his chair and that map and he's marking it with all that's happened: he marks Alison's house and where her son went missing, and he marks the search party assembling on the town square and walking into the woods, then where they had lunch and kept searching. He works out, more or less, where they finally came out of the woods yesterday then where he left his car at the lake. Martin draws his own trail through the forest, the chain he tripped over and then the tree, where the porcupine was and the copse and the bear. The sheriff and his posse and finally the jail, and when he draws the dark, heavy walls of that cell he bears down so hard his pencil goes right through the paper and scratches the table itself.

When he's done with all that, when his frantic sketching and scribbling have stopped, the map is so marked up it's become hard to read. So many new lines and so many smudges where his fingers and the side of his hand have dragged graphite around. He tried so hard to get it all down that none of it makes any sense.

Martin undresses in the middle of the room, bumping into furniture and walls that seem closer, somehow, as he flails his way down to bare skin. He peels off his rank T-shirt and socks, then the bear blood-stained jeans and gray underwear dyed a deep rust where it soaked through.

It's as if he hasn't seen his own body in days. The heaviness he noticed earlier has become more pronounced, a thickness in his thighs and torso. He feels clumsy, bumping into things while he undresses, and the space of the trailer seems more claustrophobic than ever; he stubs his toes and cracks his elbows and hips on doorknobs and walls. He shrugs it all off to being tired, to being worn out, and after a hot, steaming soak with his eyes closed and a few shots to the head from the nozzle, the wall, the shelf that holds shampoo and soap, he collapses in bed with his body still dripping.

His legs hang off the edge of the mattress, dirty toenails grazing the floor. He tosses and turns for a few minutes, struggling to make himself rest, arguing with his own body about a comfortable position in which to sleep, but before long he has melted away.

This time, he doesn't dream. He sleeps, and he murmurs and growls into the thick foam of his pillow, but through the whole night not one single vision creeps into his head. He gives himself over completely, leaves mind and body all to themselves to do what they will.

He's given up on himself, or at least on this place and the possibility of belonging to it, and that's exactly where I've been trying to lead him. Driven away from the league of his kind until he's no more at home in the world made by men than he was last night in the woods. He's a dropped signal and belongs nowhere, now, except in his own dreams; it's the only place he can be himself. He's so tired that he's longing for nothing but sleep, a rest so long that by the time he wakes up his world will have righted itself—all the suspicion and all his own feelings of guilt, the lost child and his thwarted hopes about the boy's mother, will have washed away. He wants, more than anything else, to have his questions answered—he wants to know once and for all how he fits into this world where he has tried to make a home for himself. Or, better yet, he wants to not ask those old questions of his any longer.

But hours have slipped by while we've watched him sleep, and already his body is stirring. We don't want him to see us here at his window with our claws scratching again at his screen. Duck down. Lie low. Hide the shine of your eyes and we'll leave what is coming to come. We'll see what answers he's found to those gnawing questions that will no longer keep him awake.

22

ITCHY SUN FALLS THROUGH THE SLATS OF THE WINDOW AND across his face, and he mumbles and twitches his nose. He rolls over, still sleeping, with a groan that builds from his belly. His body shifts to one side and suddenly tumbles, spilling him to the floor with a thump that rattles the cabinets. One leg of the bed has broken, tipping the mattress, and his blankets and pillows are piled in a heap where the collapsed corner rests on the floor. His body sprawls tangled among them.

The impact snaps him awake and he growls some kind of reply, swings an angry arm out and when it connects with the wall it hits hard enough to shake the whole trailer. Where he strikes the flimsy faux-wood paneling, his claws leave jagged stab wounds in the surface. Then those same claws reach back to their body, toward the long snout, and scratch at the glistening black nose where it still itches from tickling sun.

He stretches, and folds of orange-streaked fur over late-summer fat shake in shimmering ripples. He pushes the blankets away with stretching legs, and where they cling to his claws the bedclothes rip and tear. He sits up, and the motion throws him off-balance as if he expected his center of gravity to be somewhere else, the shift of his weight to be different. The bulk of his shape tilts forward and he nearly topples onto his face, but a heavy paw pressed to the floor blocks his fall. The paw flexes and relaxes, expands and retracts on the floor, and its claws pluck at synthetic threads in the tight weave of carpet.

The bear stands on all four of his legs. He dips forward, raising his hind end into the air and releasing a satisfied groan. Then he shakes his head so a long string of drool slings across the floor and the wall of the room. He lumbers the length of the trailer with stiff, unsure steps. The bear walks like he hasn't walked in a while, and is regaining his feel for the motion.

He sniffs the coarse carpet, and the thin wood veneer of the walls. He pushes his nose into a basket of trash on the floor of the bathroom, and spills crumpled tissues and gauze all over the floor. His snout emerges with

195

the bright white backing of an adhesive bandage stuck to it, and the bear crosses his eyes to inspect it before shaking the small scrap of paper away. Then he bats the wicker basket with a broad paw and it bounces off a wall to land in the shower. The bear snorts, and moves toward the tiny sink and stove of the kitchenette. He spatters packets of miso soup paste and dry rice with the moisture of loud, wet sniffs, and tears open a paper canister of oatmeal so it spills all over the floor, but there's nothing the bear wants to eat in Martin's collection of food. He passes by what has passed for a kitchen with less interest than he gives to the carpet and its years of accumulated scents and forgotten spills from one temporary resident after another.

Martin's television stands on a rickety stool in front of a folding chair, and when the bear swings his body between them the chair gets in the way of his back legs. With a grumble and a growl he shakes the chair loose, toppling the stool, and the television crashes to the floor. The bear rears up and away from the sound, but when no other boom comes he moves closer, first sniffing then shoving the black plastic cube. With one forepaw he pins the TV to the floor as the other thumps at its side—not very hard, not out of rage, but as an investigation of the strange object.

When the plastic casing cracks and begins to collapse, the bear pulls his paws away and steps back, snorts again, and abandons the broken appliance. He moves to the drafting table and sniffs along the edge of its surface. The stones that pin down the building site's plans are knocked to the floor by his nose. The bear stands halfway up, leaning on the white plane of the table with the upper half of his body, and its thin legs collapse under his weight. He topples a tin can full of pencils, and they roll one by one off the edge. His breath trills the large sheets of paper, one end now unweighted, and this seems to interest the bear—again and again he blows on the pages, and watches them ripple and flap.

He backs his upper body off of the table and lowers himself to the floor, dragging claws across the black lines of ink and gray pencil notes of the map, shredding the building site and the town and the forest at once. There's a thin draft through the frame of the door, and the bear presses his nose to the seam and breathes deep. His claws scrabble and scrape at the smooth fiberglass, and against the round aluminum knob. He roars, and rears up to scratch at the door with both forepaws, and though he leaves gouges the door latch holds fast. The bear tilts his full weight against it, forepaws pressed flat and his body bouncing against them.

Hinges and springs groan and strain, and the whole trailer leans. For a second it seems the door's going to hold and the trailer will topple, spill onto its side in the mud with the door pinned to the ground. Then the latch gives with a crack and the door swings open so the bear, still leaning on it, falls toward the ground with a snort.

His paws are still in front of his face and they break his fall on the dirt. But his body crashes against the folding metal stairs with a crunch and a clang and they bend beneath the side of the trailer. The bear pulls his hind legs to the ground, takes a few steps, and then rolls onto his haunches to flutter a paw at the back of one ear.

Beige smears of mud cake his fur, and he lets out a moan, closes his eyes, and gives himself over to the pleasure of scratching. He rubs the claws of one paw across the back of his head, and his top lip curls back to show gleaming teeth. One eyelid slides open the tiniest bit and a rolled-back white shines through the space. The bear looks content to sit in the mud and scratch himself here forever; oblivious, unconcerned about what might be coming while he is swept up in his bodily rapture. He moans, low and long, like settled old floors in a house. His body is piled on itself in a heap; a shaggy black coat draped over . . . something. How can I describe the shape of a bear without calling it, simply, a bear?

At last the bear finishes scratching and gets to his feet, all four of them. His tongue uncoils to lick first his black bottom lip, then his top one. He lopes away from the trailer and toward the road, rolling forward as one shoulder at a time rises under his fur then flattens as the other wells up. The bear walks past the dormant bulldozer where a black starling perches, preening its feathers with darts of a beak. The bird doesn't even look up from its grooming as the bear passes with heavy footfalls.

This morning is only half-formed, and mist hovers over the ground. The bear walks through it primeval, a monster coming out of the fog, but he doesn't look so much a monster as he swings his head side to side in what almost seems like a rhythm; it's as if the bear is dancing in a private bear way, to a song that plays in his memory only.

Turning away from the road, the bear raises his snout to the air and takes a loud sniff. His nostrils flare, his lips curl, then he swings his body in a new direction. He crosses the mud toward the first leveled clearing, where the broad rectangle of a foundation gapes in the ground. The bear approaches the hole, leaning forward over the lip as his forepaws cling to it, and hangs as far into the ground as his body allows him. He snorts, and then sniffs again as he slides his head back and forth above the moist earth. He leans closer, but loose soil flakes away in his claws, and his weight begins pulling him over the edge. He grunts, and flexes his legs to push himself back onto solid ground. He sits for a moment over the hole, smoothing the matted fur between the claws of his front feet with a pink tongue.

He stands, and circles the foundation in a slow walk. He goes around twice, snorts, and then moves toward the road. From the gravel shoulder, he looks toward the house on the other side of the pavement, his head tilted to one side as he does, then crosses and climbs the first two steps to the porch. There's a white stoneware bowl at the top of the stairs with a spoon standing in it, and the bear stretches his body to reach it, his hind legs staying down low. He licks at the vessel, and his tongue knocks the spoon onto the boards of the porch with a clatter. The bowl spins and bounces with his hungry effort, hopping closer and closer to the edge of the porch before it finally slips off. The bear is left with his tongue hanging out as the bowl lands bottom-up on the grass by the stairs.

He grunts, then retracts his body from the rise of the steps and walks out of the yard toward the sun, stopping to sniff at a cluster of white-petaled, yellow-rimmed flowers blooming in the overgrown grass of the shoulder.

Not especially menacing, this bear, is he? Clumsy and lumbering, licking bowls of old milk . . . he's more of a clown than a monster. But don't get the wrong idea about him. He's clumsy because he can afford it; he can get away with being a clown. Who's going to stand up to a bear?

Not me. Not you, at least not in the shape you are now. And certainly not empty-handed. Bears have no need to worry about smaller bodies, only the tools those bodies might carry—it's the gun that does all the damage, not the fragile hand holding it.

So he's taking a sunrise walk into town, meandering on the side of the road to dig ants from their hills and chew blackberries out of the brambles that grow wild on the verge. His teeth and tongue are stained purple, and he sits to clean the juice from his paws before walking on toward the center of town.

23

T HE TOWN IS QUIET THIS MORNING, AS IF EVERYONE HAS
overslept, as if they're all at home dreaming of bears, denned in
their blankets and sheets. Or else gathering on the outskirts of
town to reenter the woods in search of a boy who is lost.

The grass is still thick with dew and as he weaves across it the fur of his
belly droops and drags in wet clumps. Near the bandstand and black iron
cannons, he stops, and tips onto his side to roll in the grass. Flat on his
back he swings his whole body. Head and tail move independently of one
another, each thrashing through dew on its own. The bear moans and his
long tongue unrolls from his mouth, to hang against the side of his head
and drag through the wet grass for itself.

Then he stops rolling and stretches all four legs straight up into the air,
kicking as if he's keeping a ball aloft, as if the faint, round moon still white
overhead is his plaything. At last he flops over, and climbs to his feet with
a yawn. He pants, his ribs heaving, one round black ear turned inside out
from his rolling so the pink, veiny membrane is exposed. His body drips
and glistens with dew, as a shivering shake starts in his nose and rolls the
length of his body, flinging water into the air.

The bear continues toward the café and shambles into the alley that runs
along the wall of the building. Behind the restaurant, in front of a screen
door in a white wooden frame, the bear stops and raises his snout, sniffing
with loud, wet snorts. His nose slides through the air toward the door, an
antenna seeking a signal. He pushes the screen with a wide paw and it bulges
but doesn't break. When he curls his paw into a fist the claws catch the aluminum mesh so a slight pull swings the door open. He pushes his snout, then
his head, and then his whole upper body through the opening between door
and frame, slipping from the alleyway into the restaurant's kitchen.

Inside, everything clatters—the hotel pan of bacon he chews his way
through, and the rack of steaming, clean silverware he knocks from the
dishwashing sink. The bear hardly starts at these sounds, rapt in myriad

smells and sensations—the bacon, the sausage, the frying of eggs, and the rich, greasy air of the kitchen. He drinks from a dish of warm, melted butter with tongue-slapping slurps, and shovels pancakes and scrambled eggs and fried potatoes from one plastic tub after another.

He doesn't notice the round, balding cook in his dirty white apron, aghast on the other side of the serving window, dialing a phone, or the waitress who hurries out the front door, holding her glasses to her face as she runs for help. He is only aware of the buckets and baskets of breakfast foods, being packed for delivery to those who now wander the woods. The bear hasn't been a bear very long; he's still too hung up on the feeling of being himself to worry what those others are doing. Their presence doesn't mean much to him, and he doesn't yet know what it means for him to be seen, for a bear to get caught in a space where he doesn't belong.

But they're aware of what it means for him to be there, these humans, and within seconds the wail of a siren rises above the town square, waking the few remaining sleepers as it approaches, growing louder and louder here in this kitchen. Loud enough to make even those out in the woods around town stop and look up in hope the boy has been found. The bear looks up, too, from a white tub of home fries, in time to see the sheriff and his deputy come through the front door with their guns drawn.

How would a bear, a new bear, know their intentions? How could he understand the importance of the pistols drawn in their hands and the shotgun a third man holds across his badged chest when he arrives a few seconds later?

They fan across the café with their weapons, flanking the bear, and creep toward the kitchen. The bear drops the bucket, spilling greasy potatoes all over, and the empty container bounces away on the floor. He sits on his haunches and watches the men coming closer, guns shaking in their hands—not the sheriff's, his hands are steady, but the other two men seem nervous.

The bear rises onto his hind feet, rises to his full height, and the men take a clumsy step back as if they've been hit by a wave. Something is burning under the broiler, and dark smoke rolls out with a sharp, charcoal smell. The bear surveys the ruin he's made of the kitchen, the potatoes and eggs and sausages scattered all over the floor, the silverware and chafing dishes upturned over spilled food. Then he turns away from the men and their guns, toward the screen door, lowers himself to four legs and walks out. His wet fur leaves a glazed streak across the black rubber floor mat as he passes over.

As the bear vanishes through the back door, the police officers charge through the kitchen, slipping in spilled butter and tripping on dropped forks and spoons. It would be funny if their faces weren't so deadly serious. The sheriff barks clipped commands into a radio as his men burst out the door in pursuit of the bear.

And the bear's round, lumbering rump moves out of sight at the end of the alley, the end away from the square, where a few houses cluster and the forest begins. He rambles oblivious, showing no interest in the men on his tail, his appetite sated after his impromptu breakfast, and now he's after a warm, quiet place to curl up for a nap. He feels the way all bodies feel after a big morning meal.

He rolls through a backyard without a fence where two small faces watch from a window, eyes wide and jaws dropped. A mother moves into the frame, gasps, and pulls the curtains in front of her children so they can't see the bear. Later she'll laugh at her instinctive reach for the curtains, as if the sheer fabric could deter something so large, and will wish they had watched—her children may not see a bear up so close ever again—but for now she's dialing her phone.

Other faces watch from other windows as the bear moves through their yards, and more phones dial the same number the first woman has. The bear pauses to spray a bush with his scent, and spatters the wall of a house as he does. Inside, a dog jumps up and down barking, buoyed by the barrier between himself and the bear who has invaded his turf, but the intruder doesn't even look up.

When he reaches the curtain of trees that separates the town from the forest, he plunges into the brush without a glance back. If he had looked behind him, he would have seen the sheriff and his men standing in the last yard he crossed, wrinkling their noses at his acrid scent, still holding their guns and watching the dark shape of his body fade into the forest.

They have no idea the bear was, a short time ago, Martin Blaskett. No idea Martin dreamed of being a bear while he was locked in their cell, and that he has now become one. He's an ordinary creature, as far as they know, and they hunt him as they would any other.

And he is any other, now, really—Martin is not inside the bear, waiting to reemerge. He isn't aware of this change, because nothing of Martin remains to be aware, except as a faint, fuzzy memory in the bear's mind, the residue of a dream he had once while hibernating. And even that much will be gone soon.

Martin hasn't returned to some primal state he'd abandoned for his modern life. He gave way to the bear because that's what he wanted to do—he wanted to belong to this place, to these woods. He wanted his occupation of space to make sense in a way it never did while he was a man, and in a way it never could. Not as long as Martin was Martin. He struggled to build himself a home, to raise walls that could demarcate a particular space as his own as much as they would contain him. He tried so hard for so long to claim some part of the world as his own, but in the end he was unable. At least, he was unable in the shape he wore for all that time.

Don't feel sorry for Martin and what you may think he has lost, because in one single step, in the movement of the bear's foot from the yard to the forest, all that he's never had became his. Trees instead of the walls he's been building, and this forest instead of a family, but what matters most is that Martin . . . is that the bear is contented. That he isn't aware of anything missing, no more than the bear is aware Martin ever existed, or Martin is aware he no longer does.

His impotent, aimless desires and daydreams have given way to ursine instincts and satisfaction. Try to imagine the Martin we've known with his face in a pan full of bacon, or rolling in the wet grass. Try to imagine our Martin giving his body free rein, and allowing his deepest desires to sing. Yet the bear does those things without thinking—he doesn't worry about whether he's happy in some vague, human way; the bear is the bear is the bear.

And he has found his way into the forest.

24

THE BEAR PLOWS THROUGH A MAZE OF BRAMBLES, PLUCKING the occasional berry and swatting black flies when they land too close to his nose. He finds a slim stream where it murmurs along beside an overgrown trail, and he leans down from his shoulders to drink with a satisfied smacking of lips. Then he crosses the stream, away from the recognizable path, and ambles into the trees.

He walks with a musical lope, and makes frequent stops for sniffing this leaf and scratching that log, to rub this tree with his scent. The bear walks until he comes to the face of a cliff, a high, gray bluff bright with early sun. In the warm shelter of the rock face he curls up, eyes squeezed shut and head resting on his own back as his body curls around itself. And with rattling, rumbling snores and spasmodic twitches and jerks in his legs, the bear takes his mid-morning nap.

When the bear dreams, he dreams of being a bear. Of being himself, and of what he will do when he wakes, the fish he will paw from the water and the plants he will find in his path. The place where he will take his next nap. The bear dreams of his life more or less as it is; the honey may be a bit sweeter and the grubs a drop juicier, but no differences greater than that.

There's a sound in the trees near the bluff, a footstep and the brushing of fabric on branches. The bear snaps awake and onto his feet, a motion quicker than his slow, heavy body looks capable of. He looks into the trees, snout in the air and sniffing loudly. The wind in the leaves could be a hunter's canvas passing by brambles; acorns rattling their way down through branches are the footsteps and snapping twigs of something's approach. The bear sniffs the air then paces the rim of the clearing before yawning and moving back toward his bed.

A loud crack shakes the birds from the trees in fluttering clouds, and the echo rolls through the woods. The bear's body jerks to one side; his left hind leg folds beneath him and his body crumples onto the ground. He moans and roars in one sound, a gurgling note full of pain. The leg that buckled bleeds crimson streams through his fur, quickly crusted with dirt. The bear twists his back so his tongue can reach the wound. He pushes himself to his feet and lumbers into the trees, dragging the injured leg.

The gunman, the hunter, bursts into the clearing with his rifle leading the way. His grease-smeared orange hat is low on his head, shielding his eyes from the sun. His red, wrinkled face glistens with sweat and he's rasping and gasping for breath despite—or maybe because of—his many years in these woods, tracking one animal or another, eliminating some threat to the town.

Gil has been sent to take care of the bear, called by the sheriff and sent into the woods. He misses his quarry's departure from the clearing but the trail is easy to see—the dragging leg flattens grass and brush wherever it goes, and trails blood, and the bear is still new to all this. He isn't as skilled as he could be at covering his tracks. He isn't as invisible as he might become.

With the long, black rifle held out before him, Gil follows into the trees, moving slowly and swinging his eyes back and forth across the blood-speckled trail.

Disturbed from his nap by a shot in the leg, then chased through the woods by one of the animals that fed him before—the bear is learning fast. He's making sense of his world and learning what he needs to fear, though perhaps—like the cat that was Elmer—he is learning these things all too late.

He can't move as quickly as he could a few moments ago. His wounded leg takes tentative steps. The bullet struck his left thigh, but barely—it punctured the top layers of fat and fur but passed through without becoming embedded; the injury's painful and bloody but not serious. The bear won't be in any real danger from this particular wound, so long as he survives long enough for it to heal. So long as he gets away from the hunter.

Hurry. Keep up. Join me here on this high rock where we'll have a good view of the clash between hunter and hunted, the clash with which every story worth telling has ended since stories began. A confrontation one body or the other must win.

And here comes the bear, plowing the brush with his injured leg already taking back some of his weight. There's no trail for him to follow as he rushes along a line parallel to the bluff, deeper into the woods. The hunter keeps his distance. He's waiting for the bear to grow tired, to concede and collapse. He doesn't know how superficial the wound is—the amount of blood on the bear's trail is misleading—and he waits for his prey to give up.

But the bear runs out of trail before he runs out of blood. He doesn't know these woods yet and he's pinned himself into a corner where the cliff face ends at the top of a steep, muddy hill. The bear stands at the top of the slope, testing his footing with a hesitant paw, a motion so delicate it seems out of sync with his bulky shape. But even that light footstep is enough to crumble the soil at the top of the hill, to set a tiny avalanche into motion, and he recoils, backing his body against the rocks, squeezing into the corner as tightly as he can while still facing the trail.

The hunter steps forward, rifle raised and one eye squeezed shut as the other lines the bear up in the sights. The bear roars but stays where he is, concerned by the hot smell of the gun. A steady, calloused finger wraps around the trigger. The bear's weight begins to shift forward as if he's contemplating a charge, and the hunter steps back, but the gun remains steady as stone in his hands.

And Gil is knocked to the ground when I leap to his back from above, toppling him under my weight. The rifle spins out of his hands and clatters against the face of the cliff. The bear seizes his chance, rushes in snarling and spitting with blood on his snout from cleaning the wound in his leg.

Why did I get involved? Why did I pounce? I didn't like where the story was going. I didn't want the bear to be shot—he's been through so much to get into the woods, to become the bear that he is. This story doesn't depend upon the bear's own survival—there is one more transformation to come, though I don't really need him for that—but for the hunter to kill him so soon, with so little effort . . .

It may be unfair for me to intervene as I have, but this isn't the story of Gil or his gun. Could we be satisfied with such a fate for the bear? We already lost one bear when the story gave us no choice. Are we so willing to give up another?

And perhaps I saw a chance to take care of the hunter once and for all. To speak back to one of your kind who takes us seriously enough to shoot when he has the chance. Pragmatic vengeance against Gil and his hunting weren't my main reason for leaping in, but I can't be expected to pass up the chance when it comes.

Besides, I haven't killed him. I've only knocked the gun from his hands, and leveled the field on which this confrontation will play itself out.

Gil stretches one arm out as far as he can, fingers straining to locate the rifle, but it isn't there no matter how much he wants it to be. The bear stands above him, a broad paw on either side of his head, snarling snout pressed so close to his face that hot, blackberry breath shakes the hunter's bushy white brows.

Gil doesn't make a sound, or turn away from the bear for a second. He stares into the animal's face with granite eyes and waits to be killed. He almost looks relaxed as he reaches up toward the bear's face. He looks like he's going to touch it. The bear growls, and a heavy paw swats Gil's arm away with a crunch.

The bear's lips peel back from purple-tinged teeth, and saliva collects in the bowl of his tongue before spilling over and onto Gil's face. Then he lays a paw on the man's forehead, and his claws comb through thin white hair and down over the brow, trailing thin red lines behind them. The claws reach the man's chin and the bear snorts, then backs away from the body.

Gil lies on the ground, bleeding from cuts the length of his face, his eyes still fixed on the bear even as they glaze over crimson. His hand searches frantically for the gun, but it still lies out of his reach. His other arm hangs limp at his side, bent at an unnatural angle.

And the bear is off down the trail, leaving the hunter behind. The bear hurries, he runs, and vanishes into the forest while Gil waits to be sure he is gone. The bear will cross streams, climb up and down slopes, and in time he will go so far into the forest he passes beyond any domain the hunter might claim as his own.

In time he'll go far enough to become just one more part of the woods, another story that is taken for granted and told again and again until it takes on a life of its own: the bear who hunted the hunter, the bear who marked a man's face.

The bear who wasn't always a bear.

25

THE BEAR MOVES JUST LIKE A BEAR.

That may not seem worth saying, but to a bear who wasn't always a bear and now rolls in the grass here before us, scratching behind a round ear with his claws, what could be more important? He was a man of empty spaces as Martin Blaskett but now he has all he wanted, everything he ever asked for, and so what if it didn't come quite the way he expected it to? The bear doesn't mind, so neither should we.

I can't help but repeat that word "bear," because no other word says what it does. I could describe him to you—slightly over six feet in length and thick in the middle, teeth tinged with the dark juice of berries and scraps of half-rotten meat caught where they don't get brushed anymore. I could say he's a black bear, the most common type in this forest, instead of the towering grizzlies or polar bears that first come to mind when you think of a bear . . . I could tell you, but you'll see him only as you want him to be, so it makes little difference what species he actually is: this bear will turn into the monster that scares you the most, even if he doesn't quite fit the bill.

I could offer the finest details of science or legend, but you might still only know him as "bear." And that would be fine, because sometimes a name is worth more than anything else, a name with the full weight of fear and awe layered upon it by generations both past and yet to come. Your kind haven't grown any larger over the years, at least not so much that it matters, but the bear always gets bigger; the bear always comes to mean more every time you cross his path in the woods.

It doesn't much matter if he's any one kind of bear or another, he isn't the name hammered into his body with the sharp spikes of Latin and science and lies. He's this particular bear and he's all bears at once, as every bear is. The ur-bear. He's dangerous because stories have made him that way. You call on him to fill the bear-shaped space in the back of your mind, to provide a ready answer to so many questions: all the reason you need for bigger boxes and higher walls, faster cars and louder alarms to remind you what you're afraid of and what goes on beyond the bright reach of the spotlight above your back door.

He's the story parents won't tell their children and that children tell each other instead. The bear is the reason for all you've accomplished, the source of your stories and the old mysteries you cling to for fear of becoming bored with the world. So he will always be here, in these woods, perhaps even after the forest is gone as I'm sure it one day will be. I know your kind well enough to believe the bear will always remain as the shadowy shape your eyes can't make sense of as it rumbles along in the dark.

Do you feel the air turning? The crisp tang of fall closing in? There's enough time for this bear to fatten himself before cold weather comes and brings with it his hibernation. So let's leave himself to himself, to the juicy berries and succulent grubs that will carry him over to spring, and to an afternoon nap in a particular clearing where an old rotten log surrounded by growth is the right shape and size for his body, and catches sun in just the right way. Its thick mattress of moss takes the bear's weight the way nothing else could.

I'm going to shed my shape, too. There's a particular hole in the world I'm interested in, about the size of a man, one I've been meaning to fill. I'm going to leave these woods for a while and get away from this part of the world—Martin may not have murdered the boy, but he isn't as welcome in town as he once was, and how would I explain to people who think they recognize him that Martin isn't Martin at all? How much more welcoming would they be of me, the monster who has been at the backs of their minds for so long? Would they want me in town any more than they'd want the real Martin, even if they could tell us apart? Or if they knew I was gone, had left them alone, would their way of life fall into ruin?

I wouldn't have gone to all this effort just to stay here. What do I care about building houses? Why would I want to knock down more trees? There are other things I can do with his body, things he never did with it himself. I don't care what it was to be Martin. I want to know what it could be, if Martin wasn't so much like himself and if he was more like the bear.

I expect you'll find your way out of that body in time, and back into your own. Then you'll find your way out of this forest. And if you don't, no harm done. These woods could use another coyote, the same as there's always room for another nurse log and the new stories that grow where it falls. I'm sure there's another voice eager to speak in the silence you'd leave behind.

ACKNOWLEDGEMENTS

With gratitude to Michelle Bailat-Jones, Laura McCune-Poplin, Mary Kate Hampton, Jessica Treadway, Lise Haines, Rick Reiken, and everyone who read the earliest version of this book at Emerson, and to the Writers' Room of Boston and Robie and Julia Harrington who provided a space to work on it; to Michael Kindness, Ann Kingman, Kevin Fanning, Rob and Karissa Kloss, Amber Sparks and Chris Backley, Kate Racculia, Roy Kesey, and Lori Hettler, who walked these woods along the way, and to anyone I've inadvertently left off this list and now owe a beer; to Richard Thomas, Alban Fischer, and all at Dark House/Curbside Splendor who gave it a home; to my parents, and to Tim and Pete and Theresa, and to Sage and Gretchen, of course; and to the bears and to everything wild in the woods.

STEVE HIMMER is the author of the novels *The Bee-Loud Glade* and *Fram*. His short stories, essays, and reviews have appeared in *The Millions*, *Ploughshares* online, *Post Road*, *Los Angeles Review*, *Hobart*, and other anthologies and journals. He edits the webjournal *Necessary Fiction* and teaches at Emerson College in Boston, Massachusetts.